LAST PROMISE

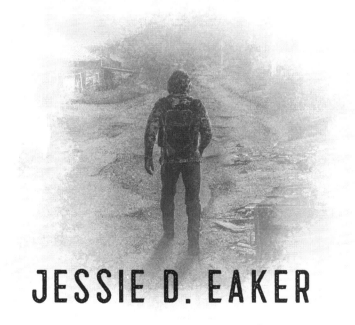

JESSIE D. EAKER

Cover designed by MiblArt

Last Promise / Jessie D. Eaker — First edition

Library of Congress Control Number: 2025908788

ISBN 979-8-9857335-8-7, Hardcover

For Becki

Contents

CHAPTER ONE

A TWIG SNAPPED.

I froze at the unexpected sound behind me. I listened, waiting for another—but none came. It was likely a curious raccoon or maybe some surviving pet looking for a handout. But I had seen evidence of a bear three days ago, so I thought it best to grab my gun before confronting the beast.

I carefully closed the book I had been reading, clutching it protectively to my chest. Then, I slowly reached toward my holstered gun sitting beside me.

But before my hand traveled an inch, there came the unmistakable *cha-chank* of a shotgun pump chambering a shell. The sound was thunderously loud against the quiet of the night, startling the crickets to silence. That one action announced it was not an animal but something far more deadly.

My heart pounded as I instantly realized how exposed I was. In my preoccupation with the book, the shotgun's owner had positioned themselves directly behind me. With my handgun out of reach and my crossed legs partially numb, there was no other way to say it.

I was screwed.

I had camped inside a ring of pine trees to shield my tent and conceal my tiny campfire. The flames provided barely enough heat to warm my tea and just enough light to read a few pages from Wendy's book. Not that I needed to see the ornately printed text. By now, it was ritual. Its chapters had long since been committed to memory in an attempt to ease my heart's pain. But the volume's words did nothing to fill the void of my loss. Only one thing would do that. And the time was near.

The peaceful evening had lulled me into a false sense of security. Despite the growing early November chill, a few hardy crickets had managed an evening serenade. They were doomed by the season's first frost—only days away. Yet, the males bravely serenaded the females, hoping for one last fling. I had to admire their tenacity, but unfortunately, I did not share their optimism. God's judgment waited for no one: cricket or man.

Although I'd passed a few small farms, I did not expect to be bothered. Their houses were dark, empty, and devoid of activity—husks of a life now gone. By habit, I hid anyway and assumed a curious animal would be my worst potential problem. This part of the Appalachian Mountains was sparsely populated even before the disaster. Now, everyone was dead.

Well, almost everyone. A handful of people had survived.

Like me.

And the one holding the shotgun.

"DON'T MOVE, MISTER!" ordered a female voice from behind me—the first human words I'd heard in months. "And keep your eyes dead ahead, or I'll put a hole in you the size of a barn!" She spoke with the Southern drawl of a local. At one time, I would have thought her accent was cute. But those times were long gone.

My thoughts raced. *Is she one of the crazies? God help me if she is.*

She stepped closer. I cut my eyes hard to the right, straining to see my gun. Slowly, my hand crept toward it. If I could just reach—

The shotgun exploded directly behind me, and I jumped in shock. A rain of pine needles and twigs peppered me from above while the scent of spent gunpowder assaulted my nose. The shot had been aimed into the branches over my head, but it could have just as easily blown my head off.

"Who did you think I was talking to?" yelled the woman behind me. "The birds 'n' the bees? Do that again, and my next shot won't miss."

I turned my head slightly to the right to get a better look at my assailant, but a loud crackling of brush to my left made me instinctively glance that way. Suddenly, a cloth bag was jerked over my head, and its drawstring pulled snugly around my neck. It effectively blinded me. I gasped and stiffened, but a gun barrel poked me in the back—its hardness unpleasantly warm even through my light coat.

"Don't move an inch, mister." The female voice came from directly behind me now. "Do as I say, and we won't hurt you. Now, lie flat on your stomach. And no monkey business." When I hesitated, she barked loudly, "NOW! On your stomach!"

I was at a complete disadvantage. The bag over my head was a thick burlap, rough and scratchy, with the faint scent of onions. Only shadows made it through. I set my precious book aside—hopefully out of the way—then slowly lay on the cold ground.

Bushes rustled behind me, followed by the soft scuff of approaching boots. I flinched when the gun's barrel was jabbed between my shoulder blades.

"Don't even think about moving," she said. "My friend Aaron here has his gun on your spine. Give even one twitch, and he'll separate your vertebra for you. Now put your hands behind your back."

I did as told, and she called to her partner. "Keep that shotgun on him. We don't need him getting any ideas."

I grunted in surprise as the woman sat right down on my rump. The unexpected weight pressed a rock into my leg. Damn, she was heavy.

I felt cold metal against my wrists, followed by two clicks. It didn't take a genius to figure out she was using handcuffs. She groaned as she pushed herself up. I heard the rattle of a chain and then felt her shackle my ankles. At that point, all the fight went out of me. It had just gone from bad—to hopeless.

She patted me on the shoulder as she spoke. "Now, you just lay there while I see if you've got anything worth keeping." She paused. "Aaron, you got 'em?" Another pause. "Good."

"My supplies are all in my pack," I offered, surprised my voice still worked after all these months alone. "Just take them. If you let me go, I swear I won't follow you." I took a deep breath, not wanting to show weakness but having to all the same. "But please leave my book. It's a... special edition."

She snorted. "Special to you, maybe." Then she stepped away.

I breathed a sigh of relief. Maybe she would ignore Wendy's book. The thick, special limited-edition volume was bound in black and red leather, with ornate gold lettering on the front and spine. I had given it to Wendy for our first Christmas. She'd wanted the hideously expensive book so badly that I had scrimped and saved to get it. When I gave it to her, she'd squealed in delight and made the book a permanent resident on her bedside table. She would read and reread it every night before bed.

I fondly remembered one night when I'd asked her why she loved it so much. She had given me a beautiful smile, her eyes twinkling. *"I just do,"* she'd said with a shrug. *"Just like I love you."*

The memory still pained me. I guess it was why I read from it every night since she died. I was still looking for that smile one last time, even though I knew it was no longer in this world.

I heard the clatter of my backpack's contents being dumped on the ground, and a few moments later, the rasp of my tent's zipper. I squeezed my eyes shut and fought with my indignation. *Why were they doing this?* Food was the only reason I could think of, yet it seemed unlikely. While supplies were not as easily scavenged now, plenty were still available if you knew where to look—and weren't afraid of the bodies. Everyone dying had left a few.

The disaster had happened so fast that no one had time to name it. My brother had called it God's Judgement, so that's how I thought of it. And I must say, God had been very efficient about it. Why mess with fire, or flood, or even ice when you can make them all go mad and kill themselves? Some quite creatively. Humans can work wonders when they put their minds to it.

Almost everyone was gone in three days.

Wendy lasted four.

There had been a few survivors. My captors were likely connected to the older teens I'd seen from a distance a week or so back. I had studied them through my binoculars, but their actions hadn't impressed me—especially when the leader had casually backhanded a girl in his party hard enough to send her sprawling and then shot the young man kneeling beside her. But it was what came afterward that made me turn and walk the other way. The gun had moved to target the girl, and she had crawled in the dirt on all fours over to his leg and kissed his boot.

Not my kind of people.

I heard a feminine sigh. "All you've got is freeze-dried crap. I wouldn't eat those if I were starving." My one camping pot clattered to the ground, followed by the crinkle of plastic. "What's with the dress shirt and pants still in the wrapper?" She mumbled. "Just a bunch of nothing."

She rooted around in the bag. "Where's the bullets?"

Damn, she found my special gun.

She was quiet for a moment. I heard the rattle of the plastic bag it was in, and then she sniffed. "I don't even think you've fired this one." I could almost hear the mirth in her voice. "Are you afraid of it or something?"

If only she knew. I wanted everything perfectly clean when I reached our cliff. Wendy's cliff. Clean clothes, a clean gun, my phone, and *her book*. I had gone through the scenario in my mind a thousand times. I just wanted this over with. Only Wendy could fill my emptiness. And there was only one way I could be with my dead wife.

But this woman was messing everything up. I needed to get rid of her. I could find another gun.

I sighed. "The bullets are in a pouch on my belt."

She made no comment but stepped over to me and once more sat on my rump. She jerked on my belt and pulled the pouch free. She unzipped it—probably checking the contents—before zipping it back and tucking it away.

Now that she had everything, maybe she would leave.

But then I felt her shift in the direction of my book. I stiffened.

"What's this?" she asked in surprise. "Wow, you weren't lying when you said it was a special edition. I thought you were talking about some trashy paperback."

I cringed when I heard a page turn and then another. *That's Wendy's book!* My hands curled into fists. *She has no right!*

She stepped closer to the fire. "Are you kidding me?" she asked. "After what happened, you're reading a fuckin' *fantasy?*"

"I read to be close to my wife!" Anger overcame my fear. "*The Paladin's Last Command* was her favorite."

She paused. The silence stretched. "You were married?" Her question was soft, barely a whisper, almost reverent.

Her shift in tone further angered me. *It's none of your damned business!*

"Children?"

I froze. The word sliced into my broken heart, opening a raw wound. Wendy and I had bought a house three months before the disaster. In another month, we planned to start trying for a family. I opened my mouth to answer, but my throat closed up, and only a sob came out. Answering meant acknowledging she was gone and our dreams were dead.

"Mister," the woman repeated, her irritation growing. "I asked you a question. Did you have children?"

I gritted my teeth and finally croaked out, "No."

There was a long pause. Heartbeats passed. She kept completely still—not a sound. The silence stretched out, making me wonder what she was doing. Was she considering me? Was my life being decided in these few moments?

My assailant burst into activity—clothing rustled, things were shoved into a backpack, and a zipper closed shut. Then I heard the unmistakable *cha-chank* of the shotgun again. *She's going to shoot me.*

I sagged in despair and rested my forehead on the ground. So this was it. She was stealing my stuff and killing me. I wasn't surprised. The universe had conspired to take my home, my parents, and my one true love. Why should my plans to rejoin Wendy be any different? I was actually glad. I'd get to see my wife all the sooner. Not quite the way Wendy wanted, but I'm sure she would understand it wasn't my fault and still welcome me.

"Aaron, you ready?" the woman yelled. There was a pause. "Let's do this."

I closed my eyes and waited for the gunshot. I wondered what it would feel like—would it hurt, or would I just pass on?

I was momentarily confused when the woman grabbed my arm and pulled it upward. "Stand up," she commanded.

"What?" I asked in confusion. "Aren't you going to kill me?"

She chuckled. "Don't tempt me. Now, stand up. We're going for a little stroll." Strangely, her tone had softened. It was still firm, but she had dropped the condescending mockery of before. The change threw me. *Why?*

I slowly got to my feet and was immediately shoved in the back with something hard. I could only assume it was the shotgun. I staggered and would have fallen if the woman hadn't steadied me.

"Quit it, Aaron. Shoving won't make him go any faster. So just keep your shirt on."

She fumbled with something for a moment, then leaned close. "Mister, I'm leaving your tent and your sleeping gear. But I've got your pack and the rest of your stuff."

I was nudged in the back with the shotgun again.

"Aaron, dammit," she called out. "Leave him alone." There was a pause, then confusing sounds of movement behind me.

She put a gentle hand on my arm. "He might just use the business end of his shotgun on your head." She tugged gently. "Now, step forward."

I didn't take three steps before the chain on my feet caught on something, and I tripped. The woman grabbed me hard and steadied me. I was impressed with her strength.

"Hold up for a minute," she ordered. I felt her do something to the chain on my leg and attach something to my pants. "Let's try that again." She took my arm and urged me forward. Whatever it was, I didn't trip again.

I was completely lost after the first dozen steps. I could tell we were going generally uphill, which likely meant west or east. I had camped at the bottom of a wooded hollow, so it was likely one of those directions. Regardless, finding my way back to my camp would be very difficult.

After what I guessed was a little over a mile, she spoke softly, "Take little steps. We gotta get through some short brush, and then we'll be on the road. It'll get easier after that."

I did as she suggested, and sure enough, I stepped out onto something hard. *Pavement?* I wasn't sure. But the woman steered me to the right, and we continued uphill.

The road gradually got steeper, and the woman beside me began to breathe a little harder. I wondered if this was a longer walk than she was used to. I tried to imagine what she looked like. I couldn't figure out her age from her voice, but something in her tone spoke of maturity. In my head, I couldn't help but imagine her as some round, old lady who sat around smoking cigarettes all day. I frowned. No, I was sure that was wrong. And that Aaron guy. The way he never talked freaked me out.

We must have traveled at least two miles when I heard the unmistakable whine of a dog in the distance. It didn't sound hurt or upset, but happily excited. *Could it be hers?*

Pets had fared somewhat better than humans during the craziness—but not by much. Those that did survive were now well on their way to turning feral. I had seen a few skittish cats and timid dogs, even tempted them with treats. But only a few had accepted, and even those had immediately left. I guess they had lost their trust of humans since we had betrayed them so badly.

My guide pulled me in a different direction, and the pavement transitioned to loose gravel, which crunched loudly under my feet. The dog's whine got louder and turned into an excited bark.

The woman made kissing sounds and pitched her voice higher in baby talk. "Hiya, boy. Did you miss me? I'm sorry I had to leave you behind, but you're no good at being quiet." The mutt whined in response. I could almost see the dog in my mind, wagging its tail—any wrongdoing already forgiven.

She tugged on my arm. "Wait here," she commanded.

"Aaron, watch him." I heard the gravel crunch as she stepped away. The dog continued to bark happily.

I lowered my head and hoped I gave Aaron the impression of being defeated. But I wasn't. I needed to get away.

My apprehension had grown with each step. Aaron's silence unnerved me, and the woman had switched to being halfway nice. They wanted me for something. Something I wasn't going to like.

I had to make my move soon—the woman's dog was here, so they must live nearby. Knowing Aaron's location was going to be key to getting away. *But where the hell was he?*

I held my breath and listened.

Nothing. Not even the whisper of his breathing.

The bastard must be part ghost. For all I knew, he could be right behind me with his shotgun aimed at my head.

A short distance away, I heard a chain rattle and a delighted laugh. "Hold still, you mutt," she said, affection obvious in her voice. "There you go." It was such a contrast to how she bossed me around.

I heard the dog gallop toward me and then sniff around my feet. Unexpectedly, he shoved his snout right into my crotch. I jerked back in surprise and nearly tripped.

She laughed. "Well, Sammy didn't bite your man-parts off, so he must like you. But don't push your luck. My dog's fast." She paused. "And he loves to hunt."

I got the message.

She took me by the arm and led me forward but stopped after only a dozen steps. Maybe it was a change in acoustics, but I got the impression we were standing next to a large structure. *A house, maybe?*

"Okay, we're at the hardest part," she said. "We're going up five steps. Take your time, and start with your left foot. I'll be right here with you."

I was running out of time.

She urged me forward, and I took the first step. It had a hollow sound like wood. She stepped with me. Then we took another. I felt her dog brush past me, going ahead of us.

I paused. She tugged me forward again, but I resisted.

"You're doing good," she said. "Just a couple more."

I strained my ears, listening for Aaron. I could hear the dog panting, her clothes rustling beside me, but I didn't hear the bastard. I could only pray he'd stepped away. I didn't think I'd get a better chance.

She led me up another step.

"Two more," she said gently, like a proud parent teaching her kid to walk. Only this kid had had enough.

Now's my chance.

I lifted my foot but instead shifted my weight. I lowered my shoulder and shoved her hard. She fell away and cursed, landing with a thump and sending something crashing. The dog went into a barking frenzy.

I quickly walked backward down the stairs and then did a short-step walk downhill as fast as the leg chains would allow. I tried to retrace my steps and was rewarded by gravel crunching under my feet. As I searched for the connecting road, I rubbed the hood against my shoulder, desperately trying to get it off. If I could lose them in the darkness, I might stand a chance.

The dog galloped after me and nipped at my ankles. I sidestepped, but something large hit me in the back. I stumbled and fell hard—my shoulder taking the brunt of it. I rolled to get up, but the dog moved to growl in my face. I wondered if he trusted me now.

I managed to turn over when someone stuck a gun barrel into my chest. They were panting. "You *idiot!*" spat the woman, her breath coming hard. "That was just plain stupid. You could have broken your fuckin' neck!"

I'd totally pissed her off. I had been transitioned back to asshole status.

"I should have just shot you," she ranted. "But then I'd have to clean up the mess and bury you." She pressed the shotgun more firmly into my chest. "Don't do that again. There will not be a second chance. Get it through your head that I *own* your ass!" She poked me hard with the gun. "Now on your feet!" I heard her take a step back. "Aaron! Get your butt over here!" she shouted.

With no help this time, I rolled to my side and slowly managed to stand. She directed me back to the stairs using prods from the shotgun until we were once again at their base. I briefly considered running again—but didn't. What was the point? She was right. She did own my ass.

"Now let's try this again," she said in irritation. "The step is right in front of you. Left leg up."

I raised my leg but jerked back as a deep growl came from in front of me.

"Sammy!" shouted the woman. "Sit. I don't need you acting up, too. He's not gonna hurt me again." I felt the gun nudge me. "Are you."

His growling suddenly stopped, and I could tell she was patting him. "That's a good boy. You're my protector." The dog growled again. "Yeah, I don't trust him either."

This time, the woman stayed safely behind me and let me stagger up the five steps alone. It was childish, but I took a wicked satisfaction at the newfound caution she now showed for her prisoner. I hoped her fall hurt as much as mine did.

I emerged onto some type of porch. The floor had a hollow sound, and a few of the boards squeaked. She ordered me to one side and climbed the steps behind me. Strangely, there was only one set of footsteps. *Where was that Aaron guy?*

A hand touched my shoulder, pushing sideways. "Lean here," she directed. I shifted against what I felt like a wall. "You're not going in my house with those filthy boots."

Her house? Not hers and Aarons. Not his even. But *her* house. I had expected to be locked in a barn or shed, but not this.

What did she want with me?

The grip on my arm returned. What sounded like a screen door creaked open, followed by a doorknob rattling. Warm air welcomed me, pushing aside the cold of the night. The dog trotted ahead like it owned the place—his nails clicking on a hardwood floor. I could hear a ticking clock somewhere close by.

It took a moment to penetrate the bag over my head, but familiar scents teased my nose: wood polish, a past meal, and baked bread. And was that *cinnamon?* The smells were familiar, so *home.*

I was pulled forward. But I resisted.

I ached as I was reminded of a life filled with the love and laughter of my wife.

But that life had died with her.

And it was never coming back.

I cocked my jaw. The hand tugged one more time, and I followed, stepping inside.

She guided me through some confusing turns but finally drew to a halt. Something slid into place behind me and touched the back of my knees.

"Sit," she commanded. "There is a chair right behind you." She put a hand on my arm, and I slowly sank into a hardback chair. It squeaked as it accepted my weight, and with my hands behind me, I could feel it had a slick finish. I thought it might be part of a dining room set.

I heard quick steps moving away, stuff being moved, and then quick steps back. I jumped when she grabbed my jacket and unzipped it, opening it wide. I stiffened as she slipped a hand inside and probed the shoulder that had taken the brunt of my fall. The fingers that ran over my shirt were firm, almost professional. Her probing expanded, and she ran her hands over my chest, feeling my ribs.

What was she doing?

She stepped back. "Your jacket protected you when you fell." She tugged it back into place but did not zip it. "Are you hurt anywhere? Anything broken? Cuts or scrapes?"

I didn't say anything. I couldn't understand why she was suddenly concerned. None of this was making any sense.

She snorted. "Listen, mister. In case you haven't heard, 911 doesn't work anymore, the closest hospital burned to the ground, and the last doctor has died. So if you're hurt, we need to treat it now. Because later..." She paused. "...it will kill you." She took a deep breath. "So, I'll ask again. Are you hurt?"

"I'm fine," I huffed.

She paused, seeming to evaluate my answer. "Good."

I heard a chair creak next to me, what sounded like a bottle unscrewing, then a medicinal smell. I jerked back. *Was she going to drug me?*

"I said I wasn't hurt."

She didn't answer at first. "Okay." I heard the cloth moving and then a grunt of pain.

Oh. She must have been hurt when I pushed her. My prior satisfaction with her fall suddenly seemed stupid. While she had taken me captive and threatened me, she had actually taken pains not to hurt me.

"Sorry," I mumbled.

The movement suddenly stopped. I'm not exactly sure why I felt it, but I could swear she was staring at me.

After what seemed like forever, she finally spoke. "I should have expected it."

Her chair scraped back, and then steps moved away. Cabinet doors opened and shut, followed by a metallic banging. *What was she doing?*

I had my answer a few moments later when I recognized the sound of sizzling and the smell of ham frying. Probably canned, but it did smell good. My mouth watered, and I tried to remember the last time I'd had something other than beef jerky or a power bar.

Sammy knew what was happening. He padded over to where the woman had sat and began licking his lips. Loudly.

There was the sound of more cabinets, and a short while later, the sizzling stopped. She returned and set down what sounded like two plates. I snorted. I was sitting at a dining room table and hadn't even known it.

She groaned as she sat across from me. I think someone was going to be sore tomorrow.

"I fixed myself a ham biscuit," she said. "My momma always taught me to share, so I fixed you one too. If you promise not to bite my hand off, I'll lift your hood enough to feed it to you."

It smelled so good—hunger gnawed at my stomach. It would be so easy to just accept the kindness. But I stiffened my resolve. I was a prisoner, not some disabled guest. Sammy might like eating from her hand, but I did not.

"No thanks," I stated flatly.

She sighed—the barest hint of sadness and disappointment escaping with it. But she hardened. "Suit yourself. Sammy will love having it." She switched to what I was beginning to think of as her dog voice. "Wouldn't you, my little baby?"

The dog whined and gave a short bark.

I heard her pick up the plate. "Last call before it becomes dog food."

I remained silent.

She sighed, and then the plate was moved. The sound of chomping quickly followed.

She laughed. "Sammy, you must be part pig."

I heard licking and the plate scooting across the floor. He whined again.

The woman got up and put a hand under my arm. "Come on. Let's go." She sounded disappointed.

She led me further into the house, and I could tell we had entered a different room. She abruptly stopped.

"Hold still," she commanded. "I'm gonna take your leg chains off. Move, and Aaron over there'll be happy to shoot you." I could almost hear the grin. "But please don't. Blood is a bitch to clean."

She messed with my ankles, then something hard and cool was pressed into my palm. She rapidly stepped away.

"All right, mister," she said from further away. "I just put the key to the handcuffs in your hand. Don't drop it. If you work at it, you should be able to unlock them. Once you do, take off your hood."

It was awkward, but she was true to her word. I managed to get the key in the lock and free my left wrist. I immediately jerked my hood off.

I found myself alone in a small bedroom. A single solar lantern on the dresser provided barely enough light to see. But it was enough to tell that the doorway was open.

Yes!

I immediately ran for the exit. But I only got two steps before my left leg caught on something, and I fell flat on my face about a foot short of the door. Spitting mad, I looked back to see what had caught me and discovered a manacle on my ankle—stainless steel with a length of high-grade chain attached. It went through a hole in the floor in the exact center of the room. I stood and pulled on it, putting all my strength into it, but it didn't budge. The other end was bolted to something solid, and the hole was too small to see what it was. I was not going anywhere.

"Shit!" I jerked on the chain in frustration. The bitch had swapped one ankle chain for another.

I surveyed the room, searching for something I could use to free myself. The room had been done in a rustic pine paneling and had a bare hardwood floor. The room's only furniture was a twin bed and a little three-drawer dresser off to the side. An old-fashioned metal washbowl and pitcher sat on top of the dresser. The little four-poster bed had been made up to perfection using a handmade quilt with a pattern of eight-pointed stars and matching sham-covered pillows. The room would have been suitable for a bed and breakfast before the Judgement.

I quickly tested the length of my chain, walking around the room. I found I could reach the dresser and the bed but not the closet, the window, or the door. I wondered about a bathroom until I spotted a bucket and toilet paper in the corner.

I stared at the toilet paper. I shook my head in denial, but there was no mistaking it. Someone had spent a lot of time preparing for this. My capture had not been a spur-of-the-moment thing. It had been deliberate. Someone had noticed me and decided I was worth keeping. *But for what?*

The enormity of my situation finally crept into my skull. It was late. I was hungry. I was exhausted. And worst of all, I was a prisoner.

Despair weighed on me. I sank to the floor and put my head in my hands. Rejoining Wendy just seemed so out of reach.

Steps came from the other room. I peered into its darkness, but whoever it was stopped just beyond the light.

"The water in the pitcher is clean," the woman said. "It's from the well out back. I drink it myself, and it hasn't killed me yet. You're also welcome to use the bed, but try not to get the quilt too dirty. It's a bitch to clean."

She paused, waiting for a response, but I didn't say anything.

"I'm sorry," she said softly.

My anger became too much. "What do you want with me?" I shouted, jumping to my feet and walking toward her, halting only when my chain drew short. "Just let me go. I wasn't going to hurt you or steal from you. I was just passing through while I looked for something."

She was silent for so long that I thought she had stepped away.

"Listen, mister. I'm exhausted, and I need some sleep." She gave a heavy sigh. It almost sounded like the weight of the world was on her shoulders.

I pulled on my chain and tried to see into the darkness of the other room. But I could only see shadows.

She drew a long breath and let it out slowly. "I promise we'll talk in the morning. Nothing will happen to you as long as you don't do something stupid."

I jerked on my chain in frustration.

I heard steps walking away, but the woman said nothing more.

"What about Aaron? Am I safe from him?"

The footsteps abruptly halted. All was silent except for the ticking of the windup clock. Long seconds passed. Finally, she answered, her voice barely above a whisper. "I was lying. There was no Aaron. It was just…"

She took a ragged breath.

"Me."

CHAPTER TWO

I LAY ON THE FLOOR, looking up at the dark ceiling. A dim illumination came from outside my room and around the corner. I assumed it was a battery nightlight. I briefly wondered where she charged it and why she wasted the energy. Such things were precious now.

I had tried the bed but found it too soft after sleeping on the ground for so long. So, I pulled the blanket off and lay on the floor, but ended up going back for the quilt because the floor grew cold. Sleep, however, wouldn't come. The events of the past day kept playing through my mind.

Until a few hours ago, I had been in control of my life and needed only one last thing before joining my wife—to locate Wendy's special spot.

Then, that strange woman made everything fall apart.

What could she want with me?

The question rolled around in my head. From the looks of it, she had everything she needed—a nice home, food, a way to cook. Hell, she even had a dog. And if she was searching for male companionship, taking it at gunpoint seemed an odd way to get it.

I rolled over on my side and tried to get comfortable. No, this was something different. Even with all her planning, it could have gone wrong in so many ways. What she did was risky.

It spoke of desperation.

I frowned. Regardless of her motive, she now had my wife's book, and not having it, made my fingers twitch. It was the one connection to Wendy that had survived. I smiled to myself. I could see my wife in my mind—propped up in bed, a book resting on her knees, her eyes darting across the page. She had been a sponge for information. I used to kid her that she loved books more than me.

"True," she'd respond without even looking up. "I only married you for your hot bod."

I'd pout. "So I'm just your play toy?"

She'd carefully mark her place and set her book aside, then quickly roll on top of me, grinning. "Yeah, and it's playtime."

A tear rolled down my cheek. Those intimate moments were the ones I missed the most. But I longed for the quiet moments, too. I could remember waking up beside her, our faces just inches apart. Strands of her brown hair lay across her beautifully relaxed face. And if the sun caught her hair just right, it almost made her look like an angel. I frowned, trying to remember the last time I had woken up beside her.

It was the morning that everything fell apart.

It was a Saturday. We had arrived late the previous evening and were sleeping in my old bedroom at my parents' house. Dad's birthday was on that Sunday, and since he was hitting the big five-oh, Mom had planned a not-so-surprising birthday party with a few friends and family. Even my older brother Geri was supposed to make an appearance.

I had been watching Wendy sleep when there was a knock on our bedroom door.

"Are you guys up yet?" Mom had asked from the other side. "I've got breakfast ready. Didn't want it to get cold."

"We'll be down in a minute, Mom," I called softly.

I turned back to my bride to find two lovely brown eyes watching me. She smiled and stretched. "Morning."

I couldn't help but return her contented smile and give her a quick peck. I pulled her closer and snuggled in, slipping a hand into the back of her pajama bottoms. I did it just to get a reaction, and I did.

"Not going to happen," she said playfully while pulling out the offending limb. "Especially with your mom just outside the door. Don't even think about it."

I chuckled. "I can think about anything I want. We are still newlyweds, you know. Can I help it if I married the sexiest woman in the world? Besides, aren't we going to start on that baby soon?"

She rolled her eyes, knowing what was coming but playing along anyway. "You know I don't go off my birth control until next month."

I pulled her closer. "But we could still practice."

She shook her head and gave a dramatic sigh. "Men, all you think about is sex." She pulled away, and I reluctantly let her go. She started toward the bathroom.

I gave her a mock frown. "Are you going to tell me you never have those thoughts?"

She reversed course and leaned over me, her hair gently caressing my face—her eyes twinkling in mischievous delight. "A woman has her secrets." Then she kissed me.

I reached for her, but she lept back, giggling, and continued to the bathroom. *I loved her so much.*

We went downstairs, still in our pajamas, and sat at the table while Mom scurried about, getting everything ready. As usual, she had gone all out and prepared a massive Southern-style breakfast of bacon, hash browns, eggs, and biscuits. She even had gravy.

I caught Wendy's eye and subtly patted my stomach. Her eyes twinkled as she nodded. We were trying to prevent our newlywed waistlines from expanding any further, so we usually stuck to something with a lot less fat and carbs. But since no cholesterol had been spared, we were going to have to suffer through it. Not that it was *that* much of a hardship.

Dad hadn't made it to the table yet. Frowning, Mom stepped toward the den and called him. "Cory, come eat. It's getting cold."

Mom worked hard to make sure everything was piping hot and got really pissed if you didn't come to the table when she called.

"Just a minute," he answered. "There's something weird going on in New York. Some kind of riot."

Mom was clearly not convinced. "Don't blame me when your food's cold." Then she mumbled under her breath. "Or that I worked my ass off."

"I'll be there in a minute," he called.

Mom harrumphed, clearly not pleased. Hot food trumped hot news every time.

Wendy and I fought to keep a straight face.

Mom sat down and gave us a strained smile. "Dig in. He'll just have to eat it cold."

Wendy and I didn't hesitate.

Dad called from the den. "There's also riots in DC."

Mom set the bowl of eggs aside and frowned. "Isn't that close to where Geri works?"

"Not sure," he called back.

She looked over at me. "What's the name of the place your brother works? Nato-natto something?."

I put a biscuit on my plate and passed the bowl to Wendy. "It's NanoNeural Engineering, Mom. And he works in Vienna, which is outside of DC."

Mom nodded. "Thank you, dear. I'd forget my name if it wasn't on my license."

Wendy and I shared a glance.

A few moments later, a soft "I don't believe this" came from the den.

For the first time, I began to wonder if something bad was happening. Dad's delay was unusual. He normally wouldn't risk incurring Mom's wrath.

"Guys…" concern in his voice, "…you need to see this."

I took Wendy's hand, and we went to see what was happening. Reluctantly, Mom followed a moment later.

As Dad's oversized screen came into view, I froze, unsure how to process what I was seeing. A bold caption announced *Riots in DC* overlaying an aerial view of a street filled with screaming and fighting people. The crack of gunshots, both near and far, echoed over the crowd's roar. There seemed to be no order, no objective—just destruction.

A lone man broke free from the angry swarm and pointed a rifle at the camera. The scene cut to static.

The picture immediately switched to a harried news anchor sitting behind a desk. "We are having some technical difficulties," he said, glancing down at his notes before looking back into the camera. "For those that joined late, we are covering the New York and DC riots. They started in the early morning and have been spreading to surrounding communities. From what we can tell, no group has claimed responsibility, and the rioters are not making any demands. The governors in the affected regions have declared a state of emergency...." He paused and put a hand to his ear. "It appears riots have also started in Atlanta around Hartsfield-Jackson International Airport. Reports are unconfirmed, but it appears to have started after the emergency landing of a flight from New York. This matches the information we've received from London and Paris." He looked away, listening. "We just got a report of similar riots starting in San Francisco."

Wendy turned to me, eyes wide in disbelief. "What's going on?"

A low throbbing came from outside, which grew until the house started rattling. I ran to the front door and threw it open in time to see five military helicopters flying low and heading north. Wendy and Mom followed me out.

"Should we try to get back home?" Wendy looked panicked.

I thought that sounded like an excellent idea. Our little house was outside Norfolk, so I doubted the riots would reach it. We might even get Mom and Dad to come with us.

I ran back inside, yelling instructions, intent on grabbing what I could. But as I entered, the phone in my pocket lit up with the shrill alarm of an emergency warning. Everyone else's phone did the same.

With dread, I pulled out the device. *"MARTIAL LAW DECLARED. THIS IS NOT A TEST. UNTIL THE EMERGENCY IS CLEARED, A CURFEW IS NOW IN EFFECT FOR ALL STATES AND COUNTIES. ALL RESIDENTS ARE ORDERED TO STAY INDOORS WITH YOUR DOORS AND WINDOWS LOCKED. DO NOT VENTURE OUT UNTIL LAW ENFORCEMENT CAN RESOLVE THE SITUATION."*

The others ran in behind me. Dad had never left the TV and sat staring at its live feed. "Oh shit," he whispered.

The newscaster's eyes went wide, and he fled off-screen. A moment later, we heard off-camera shouting and then automatic gunfire. The studio camera spun to catch a man running toward them, spraying bullets indiscriminately. The shooter was grinning from ear to ear and shouted, "Don't worry, people! I'm here to stop the voices!"

Abruptly, he stopped and cocked his head to one side like he was listening to something we couldn't hear. He then nodded and calmly pulled a handgun from his pocket and aimed it at his head. He smiled, and I saw his finger tighten on the trigger—

The video went out.

We looked at each other in horror. *What was going on?*

A jet zoomed over our house, rattling the windows. Once more, I ran outside to see it circle and then climb. Another jet roared toward it, and they collided mid-air, exploding into a cloud of smoke and flames, with debris raining down over the area.

It was all happening so fast I didn't know what to think. I

remembered the text message to take shelter and thought it sounded better by the second.

Mom put her hands over her mouth. "Oh, God."

I jumped when something crashed loudly behind me. I wheeled to find a faded black pickup had mowed down the mailbox and plowed into my white sedan in the driveway. I recognized the truck—it was my brother's.

The driver-side door swung open before I could get to it, and my brother staggered out. He had a hand clamped to his left side, which was slick with blood. His other arm hung loose, but he held something in his hand.

"Geri!" I called and ran toward him.

"I've got to help you," he said breathlessly. "The voices are telling me I have to."

I took his good arm to steady him, but he staggered, and his legs gave out. I managed to partially catch him and lower him to the ground.

"Call 911!" I yelled over my shoulder.

"I am!" Mom shouted back. "But I'm only getting a busy signal."

I turned my brother on his back and put pressure on his wound. "Get me something I can use for bandages!"

My brother looked up at me, his eyes wild and bright. He felt feverish—his skin had a sweaty sheen. He grabbed the front of my shirt. "They broke into the lab," he wheezed. "Protesters. They bypassed the vault's safeguards." He struggled for breath. "They let them out." He gasped. "They weren't ready." He coughed, and his grip loosened.

Wendy handed me a dish towel, and I pressed it into the wound. "What got out?" I asked. "Something you were working on?" I needed to keep him talking.

Geri pulled me close again—his grip surprisingly strong for someone so wounded. "The *Norns*. Nanomachines. But they're not finished." He licked his lips. "Things are going to get very bad." Another wheeze. "I have to save you. Their voices say I have to. The Norns are telling me to."

I shook my head. Geri was talking nonsense. "I don't understand. I'm fine."

"You won't be!" he shouted. "They are already crawling into your brain. It's what we designed them to do. Connect you up. But the Norns aren't ready. *We're* not ready."

Norns? Connect me up? What the hell is he talking about?

He coughed, and blood came up.

Dad knelt beside me while Mom fought with her phone.

Geri struggled to breathe. "I have to save you." He reached a trembling, bloody hand toward me and placed it behind my neck. "I love you, bro. Please forgive me. But I can only save you."

It was then I noticed what he had in his other hand. A small syringe. It was one of the fancy kind—a bright orange cylinder. You just pressed the button on the end, and it did the rest.

Its protective cap was off.

"Geri…" I started.

His grip tightened with unexpected strength. He jerked me down to his chest, and the arm with the syringe snaked around behind me.

"I'm so sorry," he whispered.

The needle plunged into my back just below my shoulder, and then I felt him press the button.

"*NO!*" I screamed.

* * *

I jerked awake and bolted upright, frantically looking around the unfamiliar room while I tried to control my shaking hands. Recognition gradually seeped into my sleep-dazed brain. I was in that woman's house. I must have been dreaming.

I rubbed my face and took a shaky breath. Geri had done something to me. I don't know if it was an antidote, vaccine, or altogether something different. But whatever it was, it kept the craziness away.

But it didn't stop the madness and death around me.

I had the privilege of watching my brother bleed out on the lawn. Shortly after, my dad stripped off all his clothes and ran naked down the street, saying his skin was on fire, and he had to stop the voices. My mother started singing hymns, and before I could stop her, she stepped in front of a speeding car.

And my loving wife? When I wouldn't let her stab a knife in her throat, she tried to claw my eyes out.

I managed to overpower her and tried to keep her safe. I tied her to my parent's bed as she fought, screamed, and cried for me to stop the voices. As night fell, we lost power, and I stayed right beside her as she wept.

I kept the doors locked and blinds pulled. Shouting, gunshots, and explosions kept me wide-eyed and afraid.

I watched her for three days as she talked about the voices and all the horrible things they were telling her. She screamed, saying her skin was burning off. Then, she yelled that her bones were melting. And finally, she cried in pain, begging me to kill her because bugs were slowly eating her brain.

It was hell.

On the fourth day, she calmed and became rational. She said

the voices were gone, and she was over it. I gratefully released her, and we held each other until I finally collapsed from exhaustion.

I would remember the next morning for the rest of my life. As I became aware, I took comfort in the blanket she had covered me with and reached for my wife.

But she wasn't there. Her side of the bed was cold.

Hoping I was wrong, but knowing I wasn't, I made my way through the dark house, calling her name. I finally found her in the garage where she had hung herself. A lone, overturned chair lay beneath her. On the floor nearby, a handwritten note sat atop her favorite book.

My Dearest Eyri,

I'm so sorry. I lied to you. The voices haven't stopped. And they are too painful to bear. They scramble my thoughts. I lose my words. I can only hold them off for mere moments. Even writing this is hard. Loud, so loud.

While it will hurt you, I'm taking the coward's way out. The guilt of hurting you is tremendous. But the pain of staying is horrific. They are so loud. I beg your forgiveness.

Asking me to be your wife was the happiest day of my life. And every day since has been perfect. Please think of this as just a brief parting. I will be waiting on the other side.

The voices are getting louder. I can barely think. Getting the right words is so hard. Don't immediately join me—you have much to do. SO

LOUD. Go to where you made me the happiest.
Read the words from my book. So many voices.
Promise me with all you hold dear, you will follow
the Paladin's last command. I CAN'T THINK! Read
the words. Your true love awaits. SHUT UP! You
will know what to do.

    THEY ARE SO LOUD!

All my love,
Wendy

I took a deep breath and let it out slowly. That note was why I spent the last few months coming here.

A breeze outside stirred the fallen leaves, making a scratching sound against the house—like ghosts searching for a way in.

After reading her note, I made a solemn promise that on the anniversary of our engagement, at the spot I gave her my ring, I would follow her instructions—

And I would join her.

My hands curled into fists. The woman holding me prisoner was not going to stop me.

CHAPTER THREE

THE WONDERFUL SMELLS of baking bread and cooking ham teased me awake. For a moment, I thought I was back in my cozy little house with Wendy. But that wisp of happiness vanished when I opened my eyes and found myself still in the room.

My prison.

I sat up, trying to orient myself. My room was dark, but light was spilling in from outside my door. It revealed a small den with a sofa, recliner, and coffee table. I bet if I shifted my angle, I would see an old video screen across from the recliner.

Pans and dishes clinked softly from beyond my line of sight. I assumed breakfast was being prepared. My stomach knotted in hunger, reminding me it had been a long time since my last meal.

It had taken a while, but I eventually fell back asleep. Right after the disaster, I used to have that dream every night. But as the weeks passed, the frequency had fallen off. My capture must have triggered it last night—one more reason to resent this woman.

Standing, I went to the door and found I had a watcher. A black labrador lay beside the recliner on a red plaid dog bed. He was a chunky fellow, his muzzle peppered with gray hairs and a single patch of white on his chest. While older, his alert eyes tracked my every move. This must be the dog I had heard last night. Sammy, she had called him.

I wondered if I could coax him closer and perhaps hold him hostage. I held out a hand in his direction, but his lips pulled back into a snarl, and he gave a deep growl. Well, so much for making friends.

I turned away and considered the bucket. It was strategically placed next to the closet with a little privacy curtain hanging from the ceiling so I could do my business without an audience.

I thought about pissing on her precious quilt out of spite, but rejected the idea. It might provoke her into doing something to my book, and I couldn't take that risk. I'd try to be nice for now. But if that tactic didn't work, I'd find another strategy.

I did my business and washed my face and hands using water from the pitcher. I was surprised at how dirty the used water was in the bowl. It was probably time for a bath. My last one was...

I paused. I couldn't remember.

If I counted the last rain, it was probably a few weeks ago. And if I didn't, it was that dunk in the river I took over the summer. With all that had happened, staying clean just hadn't seemed important.

When I came around the curtain, I was surprised to see the dog was gone and a tray with food had appeared. It held a water bottle and a plate heaped with eggs, canned ham, and a biscuit. A real honest-to-God homemade biscuit.

There was just one problem. It was out of reach. I snorted. So she was going to torture me after all. I refused to play that game, so I sat on the floor with my back against the foot of the bed. My stomach rumbled, reminding me again that it was not happy.

From my new position, I could see the den had a door on the right, and from the sounds, it had to be the kitchen. The dog peeked out the doorway, eyeing the unguarded plate. After glancing over its shoulder, it crept toward the food, but only made it a couple of steps.

"Stop!" came the woman's voice from what I assumed was the kitchen. "You can't have it, Sammy. That's for our guest."

I shook my head. *Guest.* I certainly didn't feel like one.

"Mister, are you on a hunger strike or something?" she asked from the other room. "Sammy's not gonna wait much longer."

I huffed. "I can't reach it." I almost added *idiot*, but decided it probably wasn't wise. "And I won't beg."

A pot slammed down. "Beg? What are you? Stupid? Use the back scratcher."

"What?" I asked in disbelief.

"The backscratcher. Surely, you've found it by now. Use it to pull the tray to you."

I stood and spotted it on the dresser behind the water pitcher—a long, thin piece of wood with curved prongs on one end, mimicking curled-up fingers. *Scratch an Itch in Eaglecliff County* was printed across it.

I laid down on the floor and reached out with it. The scratcher's curved fingers easily caught the edge of the tray, and I pulled it to me.

"No fork?" I called.

"Do you think I'm crazy?" she shot back.

"You're the one that held a shotgun on me, put a bag over my head, and marched me halfway across the continent. I'd say that qualifies for crazy."

Surprisingly, she chuckled. "Yeah, I'd have to agree with that." She paused. "But I have my reasons."

I made no further comment and ate my food. The ham was canned, the eggs were powdered—but the biscuit was home-made. And damn good. As I savored my first bite, I was instantly reminded of Mom, my eyes welling with tears. I stubbornly blinked them back. I refused to let my captor see me cry.

After finishing, I washed it down with the water and felt quite satisfied. I didn't want to admit it, but it was the best meal I'd had since the Judgement. It made me wary. She was likely trying to soften me up. Something must be coming that I wasn't going to like.

Sammy returned to his sentry position with a chew bone. He flopped down in his bed and gnawed on it while keeping a watchful eye on me. Yet my mysterious captor refused to make an appearance. I heard movement, so I knew she was there. Was she avoiding this discussion?

Well, I'd had enough.

I called to her. "You said we were going to talk this morning."

"We will," came the reply. "Just as soon as I put on this pot of beans. I now have another person to feed, and that doesn't happen by itself."

"You could let me go."

She didn't answer. But it sounded like I'd at least get to live through lunch.

While the light outside my room had gotten brighter, my room was still dark. Curious, I pulled the drapes back to find the glass painted black. Odd. I glanced at the den windows and noticed they also had a strange absence of light. Sunlight only seemed to come from the back of the house. I wondered what that was about. Maybe this lady was crazier than I had thought.

I heard a deep sigh from the other room, sounding like someone about to do something they really didn't want to. "Are you ready to talk now?" she called.

"You sort of have my undivided attention." I took my place, sitting on the floor at the foot of the bed. So I was finally going to see my captor.

A *shick-shick* sound of slippers slowly sliding across the floor started my way. Sammy's head popped up, and he gazed expectantly toward the kitchen, his tail beating a happy rhythm against his bed.

Unbidden, I remembered a movie where a woman kidnapped an injured man just to torture him. I could just imagine an evil-looking middle-aged woman coming through the door. Someone I would be able to easily dislike.

But it wasn't like that.

My eyes widened as a much younger woman came into view— twenty, if that. Easily a college student. She was a little shorter than average and had a slender build with short, dirty blonde hair that hung in loose natural curls around her pleasant face. She wore no makeup, unless you wanted to count the smudge of soot on her cheek, and was dressed in a long-sleeve camo t-shirt and bib overalls. Her thick yellow socks and pink bedroom slippers were the icing on the cake. Comfort seemed to be her style. Behind her, she dragged a wooden dining room chair. While her cheeks had a healthy glow, she projected a resigned sadness, like she was the prisoner instead of me.

But what I couldn't take my eyes off was her belly. I stared at it in shock. It was huge on her petite frame. The words tumbled out before I could stop them.

"You're pregnant."

She chuckled, and for the barest moment, her bright blue eyes twinkled. "No shit, Sherlock. I figured that out about seven months ago."

A pregnant woman had captured me? It didn't seem possible. How had she managed it? And she did it alone? Was she a superwoman or something? I had imagined all kinds of horrid things, but never this. I thought my brain was going to explode. I couldn't look away from her.

She placed the chair next to Sammy and lowered herself carefully into it. Settling back, she folded her hands across her belly. She was amused. "I can pull up my shirt so you can get a better look. It might help you put your eyes back in your head."

I blushed and glanced away. "Sorry."

"Don't be. It does kinda stand out."

I wasn't sure what to say.

The chair creaked as she shifted and tried to get comfortable. "Let's cut through some of the crap, shall we? My name is Trudessa Goodman, although I prefer Trudi. I was a sophomore at JMU until all this mess happened. And since I know you'll ask, I'm about thirty weeks along." She reached over to give Sammy's head a scratch. The dog leaned into it, loving the attention. "And this is Sammy. He's my protector. Aren't you, boy?"

His tail beat a happy rhythm against the floor, and Trudi's eyes shone warmly with affection.

But her gaze chilled as her attention shifted back to me. "What about you, mister?"

"Eyrian Dreal. I lived in Norfolk, although I was at my parents in Richmond when everything went crazy. I worked as an electrical engineer for DVA Power. A lot of good it does me now."

Her expression was flat. "I was a nursing major. Wanted to get my RN and go into pediatrics."

I nodded. "At least you had training in something useful." I leaned forward with a wry smile. "Engineering jobs have dried up recently."

The corner of her mouth curled up with the hint of a smile, briefly cracking her stoic expression. "I can imagine." But she quickly disciplined herself. Her eyes traced over me—assessing me, no detail missed. Not in a malicious way, but more like a farmer sizing up a horse or a sheep. Then it hit me. This was an interview, and I had no idea what the job was. Not that I cared. I had my own agenda.

"I'm sorry I was on your property," I said. "I'm just passing through and didn't know this had been claimed. If you let me go, I'll be out of here before you know it."

She ignored my question. Instead, she reached over and gave Sammy a few more loving strokes. I found myself wishing she would hurry and get this over with.

"Where's the rest of your group?" she asked without looking up. "The few survivors I've encountered have been banding together."

I shook my head. "I don't have a group. I've been traveling alone."

She looked back in my direction. "Kicked out?"

"No, joining up with others wouldn't work for me. I've got something I need to do."

"And what's that?"

I considered telling her but decided it was between me and my wife. "It's private."

She settled back in her chair, suspicion flickering across her bright blue eyes. "How did you survive the crazies, then, Mister Dreal?"

"You can call me Eyrian."

Her expression remained flat. "I'm not sure we're to that point yet, *Mister* Dreal."

I frowned. "And why not, *Miss Goodman?*"

She leaned forward. Her eyes probed mine like she knew something more was there. "You're deflecting, Mister Dreal. Now, how did you survive?"

I paused. I wasn't about to tell her about Geri. "Hid mostly. I was close to the center of whatever happened, but it was mostly over in a couple of days. I hid out with my wife until things settled."

"What happened to her?"

"The craziness got her."

The young woman nodded in understanding.

"What about you?" I asked.

"My brother and I were at JMU when it happened. We thought coming back home would get us away from all the destruction."

"Where's your brother?"

She inclined her head to her left. "Out back."

I frowned. "I thought you said you were alone?"

Trudi considered me—sadness flicked across her face. "He's under the oak tree in a grave as deep as I could bury him."

"Did the craziness get him?"

She shook her head. "Aaron was shot."

I hadn't expected that. "I'm sorry."

She shrugged, her expression unchanging.

"Who shot him?"

"The baddies."

We studied each other.

Baddies. I remembered the people I'd observed not too far from here. The name certainly fit. I wondered if they were the same.

I gazed at her levelly. "I'm not one of those."

She gave an angry frown. "I'm not sure I believe you, Mister Dreal." She slowly got up from her chair. Sammy's tail started thumping against the floor again.

"Please," I begged. "Just give me my things, and I'll be out of here in no time."

She ignored me and walked out of sight into the kitchen. A moment later, she returned carrying my backpack. I tried not to show any emotion.

Easing back into her chair, she set the bag in her lap and picked through its contents—beef jerky, power bars, and extra clothes were tossed on the floor. Sammy took this as an invitation to investigate.

Trudi didn't even look up. "Stay."

The dog promptly sat but continued to eye the jerky.

Digging in one more time, she pulled out my mobile phone. My breath caught. It held my only pictures of Wendy.

Trudi hunted for the power button.

"Don't!" I leaped up. "The battery is almost out, and I don't have a way to charge it."

But she pressed it anyway—it beeped as it started up.

I clenched my fists.

She looked up when it came to the unlock screen. "What's the passcode?"

I just scowled at her.

She rolled her eyes. "What are you afraid of? That I'll wipe out your checking account or post your dirty pictures." She snorted. "Or maybe I'll just text the President."

I looked away.

"All right," she said. I heard a series of clicks and then a beep. "That's one."

My head snapped back in her direction. There was no way she could guess it.

She did it again. "That's two." She lowered the phone. Her gaze was colder than ice. "You realize all I have to do is enter a fake password eight more times, and it will lock. And I happen to know the support number no longer works."

I went to the limit of my chain. *Wendy's pictures will be lost!*

Trudi held my gaze as her thumb typed in another random code. It beeped again. "I think that's three times. Seven more to go." She started typing again.

"Wait!" I said, shaking in frustration.

Her thumb froze. Her unwavering blue eyes locked with mine. There was no malice, only a grim determination. And I knew she would do it.

I sighed and gave her the code.

One of her eyebrows went up. "What's so special about November 25th from two years ago?"

I just looked at her. I didn't want to answer—but was afraid not to. "It's the date I proposed to my wife."

She nodded and turned back to the phone, entering the code and flipping through it. She paused, studying something on the screen. "Was this your wife?"

She flipped the phone around, displaying the last picture I had taken of Wendy. It was at a restaurant the night before things had gone crazy. My parents had taken us out, and I just thought she looked beautiful. Seeing her made my heart ache.

"Yeah," I studied the floor, ashamed of my weakness and the longing the picture invoked.

She turned the phone back around and examined it a moment more. "Your wife was pretty." She swallowed. "She looked like a nice person."

"She was," I said softly.

Trudi scrolled a few more times and then hit the power button, turning off my phone.

She carefully set the phone down and pulled out the last item. Wendy's book.

I held my breath as she carefully opened the cover and read what was written inside. I knew exactly what it said. "To my dearest love."

"You gave this to your wife?" she asked gently.

"Yes," I whispered.

She closed it and looked up at me. "You must have loved her a lot."

"I did."

Her expression grew puzzled. She cocked her head to one side. "This doesn't make sense. What are you running away from?"

I shook my head and glanced down. I'd shared as much as I wanted.

She kept staring at me. I fidgeted in discomfort. Her scrutiny was unnerving in its intensity—like she refused to let any secret stay hidden.

"Just let me go," I pleaded. "I don't want any trouble."

Trudi pursed her lips. "Listen, Mister Dreal. I'm sorry, but I'm trying to decide whether to keep you or shoot you. And honestly, shooting you would be a lot safer. You wouldn't be my first."

A wave of panic washed over me. *Keep calm.* I told myself. *You can do this.*

"Just let me have my phone and my book. You can keep everything else. Just let me go."

She pursed her lips—that same stubborn determination hardened her expression. "Mister Dreal. Would you say that your wife was the most important thing in the world to you?"

I blinked in surprise. "Of course. She was my everything."

"If it would have kept her alive, would you have killed for her? Murdered someone to keep her alive? Would you have gone that far for her?"

My mouth opened, but no words came out. The question took me completely off guard, but there was no hiding from the answer. I considered lying and giving her my pre-Judgement answer. But I felt she would somehow know. "Yes," I finally answered. "I'd hate to do it. But I guess I would."

Her chin came up slightly, and her bright eyes misted for just a moment. "As would I."

She returned everything to the bag and stood, clutching it to her chest. Sammy trotted over, and she gave his head a loving pat.

"I have to think." She stepped toward the kitchen.

I rushed forward to the extent of my chain. "Please! Let me go," I begged. "I swear I won't hurt you."

She froze in place—her grip on the bag tightened. "You see, Mister Dreal. That's the problem. I've been told that before." She stepped out of sight.

"They lied."

CHAPTER
FOUR

SHORTLY AFTER OUR discussion, Trudi placed another tray outside my door containing two peanut butter and jelly biscuits, a water bottle, and a sealed bag of chips.

"Lunch," she simply said and walked away.

I was puzzled at first. We'd just eaten breakfast. But when I heard a heavy door slam, I knew. She and Sammy had left me alone, chained, and with only a ticking clock for company. I nearly panicked. *What if she doesn't come back?*

But I calmed when I looked at the chair Trudi had used when we talked. It sat exactly where she had left it, meaning she would be back. There was unfinished business. Her leaving was a power play to show she was in charge and to make me easier to handle.

I took a deep breath and let it out slowly—my resolve strengthened. She'd find I wasn't so easy.

The hours passed slowly as I waited. Very slowly. I watched the shadows grow as the sun moved from morning to late afternoon.

I spent my alone time going over the room yet again, looking for anything I could use to escape. I pulled out the dresser drawers, searched in the corners, and even crawled under the bed. Nothing.

It wasn't until I lifted the mattress that I found something. A single sheet of notebook paper with a note written in a looping, feminine scrawl—*Made You Look!* She had even drawn a heart on it.

I couldn't help but laugh. The bitch. She knew I'd search there. It spoke volumes about her ability to plan. She might not be old enough to drink, but you had to admire her intelligence. I was no dummy, but Trudi was on a whole different level. In one brief conversation, she discovered all my weak points while giving up none of hers. I sighed. If I was going to escape, that needed to change. I needed to seriously up my game.

With nothing else to do, I lay on the bed and thought about my captor. She still hadn't told me what she intended. Only that she had her reasons.

I still couldn't get over her pregnancy. She said thirty weeks, but it had to be more than that. Her belly looked like it was about to explode. She must have miscalculated. That timing would mean she got pregnant about a month after the Judgement. Had her boyfriend been shot along with Aaron?

And why was she alone? She'd asked why I hadn't joined a group, but a better question might be, why hadn't *she* joined one? In these times, a pregnant woman by herself seemed like suicide. There must be more to her story.

My musings were interrupted by a door opening. A few minutes later, Sammy trotted into the den and flopped down in his bed, resuming his watch. Trudi did not make an appearance.

Pots clanked in the kitchen, and a short while later, my nose was teased by the most wonderful smell. *Was that fried chicken?* The last fried chicken I'd had was at the restaurant the night before things went crazy. I'd given Wendy a bite—

I shoved the memory away. *No! I needed to focus.*

But the memory fought back. I buried my head in my hands and sank to the floor—my breath came in gasps, and my pulse pounded in my ears. You'd think that after all this time, the pain would have subsided. But it hadn't. It seemed to have gotten worse.

I flashed back to that day. I was *there* as I opened the door to the garage—Mom's ancient minivan, drips of oil on the gray concrete, the musty smell of things stored for too long. Then, finally, looking up to see Wendy hanging there. Lifeless. Dead. Her neck at an angle it shouldn't be. The sense of failure that crushed my heart and drove me to my knees.

I hadn't been strong enough to save her. I should have strung up a rope right beside her and joined her.

I had to make it right. I had to follow her wishes and be with her again.

I promised!

Trudi's voice jerked me back. "Are you all right?"

I looked up with tears on my face. Trudi stood just outside the door wearing a concerned expression and holding a plate with something fried, a piece of bread, and beans.

I looked away, wiping my eyes with the back of my hand. "Sorry, the smell must have been hurting my eyes. Frying chicken does that sometimes."

When I turned back, her eyes were sad with understanding. She knew exactly what I was feeling. The loss. The pain.

"Don't worry," she said, her stoic face returning. "It's not chicken."

Her statement distracted me. *What?* I looked at the plate more closely.

"Rabbit," she explained. "I haven't seen a chicken in months. We bred the intelligence right out of them. And the ones that did survive stay clear because they know they taste pretty damn good."

She set the plate on the tray in front of the door. "Eat. Before Sammy decides it's meant for him." She used her back scratcher to push it toward me.

She joined me in her chair while I sat on the floor, and we ate in silence, almost reverently. It's amazing the memories that are connected with food—the time Dad brought home a bucket of chicken after a winning game, or when Wendy and I split the last piece the store had. Good memories.

I glanced at Trudi, her head bowed over her plate. I wondered what memories she was having. They were likely a mix of good and bad, just like mine.

When only the bones were left, I set my plate aside. "Thank you for the food," I said. "You're a good cook."

"I've had to learn." She pointed to my plate. "Push your tray to me. I don't dare trust Sammy with those bones."

I did as she requested. As she turned away, I couldn't help but ask one more time. "Please let me go. Just give me my phone and book. I promise not to bother you."

She considered me for a moment but then went to the kitchen without a word.

I thought our conversation over, but she quickly returned and sat back in her chair, resting her hands protectively over her pregnant belly. As she settled, her gaze locked solidly with mine, lips pursed, and a subtle tension stiffening her neck and shoulders.

"What if I need you to stay?" she asked softly.

I blinked at her as the words sank in. "Why?"

She squirmed in her seat. "I'm due soon. While I don't know for sure, I think I'm carrying twins. And with two, there are often times… complications. For both me and my babies."

I shrugged. "So what's that got to do with me?"

Those bright blue eyes seemed to look right into my soul. "I need you to help me deliver my babies."

I blinked at her in shock. "*What!* No. Absolutely no way. I am *not* a doctor and know nothing about having babies."

"I'm not much better," she said calmly, holding my gaze. "But my babies are more important to me than anything, and I'm gonna do my best to ensure they survive. If that means I have to maim or kill, I will." Her eyes narrowed. "I'll even hold someone prisoner if I have to."

Her words were chilling, but comments from the day before suddenly made sense. *Would you kill to save someone you love?* I shook my head. My finger stabbed the floor beside me. "This is insane! I can't do it. There's got to be someone else. Even if I agreed, I'd end up killing you."

She looked toward the front of the house. "Since I found out, I've been waiting and hoping for somebody to help me. I had almost given up." Her gaze returned to mine. "Then I saw your campfire. I won't get another opportunity, Mister Dreal. It has to be you. I'll deliver in only a few weeks, so there is no more time."

I shook my head in frustration. "*A few weeks!* I can't stay that long. Wendy is waiting for me."

Her eyes drew down in puzzlement. "I thought you said your wife had died."

I stared at her without offering an answer, but damn her, she figured it out anyway.

Her eyes grew wide in realization. "You're gonna kill yourself to be with your dead wife."

There was no point in remaining silent. I took a deep breath and let it out slowly, trying to control my growing agitation. "I kept Wendy safe for three days, but on the fourth, I passed out from exhaustion, and Wendy hung herself." I met her steady gaze head-on. "She left me a note that said we'd meet at the place where I proposed on our special day. That's where I'm headed. I made a promise."

Trudi frowned, looking like she was working on a complex math problem. "Something's not adding up. I'm missing a piece." She thought for a moment, then snapped her fingers. "You can't find the place."

I groaned. *Could I keep no secrets from this lady?*

I crossed my arms. "A blog listed it as an unusual location to propose, and if it hadn't listed the GPS coordinates, I wouldn't have found it." My hands curled into fists, my frustration growing. "But the crazies fried the damned GPS satellites and destroyed all the landmarks. So, yes. I'm having trouble." I again stabbed the floor with my finger. "But I *will* find it. I know it was in a federal reserve with a cliff facing the west—"

Trudi interrupted. "Did the trail pass between two huge boulders and take you over a stone bridge with a small waterfall?"

My mouth came open. "Yeah, it did."

She must know where it is. But I refused to ask her to take me there. That would just give her even more to hold over me.

Trudi cocked her head to one side. "So, you were gonna throw yourself off the cliff into her arms?"

I gritted my teeth. "No. That's what the gun was for. If I jumped, I might end up breaking my back and spending days in agony before passing. I wanted something I could count on."

Her eyes softened for just a moment. And it infuriated me. I didn't need her pity. *I was going to join Wendy!*

But her expression immediately hardened. "Is that why your phone and that book are so important to you? Are they part of your suicide ritual?"

I knew where she was going. She wanted to use those against me. I glared at her without answering. A full minute passed as we stared at each other, neither giving an inch.

I finally broke the silence. "I'm sorry about your babies, but I can't help you. So just let me go be with Wendy."

Trudi cocked her jaw, and her eyes narrowed. She stood and went to the kitchen, returning a moment later with my backpack and a steel bucket. The clang of the bucket sounded ominous as she placed it in front of her chair. She sat and pulled out my book, laying it across her knees. I eyed it nervously, knowing this couldn't be good.

"I haven't got time for your suicidal nonsense. I'm not a shrink, so I can only see one way to do this." She frowned as if tasting something sour. "Mister Dreal, I have no other options. You're gonna help me deliver my babies…"

She paused, her face devoid of emotion.

"Or I'll burn your book."

I sucked a breath in horror. I jumped to my feet. "Don't…"

Holding up my book, she pulled a little plastic lighter out of her pocket. She flicked it once, and it brought up a tiny flame, bright in the dim room. It cast a dark shadow over the delicate curves of her face, turning it into a mask of grim determination. She took no pleasure in this, but she would do it for the one important thing in her life—her babies.

"It's just a book," she said softly. "Not even an important one."

My eyes flicked from the book to the flame. The gold lettering of its title flashed in the light. "Please don't..."

She moved the flame closer to the book.

I leaped toward her, but my chain caught, and I fell hard on the floor.

"Stop!" I yelled, reaching for her. "Don't do it."

The flame moved closer.

In panic, I blurted out, "I'll stay. Just don't..."

She flicked off the lighter.

She set the book gently on my backpack and nudged the bucket away with her foot.

"Here's the deal. I'm gonna hide your phone and book in a place you'll never find. After my babies are born, I'll give them back, and you're free to go. And to sweeten the bargain, I'll take you to your cliff. I know exactly where it is. So you have a choice. Stay with me, and keep your book safe. Or leave, and I burn it. The choice is yours."

She stood and walked away.

"Think it over, Mister Dreal."

I sank to the floor and put my head in my hands. I couldn't imagine how this could get any worse.

* * *

I lay on the floor with the quilt wrapped around me. The house was chilly tonight—kind of expected for late-October in the mountains. But it was the cold in my heart that affected me more.

The events of the day dredged up all kinds of feelings and memories. Some days, it felt like Wendy was whispering to me. Calling me. My fingers ached to touch the one reminder of my wife.

And it was being kept from me. A smoldering anger burned in my chest. I couldn't believe the gall of that woman to think she could blackmail me into helping her. I did feel for her. Being pregnant in this screwed-up world was terrible. But I had my own problems. My own hurt. And I wanted this pain to stop. I wanted to meet with Wendy again. I wanted out of this new world.

I realized I was probably suffering from a combination of depression and survivor syndrome. And only God knows what was in the syringe Geri used. He claimed it was to save me. I'd rather have died—just slipped quietly into my own madness.

The house was silent, save for the faint ticking of a clock. There was no wind tonight, so there wasn't even the sound of the leaves rustling. In the distance, I heard an owl hoot.

Logically, I should just tell her to burn the damn book. Wendy would surely welcome me if I didn't use it. But the thought of it being lost, or even worse, destroyed, almost made me sick. The bitch had me, and she knew it.

In the room's silence, I heard soft mumbling from outside my room, probably from Trudi's bedroom. *Great, she talks in her sleep.*

"No," I heard distinctly. "Please..." She sounded like she was begging. "NO!" And then there was the most blood-curdling scream I think I had ever heard.

I jumped from my covers and went to the door to the limit of my tether. I listened, wondering if maybe someone had gotten in the house.

"Are you all right?" I called. I tried not to be too concerned about her, but at the same time, she did have the key to my shackle. If something happened to her, I'd be in a heap of trouble.

I heard movement from her room, and then she shuffled into the den. She was nothing but a shadow and ventured a little closer to my door than she meant to. She jumped when she noticed me standing in the doorway. "Shit, you scared me." She put a hand over her heart.

I wanted to scream at her to let me go. But I forced my anger aside and tried to make light of it. "It's not like I'm going anywhere."

"Yeah." She took a deep breath and ran a hand through her mussed hair. Her hand was shaking. "Sorry I woke you. It's just—" She looked off into the distance.

I couldn't help but complete the thought for her. "The dreams."

She didn't speak for a moment. "Yeah." She started to turn away but paused. "I'm gonna fix a cup of tea. Would you like one?"

Maybe I could make one last plea to let me go. "Sure."

She shuffled to the kitchen, and I heard her shifting things around. Sammy trotted by, no doubt hearing sounds from the kitchen and thinking he might get a handout. The dog had a one-track mind.

She returned a short while later and set the mug down on the tray in front of the doorway. She pushed it toward me with her back scratcher, and I sat down cross-legged while she took her seat in the talking chair.

We silently sipped our teas.

I never cared much for hot tea, especially without lots of sugar. But I thought being nice might work in my favor. "It's good," I offered politely.

"Decaf," she said. "And without sugar, it tastes like shit."

I nearly choked. "It's not that bad."

"Yeah, it is. But I can't afford to waste sugar. The ants can smell it a mile away, and it's hard to find any that they haven't gotten to first."

We took another sip.

"Do you want to talk about it? The dream?" I asked softly.

She gave a deep sigh and shook her head. "Not especially." She took a sip of hers. "What about yours?"

"Same."

"Thought so."

She was silent for a moment. "Sucks, doesn't it?"

"Yeah." I took another sip. "It does."

We sat in silence as we finished our tea. Sammy came over, and she petted him before finally standing and stretching. "I'm going back to bed."

She turned away, but I called after her. "Is it me that triggered your dream?"

She paused. "What do you mean?"

"Holding me captive. Feeling guilty."

She shook her head. "No." I noticed her hand gently rub her belly. "It's definitely *nothing* to do with you."

She shuffled back to her bedroom, each step slow and deliberate, like the gallows awaited her. If her dreams were anything close to mine, the gallows might be just a little less painful.

When I heard the faint creak of her returning to bed, I lay down on my pallet and resumed staring at the ceiling. Trudi was such an odd character. She could be stoic and harsh, then turn right around and be caring and friendly. And the way she talked about her babies? It reminded me of the saying, "Never get between a momma bear and her cubs." Trudi was definitely the momma bear.

I sighed. Sadly, Trudi was not a bad person and was being as considerate as possible. Under other circumstances, I think I would like her. No, this messed up world was forcing her—

It suddenly dawned on me why she really needed me.

She was afraid. Pure and simple. The world had shifted under her feet, and she was terrified.

But she also struck me as a proud woman—fiercely independent and used to dealing with her own problems. Giving up wasn't part of her constitution. Then I came along and she suddenly had a way to regain some measure of control. The consequences be damned.

I lay looking at the ceiling, thinking about her offer and waiting for sleep.

Could I force her to tell me where she hid the book? Put *her* on the business end of the shotgun?

The idea was tempting—take her weapon and force her to tell me. But the picture of a momma bear came to mind. Backed into a corner, she would come out all teeth and claws to protect her cubs. And she would not stop until the threat was gone. If I went that route, I would have prepared for the worst.

I might even have to kill her.

The thought chilled me. Did I want to kill a pregnant woman protecting her unborn babies? My mind flashed to her lying with a bloody hole in her chest. I shuddered and shoved the thought away. As bad as I wanted my book, I just couldn't bring myself to go that far. I was confident Wendy wouldn't approve either.

I shook my head. No. There had to be another way. If only she liked me just a little...

My eyes widened as a new thought occurred to me.

What if I could make her think I was on her side and get her to trust me? Maybe even worm my way into her heart. She may be smarter than me, but she had human needs.

The thought of deceiving her felt wrong, but it was better than physically hurting her. Still, I couldn't afford to screw around. I only had a month before I had to be at Wendy's special place.

And while I was subtly trying to get close to her, I'd search for my book and find it on my own. It was probably under her mattress or in her underwear drawer.

I felt hope for the first time since my capture. I knew what to do. Accept her offer, but bail on her at the first opportunity. It wasn't perfect, but it would work. I couldn't help but smile.

Trudie Goodman, you've just met your match.

CHAPTER
FIVE

———————————

I AROSE JUST AS the den was getting brighter. Sammy was already in his spot, lying with his head on his paws and tracking my every move. Unlike the previous morning, the house was quiet, which meant Trudi wasn't up yet.

I did my morning business and then went to sit on the floor by the door. I passed the time by trying to get Sammy to come to me, but the best I could do was get an aggravated growl.

About an hour later, I heard the floor creak and movement from Trudi's bedroom. She came shuffling into the den in her ever-present slippers and wearing a pink housecoat. Her hair was sleep-mussed, and she looked quite groggy. She glanced my way and grunted but didn't stop to talk and trudged on to the kitchen. I smiled. Someone must have had trouble getting back to sleep.

I heard the clanking of dishes in the kitchen, and she came back a bit later with instant oatmeal and a cup of coffee on a tray. She pushed them to me before getting her own. She took her spot in her chair. It was almost comical watching the relief on her face as she sipped her coffee.

I picked up my bowl. "I didn't think you could drink coffee while pregnant." I took a taste of the oatmeal and nodded in approval. Maple walnut flavor.

She glared at me over the rim of her cup. "Ask me if I care." She took another sip.

I couldn't help but chuckle.

She set her coffee down. "I can have a cup now and then."

I took a sip of mine. It was instant but not bad. Could use a little sugar with it.

We ate in silence. When I was done, I slid my tray across the floor in Sammy's direction. He pounced on it but was sorely disappointed in the oatmeal. He half-heartedly licked it.

Trudi set her bowl down and studied me over her coffee. "Did you think about my offer?"

I studied her. "Yes, but I have questions."

She took a sip of coffee and motioned for me to continue.

"I don't understand why you think you're going to have trouble with the birth. You'll likely not have any problems."

"And you're an expert now?"

"No. That's not what I meant. From what little I know, most women deliver just fine."

She drained the rest of her coffee and set her cup aside. She leaned back in her chair and gazed at me levelly. "My family history says otherwise. My grandmother wouldn't stop bleeding when she had my mom and aunt. She had to have an emergency hysterectomy. My aunt and cousin each had problems with breech births. And my mother..." She shifted uncomfortably in her chair. "…died after giving birth to me and Aaron. She had a stroke."

I froze with my coffee halfway to my lips, staring at her in disbelief. "I'm not a doctor. I wouldn't be able to help in those situations."

She shrugged. "I know, but since I'm having twins, I want to be as prepared as I can. With the proper training, someone might be able to save my babies… and me."

I just stared at her.

She licked her lips and continued, "I've collected training materials and what tools I could find. I can show you what I learned." She smiled, trying to project confidence. "We can do this."

"You're crazy."

"No." She sighed deeply. "I'm desperate."

I put my head in my hands. *God help me. This woman wanted to put her life in my hands, and I was planning to leave at the first chance.*

I looked up at her. "Suppose I do as you ask, and you end up dying anyway? What about my book and phone?"

Her expression went cold, drained of every trace of emotion. "Then you better not let me die."

I got up and walked further into my room. I crossed my arms and stood staring at the wall. This was so messed up. I was going to feel like an ass when I left.

I thought of Wendy and the promise I made to her. I had to get my book back. I sighed. I was desperate, too. In some respects, I was no better than this crazy woman.

I faced Trudi. "I'll do it."

Her eyebrows went up in surprise. "So you agree to stay with me until my babies are born and help with the delivery?"

"Yes," I said reluctantly.

She stood to face me, her eyes searching mine. "Say it."

I blinked at her. "What?"

"I want to hear you promise it to me." She put a hand on her belly. "In this new world, spoken words have power. Promise me you will help deliver my babies."

I felt so guilty. This lady was trusting me, and I was going to abandon her. But to be back with Wendy, I would do it.

I took a big breath. I looked right into her bright blue eyes, filled with desperate hope, and gave her the words she craved.

"I promise to stay with you until your babies are born. And I will do my best to help you and them survive."

She didn't hesitate. "And in exchange, I promise to give you your phone, book, and the cliff location."

Her head tilted to one side as she gazed at me, one hand absent-mindedly stroking her belly. I tried to keep my face neutral—afraid she would see the lie.

She abruptly picked up the tray and took it to the kitchen, returning a moment later with the shotgun. I grew concerned. *Was this lady that crazy?*

She stopped in front of me, but her stance was nonthreatening, and the muzzle pointed at the ceiling. She tossed me a key. "These are to your shackles."

I knelt down and unlocked the leg cuffs. I wasn't sure what she was planning with that gun, but I thought it best to rush her and take that weapon away from her. But to my surprise, she stepped forward and held it out to me.

"Let's get this over with. I know you were lying about staying with me. I can feel it. My best guess is that you're gonna take my gun and then threaten me with it." Her eyes were so bright this close—they had a weary sadness in them.

I wasn't sure what to do.

"Go ahead." She held it closer. "Take it. It's what you want."

I cautiously wrapped my fingers around the cold weapon, making sure it was pointed safely toward the ceiling.

But she stepped closer and gripped the barrel, angling it down until it was tucked under her chin. "Go ahead and pull the trigger. Put me out of my misery. I can't watch my babies die."

Her bizarre behavior unnerved me. I wasn't sure what to do except keep my finger well away from the trigger.

She stepped closer, the barrel tightening against her throat. "I've got a ticking time bomb in my belly, Mister Dreal." Her voice was just above a whisper. "I just *know* something is gonna happen during childbirth. Without your help, I'm a dead woman. So if you're gonna do something, just do it now and get it over with. If you don't want to use the gun, there are knives in the kitchen. And you can beat me if you want. I've been beaten before." Her gaze hardened, and her lip trembled. "But I swear to God, I won't tell you where your book is. It will die with me, and you will *never* find it."

This was not how I imagined this conversation going. She stared into my eyes without a trace of fear. Death didn't scare her. I wondered what had happened to make her this way. You had to admire the courage of someone who could look death in the eye and not budge.

I pointed the muzzle away from her. "You are one crazy pregnant lady. But I won't hurt you. I'm not one of your baddies." And to emphasize the point, I handed her the gun.

She gave a sad smile as she took it. "I know. You can still leave, though."

"Not without my book."

She nodded. "I will keep my word."

I could detect no hint of a lie in her gaze. "Then I guess we have a deal."

I held out my hand to shake, but she eyed it with disdain and made no move to take it. Her eyes returned to mine. "I'll shake, but let's wait a little bit. There's one last thing we need to take care of."

I frowned. "Oh? What's that?"

"You're filthy, and you smell worse than a dead skunk."

Before I could say another word, she directed me down a hallway to a simple but well-decorated country bathroom. The room's bright yellow walls had been stenciled with spring flowers, and the air scented with lavender. On the sink counter sat a bar of soap, clean towels, deodorant, and two types of shampoo. But there had been a few post-Judgement changes. The one high window had been painted over like the one in my room, with a small battery lantern providing light from the corner. A water pitcher rested beside the sink, and three water-filled buckets sat in the standard white bathtub.

Trudi faced me. "Bend down," she ordered.

I hesitated, unsure of what she wanted. When I didn't move, she rolled up her shirt sleeves and pulled my head down. She picked through my hair. "Ew... gross. I knew it. You've got lice."

"What?" I said, jerking away from her. I cringed at the thought of little crawlers in my hair.

She immediately used the water in the pitcher to wash her

hands in the sink. "Use the medicated shampoo and make sure all the water goes down the drain and not on the floor. Rinse your head well, and don't forget to shampoo down there, too."

"Down where?"

She rolled her eyes and patted above her crotch. "Down there. From your appearance, I'm assuming you're not the kind that likes to go bare."

I blushed.

She stepped toward the door. "If you use the toilet, pour some water in it to make it flush. Thank goodness the septic tank still works." She pointed to the bathtub. "Put your clothes in one of the empty buckets. We'll wash them when we do your bedding. And clean up after yourself. I'm not your maid." She marched out the door, closing it behind her.

I blinked after her, not sure about the whirlwind that had just gone through.

It was then I noticed the full-length mirror on the back of the door. I froze. A rough-looking man with a scruffy beard and snarled oily hair stared back at me. His clothes were filthy and hung loose on his thin body. But it was the eyes that spoke the loudest—haunted in the way of someone who had lost everything. It was a man I did not know.

If I examined myself honestly, I was surprised Trudi hadn't shot me on sight. There weren't many people left, but surely she could have found someone better than me.

I rooted around in the vanity's drawer and found a pair of scissors and a razor. I used them to remove my facial hair and shave. Then I bathed carefully, the cold water running off in brown and dirty rivulets. I scrubbed every inch of myself until my skin was pink. I also used the special shampoo despite the overwhelming medicinal smell. Twice. And yes, I did use it 'down there.' I wanted those buggers *dead*.

While I was freezing when I finished, it felt good to be clean.

I wrapped a towel around my waist and opened the door to find a neatly folded sweatshirt, sweatpants, and white socks on the floor outside. I took the clothes and dressed, glad to have their warmth in the chill house.

With dirty clothes in a bucket, I stepped outside to find Sammy waiting at the end of the hall. He watched me warily as I made my way through the den and toward the sound of vegetables being chopped.

As I entered the kitchen, the smell of baking bread filled the air, and a bright red pot bubbled merrily on the stove. Trudi had her back to me but was busily cutting up onions, and I had to say—it smelled good.

The kitchen itself would have been considered modern by pre-Judgement standards. Floor-to-ceiling cabinets lined one wall, with what I assumed was a pantry door off to the side. A propane stovetop was built into the counter, with a raised double oven beside it. Over the sink, a window with frilly, daffodil-yellow curtains let in ample sunlight and offered a view of the backyard. A dead refrigerator sat in the corner, a silent reminder that things were different now.

"Nice kitchen," I offered.

Trudi didn't answer. She glanced over her shoulder and then did a double take, her frown turning into surprise. She quickly turned away and immediately went back to her chopping. "You look better," she commented.

"Thanks." I stepped up to the big red pot. "What are you cooking?" I glanced in to find it almost full of partially heated, clear water. "Oh, and here's my clothes. Not sure what you want me to do with them."

She continued chopping but asked, "Did you clean up after yourself?"

"The bathroom? I think so."

"All water down the drain?"

"Yeah."

"Hair?"

"Down the toilet. I saved a little to flush after I was done."

She nodded and put down her knife. She went to the pantry and returned with a big plastic trash bag. "Put your bed linens in here. Including the quilt."

"Why?"

She folded her arms but had to do it over her baby bulge. "Because you contaminated everything with your bugs. Now it needs to be cleaned so you don't get reinfested." She frowned. "Or infest me." She shivered. "I'm gonna confess right now. I'm a clean freak, and bugs make me crazy."

I wasn't sure I liked being ordered around, but I was trying to play nice, so I did as she asked.

We went out on the back porch where a strange, stainless steel monstrosity sat. The laundry detergent bottle beside it hinted that it was a washing machine, but I had no clue how to use it. It had a lever attached to a tub, so I assumed you manually rocked the clothes like a cradle. I wondered where she got it.

"Since you contaminated everything," Trudi said. "You get to wash them."

I frowned, my irritation growing. "Hey, I was perfectly happy with the way I was. You're the one—"

She cut me off. "Bitch at me later. We're losing daylight, and if they don't get dry in time, you'll be sleeping on damp sheets."

She then quickly ran through how it worked and gave me instructions on washing, wringing out the water, and where to hang them to dry.

When done, she abruptly turned and left. I stared after her. Why was she being so short with me? I'd accepted her offer. Seems like she'd be a little kinder. I shook my head. How could I get close to her if she didn't even talk to me? I decided to stick with my plan and see how it went.

It took me until noon to get all the washing done and hung up to dry. It was a crisp fall day, but still cool. I wondered if the bed linens would be ready by bedtime.

I went back inside and plopped down at the kitchen table, amazed at how hard that had been. I was exhausted and surprised at how out of shape I had gotten.

Trudi had made us chicken salad biscuits, so we sat down at the table to eat. Trudi was quiet and seemed to just be tolerating me. I thought a little small talk might help lighten things up.

"Doing the laundry was harder than I thought," I said. "You must have arms of steel by now."

She didn't even glance my way, just continued to nibble at her biscuit.

I made another attempt. "So, do you have names picked out for your babies?"

"Yes," she answered, irritation in her voice.

Why was she being like this? "Are they secret?" I asked politely, trying to conceal my own irritation.

She was silent for a moment, then looked at me with her piercing blue eyes. Disappointment and anger reflected from them. "You know it's not gonna work, don't you?"

Confused, I shook my head. "What's not going to work?"

"Getting me to drop my guard. I'm not completely stupid."

I blinked at her in surprise. *Had she guessed my plan?*

"I was just making conversation," I explained. "Nothing more."

She gazed at me coolly. "You're being the perfect gentleman, hoping this lonely girl will be so *taken* with you that she'll tell you all her secrets. Sorry, it's not gonna work, *Mister* Dreal. I need you for one thing and one thing only. Boyfriend is not one of them."

I just looked at her, not sure what to say. Was this lady a mind-reader or something? I frowned. "Don't get yourself worked up. You're making me stay against my will, so I thought I would make it more bearable by being cordial."

"I liked it better when you acted like an asshole. At least you were being honest."

She crammed the last bite of her sandwich into her mouth and then snatched up my plate with my unfinished biscuit. She put it on the floor, where the ever-vigilant Sammy scarfed it up.

"Hey, I wasn't finished."

Anger flashed in her blue eyes. They were cold pools. "You are now."

Trudi stood up and leaned to within inches of my face. "I know you don't want to be here. I know you will search for your book when I turn my back. And I know you'll leave at your first opportunity. If nothing else, be honest with me and quit telling *lies*."

Tears threatened her eyes. She turned away and stomped off into the kitchen. "Damn hormones."

The woman was totally pissing me off. I yelled after her. "Well, if you keep being a bitch I *will* leave."

Sammy looked at me like I was an idiot. He sniffed the empty plate and then trotted after his mistress. A few seconds later, the back door slammed shut hard enough to shake the house.

"Shit!" I slammed my fist on the table. *Why was she making this so hard?*

I sat for the next hour, my thoughts circling. I stood up to go three times—but sat back down. I so wanted to just walk away. But then I would remember Wendy's instructions to read the passage she had marked. I'd promised.

But man, Trudi was one super intelligent fucked-up bitch. She seemed to have this sixth sense and could guess my every move. I was playing tic-tac-toe while she was playing world-class chess. *How do you beat that?* I put my head down on the table. I only had two options—leave without my book or stay and search for it. But with her intellect, I was pretty sure finding it would not be easy. No, I needed some hints or for her to slip up. Getting her to be comfortable around me was the only way. *But how?*

It was almost dark when Trudi came back in carrying the laundry. She set it down on the end of the table and gave me the evil eye. Sammy came behind her and threw himself down in his usual resting spot. His eyes flicked between us like he was hoping we'd fight again.

As I watched her, I realized there was only one way this would work—playing it straight. *And pray to God she made a mistake.*

I cleared my throat. Trudi's eyes slid in my direction, but she did not stop folding clothes.

"You're right." I leaned back in my seat and crossed my arms. "I was trying to get on your good side so you would give me clues. I want my book back, just as bad as you want your babies to live. So, here it is. The unvarnished truth."

She put down the sheet she was folding and looked at me expectantly. I stood, putting my hands on the table and leaning toward her.

"I'm terrified of this delivery thing. I do not want to do it—not even sure I can. But I will try. Just remember, I am doing this under duress. I want my book back and will search for it every chance I get. I'll also do my best to make you slip up and reveal a clue to its location. If I find it, I will leave." I licked my lips. "That's the truth and all I can offer. I promise, no more lies."

She turned to face me. Her bright blue eyes locked with mine.

"I will uphold my side of the bargain," she said softly, stepping closer. "In exchange for helping deliver my babies, I will see that you get your phone, your book, and directions to where you proposed to your wife. I understand you will end our agreement as quickly as you can. Just realize I will do everything in my power to keep you by my side. I so swear."

She extended her hand. I glanced at it, then at her. I gripped her much smaller, yet just as strong, hand in mine, and we shook.

At the touch, I couldn't help but admire this crazy woman's determination. While I was angry with her, frustrated beyond belief, I understood what drove her. Admired it even.

But my determination was just as strong as hers. And she would not keep me from rejoining the one I loved.

She was a formidable foe, but I was up to the challenge.

CHAPTER
SIX

TRUDI DECIDED WE should celebrate our bargain and set about preparing a special meal. As for me, I wasn't sure that agreeing to be her prisoner was something I wanted to celebrate. But I didn't say anything and adopted Sammy's approach—when offered free food, take it.

She shooed me out of the kitchen, saying she wanted to surprise me. I took the opportunity to make up my bed and, of course, search for my book. I used putting away the linens as an excuse, reasoning it had to be close by—she hadn't had that much time to hide it.

The linen closet was opposite the bathroom, so while I replaced the towels, I took the opportunity to explore its contents. The first thing that struck me was yellow—in all sorts of different shades and styles. Yellow towels, yellow sheets. She even had some yellow decorative soap in the back corner of the second shelf.

I stepped back from the linen closet but didn't shut the door in case she was listening. Glancing toward the kitchen, I crept to her bedroom door but found it locked—which immediately moved that room up the priority list of likely hiding places. Next time she stepped out, I would pick the lock and search there.

Sighing in disappointment, I searched through a small standing shelf with an odd collection of books, old board games, and a worn deck of cards. They were all neatly stacked, but I didn't think they had been touched in years.

When I turned, I nearly had a heart attack. Trudi stood right behind me with an *I-know-what-you've-been-doing* smirk. "Find what you were looking for?"

"I... ah..."

She shrugged. "I know." She leaned across me and pushed the linen closet door closed. "Sammy's been known to pull out my sheets, so you have to make sure the door is closed. In fact, any door that's closed, make sure it's closed when you're done." Her eyes held a hint of amusement. "Especially my bedroom. If you want to search my underwear drawer, it's the second one from the top." She turned away but called over her shoulder. "Wash up. Dinner's ready."

As I watched her walk away, I couldn't believe this woman. She *knew* where I was going to search. She was treating me like Sammy, knowing I could crap on the floor and taking steps to contain the damage. I wasn't sure how to react to that.

The kitchen table had already been set, now covered with a white tablecloth and one of those fake LED candles for a centerpiece.

I went to my usual place, and a moment later, Trudi came out of the kitchen holding two plates. Sammy was naturally right on her heels.

"Ta-da," she announced playfully. She set my plate in front of me and then plopped down in her seat.

I blinked. That couldn't be what I thought it was.

I looked up at her in shock. "Is that a real hamburger? And french fries?"

She shrugged. "As real as I could make it. I had some canned beef and canned potatoes I'd been saving. I thought this would be the perfect occasion to have it. I even put ketchup, mustard, and a pickle on it." She sighed. "Though the bread is all mine."

I leaned down and inhaled, letting the scent wash over me. "It's... wonderful."

She grinned. "Well, dig in."

And I did. The first bite had a different texture than I expected, but it was definitely a hamburger. I chewed slowly, savoring the flavor. Wendy and I had shared a burger on our first date—a spur-of-the-moment invite that reshaped our lives. It was a good memory and made me miss her.

I reverently tasted a fry. I couldn't help but comment. "All we need now is a shake."

Trudi snorted in amusement. "Chocolate for me. I've been craving them since my fourth month." She sighed. "But that's not gonna happen. It'll be a long time before we have that again."

Something in my engineer brain clicked. I saw how it could be done. I kept quiet because I wasn't sure how Trudi would react. She might think I was trying to manipulate her. But I filed that thought away in case I needed it.

After we were done, I helped her clean up, and she took the opportunity to show me where everything was in the kitchen. It was highly organized. Maybe a little too organized. But she seemed quite proud of what she had.

I thought it couldn't hurt to help out a little. "How about I cook dinner tomorrow night? You've been doing all the cooking. I bet you'd like a break."

"It would be better if I continued doing it," she responded matter-of-factly.

I huffed. "I promise not to poison you."

She stared at me a moment. "At least not intentionally."

She took the lantern into the other room, leaving me standing in darkness. *She was not making this easy.*

I sighed and followed. Trudi set the lantern on the dining room table. From a desk drawer, she pulled out a laptop. "I was able to charge my computer yesterday—"

I interrupted. "Wait. You have a way to charge stuff?" I immediately thought of my nearly dead phone.

She nodded. "I use my truck. It's not the most efficient, but it works. And before you do something stupid, yes, I'll let you use it to charge your phone."

I paused. I was becoming more and more convinced she was reading my mind. "Uh… thanks," I simply said.

She nodded, not seeming to notice my controlled response. "Like I was saying, my laptop is charged, so I was gonna watch a movie. Do you want to watch with me? I only have the six that were on my laptop when everything happened."

I nodded knowingly. "And I bet you've seen them like a zillion times."

She gave a weak smile. "At least twice that."

I remembered the games on the shelves I had stumbled across earlier—a plan began forming in my mind. "What about a game instead?"

Her eyes brightened. "Good idea. There's a couple of old board games on the shelf. I think they have all their pieces."

I remembered the deck of cards and thought of a game I'd played in college. This might be the perfect opportunity to get her to lower her guard a bit.

"I saw some cards." I pointed over my shoulder.

She looked thoughtful. "That would be okay. The cards are old, though. Aaron and I used to play with them as kids."

I got the cards, and we sat at the table across from one another.

"Want to play gin rummy?" she asked, picking them up and shuffling them.

I shook my head. "How about a real game?"

Her eyebrows went up. She continued to shuffle them while looking at me, waiting for me to explain.

"Let's play poker," I suggested.

"We don't have any chips," she protested. "And money's not worth anything anyway. I guess we could play for chores." She frowned and stopped shuffling. Her eyes narrowed. "And I'm not playing strip poker. I'm eight months pregnant, for God's sake. I won't even let Sammy see me naked."

I couldn't help but grin. "How about playing for something more in line with what we talked about earlier? Something much more valuable."

Her eyes sparkled. She leaned forward, clearly interested. "And what is that?"

"Secrets. We play for secrets. The winner of the hand gets to ask a question of the loser. And since we agreed to no lies, it has to be the truth."

She leaned back in her chair and studied me.

I waited, hoping she would go along with it. This might be my chance to learn a little about her and show her I could be a good guy. Someone she could trust.

Trudi leaned forward. "What's the penalty for refusing to answer?"

I've got her! I tried to keep my expression neutral. "You give me my book."

She nodded. I think she expected it. "And what if you won't answer?"

I frowned. I hadn't thought that far. *Did I have something I wouldn't answer?* I didn't think so. "What do you want?"

She thought for a moment. "Well, it has to be something worth the book." Her eyes slid to my left hand. "How about your wedding ring? I bet that's worth it."

My hand reflexively shot to my chest. She had to be kidding. Even the thought made my stomach hurt.

The corner of her mouth curled up slightly. "That's what I thought. So I guess we better play gin rummy." Her voice dropped to a conspiratory whisper. "Secrets can be dangerous."

She pulled the first card—

"Wait!" I said. "I'll do it. I'll give you my ring if I don't answer your question. But if you don't answer mine, you'll give me my book."

She nodded slowly. "I agree."

I grinned. "How about Texas Hold'em..."

"No," she interrupted. "Blackjack. I'll be the dealer. The purpose of this is to embarrass each other, so we don't need anything complex. Just plain old twenty-one will keep it simple. The winner asks a question after each hand and may ask one follow-up question, but it's got to be related. And no backing out once the hand has started. You answer, or you forfeit." Her eyes held challenge, daring me to disagree.

I stared at her for a moment. *Wow, she took charge of that quickly.* But the rules were exactly what I was thinking, so I nodded.

She tucked the card she had been about to deal back into the deck and reshuffled. Her expression cooled. "I play to win, Mister Dreal. Are you sure you want to do this?" Her eyes met mine, holding my gaze, as she riffled the cards—their fluttery hiss disturbingly loud in the quiet of the house. "You might not get what you're looking for."

I hesitated. Her sudden seriousness bothered me. *Should I be worried? Was I missing something?* I shrugged it off. It was just a game. All I wanted was to reveal some funny things about myself so she'll think I'm harmless and someone she can trust. And while I'm at it, maybe learn something useful about her to get my book back. How could this go wrong?

I leaned back in my chair and crossed my arms, giving her a confident smile. "Bring it on," I stated. "I have no secrets."

She placed the shuffled deck on the table. "Everyone has secrets, Mister Dreal." She looked into my eyes. "Everyone."

She pulled the first card but froze. "And no sex questions. I'm done with sex, and after these babies are born, I'm not having it again. Go there, and I swear I'll cut your man-parts off with a dull knife." She glared at me. "Just don't."

I held up my hands in surrender. "Agreed."

She nodded and laid a nine and a five in front of me, then a ten and an eight for her. She met my eyes with absolutely no expression—the perfect poker face.

I nodded.

She laid another card down for me—an eight, which made twenty-two. *Busted.*

She gazed at me for a moment while she composed her question. "How long have you been searching for the cliff where you proposed to your wife?"

Her question puzzled me. *Why would she want to know that?* I thought she might ask me about my most embarrassing moment or maybe sing a song. It seemed like the waste of a question.

I thought for a moment. "Well, we were in Richmond visiting my parents, so my hike started there. I knew I had some time, plus I had to gather supplies and work around all the obstacles getting here. I guess it's been around seven months."

"So you left right after your wife died?"

I shook my head. "I guess I spent a few weeks all together making my plans and finding stuff I'd need. Plus, I had to bury my family." I glanced away. "I never did find Dad."

She nodded again. "Seems to have taken you a long time to get from Richmond to here. Seven months doesn't sound like you were in a hurry."

I shrugged. "I walked most of the way. With all the debris on the roads, and some of the bridges out, taking a car wasn't practical."

"What about…?"

I grinned and shook a finger at her. "Not your turn."

"Right." She crossed her arms and sat back. "Are you ready to stop?"

I huffed. "No way. I need a turn. And I'm feeling lucky."

She dealt again. A nine and a king for me, and for her a queen and a ten. *Damn.* I asked for one more and busted again.

She smiled and sat back in her chair. She paused, choosing her words carefully. "What were you dreaming about the other night?"

I froze. I really didn't want to go there. I took a slow breath. "I dreamed about the Judgement—when everything around me went crazy. Mom and Dad killed themselves. Neighbors were running around all crazy, talking about the voices. And then Wendy..." my voice broke. "Wendy, she..." I glanced away. "She tried to scratch my eyes out and almost stabbed a butcher knife into her throat. I wrestled it away from her and tied her to the bed. I took care of her for three days. Feeding her. Washing her." I looked down. "I had to find adult diapers." I blinked as my eyes suddenly became damp. "Then, on the fourth day, she talked to me. She sounded so normal. So, I let her up to go to the bathroom, and then we cuddled on the bed. I must have fallen asleep." I wiped at the tears. "Only Wendy didn't. She was just pretending. She hung herself."

Trudi listened to my story, head cocked to one side, sadness welling in her eyes. "It's..." she blinked, and a single tear slowly slid down her cheek. Her hands curled into fists, and she looked up, blinking to clear her eyes. It was several seconds before she turned back at me. "It's horrible when you try so hard... but lose them anyway."

I nodded slowly. "It wasn't my finest hour."

Why was she crying over my loss? Did she have something similar happen?

She took a shaky breath. "What about Geri? You didn't mention him."

I stared at her. "How do you know about my brother? I've not said anything about him."

She shrugged. "You called out his name when you were dreaming."

I crossed my arms and sat back, fixing her with my gaze. She stared back without flinching. *How much did I want to tell her?* I sighed. "Geri was a researcher and must have been at the center of whatever happened. As the disaster was getting started, he came barreling down the road and crashed his car into my parents' mailbox. He'd been injured but kept saying something about how they weren't ready. Then he..." The words didn't want to come.

"Then what?" she asked.

I swallowed. "He..." I closed my eyes and forced my mouth to form the words. "He injected me with something. He said it would save me."

She nodded. "I guess it did. Any idea why he didn't give it to others, or even himself?"

"He..." I frowned. "Wait. You've already asked your two questions."

She shrugged. "Can't blame a girl for trying."

I considered her for a moment and then answered anyway. "I've wondered that same thing. He kept saying that he could only save me." I looked down at the table. "And that the voices told him to."

We sat in silence for a moment. She picked up the cards and dealt again. She laid out a pair of eights for me, then a queen and a three for herself.

She looked up at me.

I tapped the table.

She dealt me a seven. I sighed. She won again. *Was she messing with the cards?*

Trudi leaned forward. "Do you have other dreams of Geri?"

I frowned, unsure where she was going with this. "No. He only appears in my memory of that day."

She hesitated. "Do you see ghosts?"

What did she just ask?

I stared at her in disbelief. "Are you kidding?"

"Nope. Just answer the question."

"Of course not."

She nodded, reluctant to accept the answer. But didn't pursue it. "Do you want to keep playing?" she asked.

This was not going like I thought it would. I expected some things we could laugh at, but this had turned damned serious. But I thought I could still turn things around. I just needed to win one hand.

"Yeah, let's go again. I want a turn."

She shrugged and dealt the cards.

This time, I got a nine and a five, while she got a king and an ace. I asked for one more and got an eight. *She won again?*

I leaned back in my chair and rolled my eyes. "What's your question?"

She studied me—I could almost see her mind working. "Why is it important that you have the book when you kill yourself?"

"I'm not killing myself," I quickly protested. "I'm joining Wendy."

She looked at me funny. "You're gonna put a bullet in your head. Sounds like you're killing yourself to me."

I shook my head. "It's not like that."

She snorted. "Whatever," she said dismissively. "Why the book?"

I leaned back and crossed my arms. "Well, it's because it was her favorite. She read from it almost every night, and—"

Trudi cut me off. She stabbed a finger into the table. "You're avoiding the question. Tell me why you need the book when you see her again. Why is it so important?"

I stared at her. *Was I avoiding it?*

Her eyes unflinchingly met mine. Then her gaze flicked to my ring, lingering for just a heartbeat, before returning back to me.

I covered the ring with my other hand. Looking away, I took a deep breath and let it out slowly. "In her note, Wendy told me to read a specific passage before joining her. It's at the end of the book, where the hero, the Paladin, is dying. He tells his best friend that they will meet again, and then he gives him his last command—to join the one waiting for him. And then the hero... dies. I know the passage by heart."

She frowned. "If you have it memorized..." She waved the thought away. "Never mind." She thought for a moment. "Can you recite the passage for me? The command part, anyway."

I hesitated. I wasn't sure I wanted to. It was something private between Wendy and I. On the other hand, I didn't want to give up my ring and give her additional leverage over me. I began to wonder if this game had been such a good idea after all.

"All right, it goes like this." I looked up at the ceiling and began to recite. "....*The hero took a tortured breath.*

"*Thank you, my friend. My very best friend. You have sacrificed greatly for me. Before I go to meet the Great One, I give you one last command...*

"*The Second held his breath. Waiting.*

"Go to she who waits for you. Your old home is no more, but she has prepared a new one." The Paladin took one last ragged breath. *"Go to her... let her heal your heart, as you will heal hers... and be happy with her. Forever."*

I wiped a tear from my eye.

Trudi frowned, puzzled. "That's... nice," she said, stretching out the words. "But isn't it just your generic romantic bullshit?"

My eyes widened in shock. *How dare she!* I slammed my hand on the table, my eyes narrowing. "It's not bullshit! It's special. It... it..." I fought for the words, "...it means Wendy's waiting for me to join her!"

Trudi held up her hands. "Sorry, I shouldn't have said anything. I just think it's what anyone would say on their deathbed."

I glared at her, my face red hot. I settled back and fought to get my anger under control.

Seeing I needed to calm down, she scooted her chair back. "I'm getting a glass of water. Want one?"

"Sure."

She returned a moment later with a pitcher and poured us both a glass.

I took a sip. I wasn't sure I wanted to continue. This had gotten out of hand. But I needed to get my chance to ask a question.

After we had taken a few sips, she picked up the cards and raised her eyebrows. I tapped the table, and she started shuffling.

This time, she dealt me a ten and an ace. I tried to keep my face neutral, but inside I was jumping. She ended up with a three and a duce.

"Stand," I said.

She dealt herself a five, shook her head, and then a king. She sighed at the loss and looked up at me. "All right. What do you want to know?"

Finally! I almost danced. I might be able to pull this out. The game had gotten way too serious, so maybe I should ask something to lighten things up a bit. Get her to tell me a little about herself. Maybe something she'd like to talk about. I thought her boyfriend would be a safe topic.

I leaned over the table. "Tell me about your baby's father?"

Her eyes went as big as saucers. She shot up, knocking her chair over, and sending the cards flying.

"YOU ASSHOLE!" she shouted, her eyes filling with tears. She grabbed the pitcher and doused me with water before stomping off to her bedroom. She slammed the door hard enough to rattle the windows.

Sammy jumped up but wasn't sure what to do. He trotted over to her door and scratched. A moment later, the door opened a crack, and he slipped inside, but it slammed shut and locked behind him.

Well, I screwed that up. I sat there dripping wet, wondering what I had done wrong. I thought she would like to tell me about her boyfriend, but I obviously had hit a nerve. A pretty raw one.

I got a couple of towels and dried myself, then the table and floor. At least it was only water. As I worked, Trudi's warning haunted me. *Secrets can be dangerous.* How right she was.

I had just finished when her bedroom door opened, and she marched over to me with Sammy right by her side. She glared at me with red, swollen eyes.

"Mister Dreal, if I didn't need you so badly, I would shoot you. I can't believe how insensitive you are. I know you want your book, but that was cruel. I ought to—"

I held up my hands. "Stop for a minute. I don't know why you're reacting like this. I thought I was giving you a chance to tell me about your boyfriend."

She glared up at me. "My *boyfriend*? What would…?" Then she trailed off, and all her anger drained out of her. "You really don't know. I thought you had figured it out."

"Know what?"

She took a deep breath and let it out slowly. "I was raped, Mister Dreal. My rapist was their father."

Oh, shit.

CHAPTER
SEVEN

I LAY ON MY BED, staring up at the nearly dark ceiling. The house was quiet except for the occasional pop or crack as it settled. Earlier, Sammy had shuffled in to check on me but growled when I tried to pet him, reminding me I was there because his mistress deemed it important, not because he liked me. He had retreated to Trudi's room when she turned off the light.

I flipped onto my side and shut my eyes—but opened them a few minutes later. The thoughts in my brain wouldn't be quiet. The need to be moving toward Wendy's spot was almost an ache. Maybe I should just leave. I didn't actually require the book to join Wendy in the afterlife. I only needed the passage inside it, and I had that memorized. But then I remembered when Trudi held the lighter up to the book, and I just couldn't do it. No, leaving it behind wasn't an option.

And the card game had been a disaster. I'd learned practically nothing about her and pissed her off to boot. *How could I have not seen it?* No wonder she exploded. It was obvious she had been raped. No woman would voluntarily have a baby in this messed-up world. And she had never mentioned a boyfriend—I had just assumed. I shook my head, amazed at my stupidity. All I had done was make things more difficult.

My eyes finally drooped, and I felt myself drifting off. I lazily started thinking about Trudi's questions about Geri. Why *had* my brother attacked me with that syringe? And more importantly, what had been in it? Had it actually saved me from the madness? And why hadn't he used it to save someone else? What made me so special?

Sleep gradually drew me in, but it didn't completely take me. I drifted. In that in-between lucid state of some dreams, my world slowly dissolved into Mom's kitchen. I was sitting at the table, and morning light was streaming through the windows.

Before me sat the ingredients for my favorite childhood breakfast—peanut butter, jelly, and slices of sandwich bread. I grabbed my spoon tightly and dug deep into the peanut butter jar, slapping a sizable spoonful onto my plate. Then I picked up the grape jelly and, eyeballing the correct amount, scooped out a hefty serving beside it. The proportions were important—it had to be equal parts. Then came the fun part of stirring them together into an even mixture. It just tasted better to mix them together before putting them on the slices of white bread. Nobody was up yet, and Mom let me get away with making my favorite breakfast so she could sleep in.

Only in this dream, I wasn't a child. I was a grown man. The realization was jarring, and it strangely felt like maybe it really wasn't really a dream.

An adult Geri, dressed in the same jeans and shirt he'd been wearing on Judgement Day, sat across from me. He rested his elbows on the table and leaned forward. "You're almost out of time."

I stared at him, confused. "Out of time for what?"

"To decide to live."

His comment angered me. "I could have been with Wendy if you'd left me alone."

He gazed at me sadly. "I'm sorry, but I only had enough of the neutralizing agent to save one, and you were the best candidate. I wasn't even sure it would work, but it was the only way to give your brain time to adapt to the Norns." Geri leaned closer. "But unless you decide to live, it will have all been for nothing."

"Save me? By leaving me in this hell?" Anger welled up inside me. I screamed at him, "*You should have left me to die!*"

I bolted upright and looked around in confusion. Mom's kitchen was gone, and only my dark bedroom remained. *Shit!* Another dream. I tried to slow my pounding heart.

A dim light came from down the hall, and a flannel-gowned Trudi appeared at my door. "Are you all right?" she asked. "You were yelling."

I ran a hand through my hair and tried to appear calm. I really didn't want her to see how shaken I was. "Yeah, I'm okay. It was just a dream."

She came closer and perched on the edge of my bed. "What was it about?"

I took a calming breath and debated about revealing anything. But then I thought, what the hell? Maybe I'll score some points.

"It was my brother Geri."

She touched my hand. "It felt real, didn't it? Like you were there even though you realized it was a dream."

I frowned. *How did she know?* "Yeah, it was."

She nodded in understanding. "It's Aaron for me. Not all the time. Just sometimes. He talks to me and tells me things."

I frowned. "Like what things?"

She shrugged. "Crazy things."

"Are the dreams with Aaron bad ones? Do they wake you up?"

She shook her head. "No, those are the nice dreams." She got up and started toward her room. "When I wake up screaming, it's always the baddies."

I began to put together why she had nightmares.

"Trudi," I called after her.

She came back into the room.

"I'm sorry about what I asked earlier. I wasn't trying to be mean. I really didn't know."

She nodded. "I figured as much. I apologize, too. I overreacted, but I hope you understand why." She rubbed her baby bulge. "You could say it left me with unresolved issues."

I watched her hand glide over her belly. "Yeah, I can see that."

She gave a deep sigh. "And while we're apologizing, I owe you another one. I was gonna tell you after we quit playing, but we didn't get that far. You see, Aaron and I used to play with those cards a lot growing up. A *whole* lot. You might say it gave me an advantage."

I blinked at her. "You stacked the deck."

The corner of her mouth curled up ever so slightly, and then she turned away. "Why, Mister Dreal, I can't believe you would accuse a pregnant lady of cheating."

She left.

I flopped back on my bed. *Damn that woman!* She'd played me.

Again!

* * *

The next morning, after breakfast, Trudi broke the news. "Today, Mister Dreal, we begin your lessons. You have a lot to learn about labor and delivery, so we might as well start now."

"Trudi, I can't—"

She held up a hand to halt me. "Mister Dreal, you promised. Are you going back on your word?"

"What if I said I fainted at the sight of blood?"

She frowned. "Do you? And may I remind you that we agreed to no lying."

I squinted over at her. Today, she wore a baby blue sweater and a denim maternity jumper skirt, which really made her blue eyes shine. Her short hair was pulled back to one side with a simple plastic clip. As she glared at me, it struck me how cute she looked—in a crazy, pregnant woman sort of way. I averted my gaze. Wendy was the only cute one for me.

"Well?" she asked.

I sighed, knowing it was going to be a long day. "All right. Let's get it over with."

After clearing the table, Trudi brought out at least a dozen books on the childbirth process—breathing, positions, what could go wrong—you name it, she had it. She even brought out her laptop.

We looked through a few of the books, and she pointed out some basic anatomy and the birthing process. Then she switched to the laptop, and we watched several videos. But after the third one, I became a little concerned—none of them were very detailed, and they mainly focused on what to expect during pregnancy, not delivery.

After she started the fourth one, I reached across her and paused it. "Where did you get these videos?"

She sighed. "The library. I tried several gyno offices, but the crazies took a strong dislike to medical facilities."

"What about hospitals?"

"There's only one in the area, and they actually blew that one up."

I pointed to the laptop. "Trudi, there's nothing here about twins."

She looked offended. "I have a book." She grabbed it and showed me.

I tried to read the passage, but it used a bunch of medical jargon I wasn't familiar with. Getting through that was going to take time.

"Is this all the reference material you have? A lot of it is duplicate information."

She frowned and shifted in her seat. "It's not like I can go on the Internet and look it up. This is all I could find."

I held up one of the books. "These will be fine if you have a normal delivery. But you said you wouldn't. How do we prepare for that? Some kind of instruction video would be ideal."

She huffed. "Well, let me just go to the medical school and get you a tutor."

I stared at her. "I don't know if I can do this." I tossed the book on the table and crossed my arms. "What exactly are you afraid of happening? A breech birth? Will they get stuck or something?" We had just covered those.

She sighed. "Having a small pelvis runs in the family. The passage that the babies must go through might be too narrow." She patted her hips. "You've likely noticed I have the hips of a boy."

I leaned around the table. "There's nothing wrong with your hips. They look good to me."

There was that mischievous grin again. "Why Mister Dreal? Are you checking out my pregnant ass? That's not very nice."

I blinked and looked away. "That's not what I meant."

"Stare if you want, Mister Dreal. It really doesn't matter. When I'm giving birth, you're gonna see a lot more than my ass."

I was flooded with emotion. My face went red hot. "I can't... Wendy..." The words caught in my throat. I abruptly stood and headed for the backdoor. "I need a moment."

Trudi called after me. "I didn't..."

I was quickly out the door and didn't stop until I came to the detached garage directly behind Trudi's house. The crisp air felt good on my flushed face. I curled my hands into fists and looked up at the blue sky, trying to center myself.

Guilt and longing twisted my guts. If I had to help Trudi deliver, I *would* see her private parts. Intellectually, I realized it was just the birthing process—nothing crude or erotic about it. Yet, there was a certain level of intimacy to it that felt reserved only for Wendy. Not just the physical, but the whole birthing experience. I felt like I was being unfaithful—doing something reserved exclusively for my wife. Wendy and I should be sharing this experience. Instead, it was something else the

Judgement had ripped away. The loss of a future that would never be—hurt me to my core.

I'm not sure how long I stood there, just staring up at the sky, watching the few wisps of clouds. I was jerked back to reality when a coat was unexpectedly placed on my shoulders. "You'll catch a cold," Trudi said.

I hadn't heard her come up behind me.

When I turned, she looked into my eyes with a deep sadness. "I'm sorry. Things were going well, and I thought I could tease you a little and maybe get you to relax. I guess I was wrong."

"Yeah," I said without emotion.

She looked in the direction of the oak tree beyond the garage. It had to be the tree her grandfather and Aaron were buried under. "You were thinking of your wife, weren't you?"

I thought about denying it, but we'd agreed not to lie. It seemed the only thing that gave us a tiny bit of trust. I nodded.

She stepped closer, and in a mothering way, tugged my open jacket tighter around me. She looked up into my eyes and then off toward the oak tree. "Grandpa, Aaron, and I would always pal around." She chuckled softly. "Grandpa called us the three amigos, out to save the world. We had so much fun." She paused, her smile faltering as she turned her eyes back to mine. "It doesn't seem fair. I'm here, and they're not. Just doesn't seem right." She patted my arm and stepped back. "I'll try to be more careful."

I didn't know what to say.

She started back toward the house. "You can stay out here and freeze your butt off," she said. "But my skinny little ass is going inside where it's warm. Babies say it's lunchtime anyway."

I watched her leave, and then I looked up at the sky one last time before I followed. I hoped Wendy would understand I was being forced to do this. My heart was with her.

Forever.

I went back inside, and Trudi shooed me to the table, where I moved our teaching materials to one end. I didn't have to wait long before she brought out two plates and slid mine over to me. It was a canned chicken sandwich and...

"Is that a fruit salad?" I asked in surprise.

She plopped down in her chair across from me. "It's just rehydrated apples, raisins, and walnuts mixed with some mayo I made." She looked down. "I've been craving fresh fruit, but there's none close by. So, I've been making do." She sighed, sounding remorseful. "Pregnancy has its challenges."

I took a bite. "It's good."

She nodded but said nothing further, and we finished our sandwiches in silence.

I offered to help clean up, but Trudi refused, mumbling something about males being forbidden in her kitchen. As she took the dishes to the kitchen, I made a mental note to search that area for my book at the next opportunity.

When she came back, she pulled out the book we had been reviewing and dragged her chair around to my side of the table. "Let's see if we can go over a few more things."

She opened the book and turned to me.

Thoughts of Wendy flashed through my mind. The guilt was so strong. I leaned back and crossed my arms. "I can't do this. It's just too much."

Trudi frowned in irritation. "If you want your book back, Mister Dreal, you will. That was the deal." She sighed. "Look, I know this is overwhelming, but we can get through this. I don't expect you to become an expert, but you do need to know some basic things."

I pointed to her. "You know this is crazy. I haven't even had a first aid course."

Her irritation was growing. "Then what would you have me do, *Mister* Dreal? Give birth all by myself?"

I shrugged. "I guess you could. But there's got to be some other people around here somewhere. One of them would probably love to help."

She folded her arms and glared at me. "I tried that, and you were the only one who came along."

I glared right back. "I don't believe you. There's got to be someone better qualified." I leaned closer. "Forcing me to do this is just not right."

An ugly scowl came over her face, and her cheeks reddened. "Not right?" she spat, venom seeping into her voice. Her hands curled into tight fists. She stood up suddenly, knocking her chair over. She was visibly shaking. "Having your brother killed is right? *Being raped is right?* BEING FORCED TO BE PREGNANT WHEN IT COULD BE A DEATH SENTENCE IS RIGHT?" Her eyes sparkled with angry tears. "I didn't have a choice in this, Mister Dreal. So why should you?"

Her words stung like a slap, and I reflexively leaned away. I had no idea she felt that way.

She closed her eyes and took a deep breath, trying to calm herself.

She finally opened them and said through tight lips, "You have *no right*, Mister Dreal, to tell me what is fair. And no, I will not release you until my babies are born. I'm sorry if that means you can't kill yourself, but I need you alive." She poked me in the chest. "So focus. I'm doing my part, and you need to do yours. After my children are here, you can cut your own damn heart out for all I care."

I could only gape at her display of controlled anger—the rage that boiled behind those blue eyes. And rather than succumb to it, she used it to fuel her determination. You had to respect that.

She glared at me a moment more before righting her chair and sitting back down. She pulled her reference book toward her. "We were discussing—"

Sammy interrupted with a soft woof. He had been watching us from the safety of his bed, but he suddenly jumped up and trotted to the front door.

Trudi paled, her expression shifting instantly from anger to dread. Her focus snapped to where Sammy stood as an arm went protectively over her unborn babies.

"What—?" I asked, but she immediately waved me to silence.

As I listened, a distant sound tickled my ear—a growling throb that grew gradually closer. My eyes grew wide as I recognized it. *An engine?* Not a chainsaw, not a car, not an airplane. No, it had to be a motorcycle or an ATV. And it wasn't far off.

"Shit," Trudi spat. She strode quickly to the kitchen. Even in socks, her footsteps were loud on the wood floor. She returned a moment later with her shotgun and pointed it at me. "Go to your room, *now!*"

What the hell is going on? I raised my hands in surrender and slowly backed into my room. The shotgun tracked my progress until I sat on the bed.

"Do not make any noise, Mister Dreal. You do anything that attracts their attention, and I'll kill you." There was a tremor in her voice.

Without waiting for a response, she strode back toward the front of the house, out of my line of sight.

And so I waited. The noise got louder, and as it peaked, I thought I heard Trudi whispering to herself. *Was she praying?*

The noise shifted and then started to fade. Within a few minutes, it was gone.

Sammy trotted back into view, looking quite pleased with himself. He plopped down on his bed, with his eyes on Trudi as she shuffled back in and set the shotgun down on the table. She eased into a chair, leaned her head back, and draped an arm over her eyes. "They're gone."

"Who's gone?" I asked. "And why did you point your gun at me? I thought you wanted me alive."

She frowned but didn't move. I wasn't sure she going to answer, but she finally spoke. "I thought you had led them to me."

I slipped into a chair beside her. "Led who to you? You're the first person I've talked to in months."

She didn't answer.

"Trudi," I stated flatly. "What the hell is going on?"

She uncovered her eyes and glanced at me in irritation. "I thought it was the baddies, okay? They've taken up residence in Hopegrove. That's a little community about ten to twelve miles from here. They took over some big houses on the old golf course." Her voice softened. "When they... you know... caught me. I saw about fifteen people. It might be more by now."

I leaned back, considering what she said. In my travels, I

had observed other survivors, both men and women, but in small groups—rarely more than five. I steered clear of them since they would only hinder me.

But if there had been fifteen people, that was larger than any group I'd encountered. I had a chilling thought.

"On the way here," I said. "I observed a few survivors from a distance. One of them shot a kneeling man and forced the woman with him to kiss his feet. Is that them?"

Trudi sat up straighter. "Sounds like them." Her gaze shifted toward the front of the house as if she were seeing into the past. "When I was there, they practiced forced recruitment. Which is how Aaron and I came to be captured. Join or die."

I opened my mouth to ask another question, but she held up a silencing hand. "No more." She slowly rose. "And I'm done with learning today. I'm going outside."

I also rose and picked up the shotgun. I held it out to her. "You might want to take this. They could be close by."

She reached to take it, but I didn't let go. She looked up at me questioningly.

"Trudi, I get the sense there's something you're not telling me about these baddies."

She frowned. "And why do you care, Mister Dreal?"

I sighed. "Because…" I glanced around the room, hoping for inspiration. But when I came back to her guarded blue eyes, I could only think of one thing. "I can't fulfill my part of the deal if you hide things from me."

Her expression softened. "You're right." She searched my eyes—the ticking clock was thunderously loud. "They're searching for me."

"And why would they do that?" I asked, stepping closer. Her

extended belly brushed mine, but she did not move away. "Did you steal something from them?"

Her eyes searched mine. "No," she whispered so softly I almost couldn't hear her. "It was much worse than that."

CHAPTER
EIGHT

IT WAS DARK when Trudi came back. Her eyes were red, and exhaustion weighed on her shoulders. Even by her standards, she was unusually quiet.

I had wanted to start dinner but was reluctant since I'd been warned off the kitchen. So instead, I spent the time searching for my book—with no success.

She immediately set about fixing dinner—pulling out the leftover chicken salad, putting some biscuits in the oven to warm, and then setting out two plates for the food. I offered to help, but she just glanced at me and shook her head.

I sat at the table and picked up one of the reference books, pretending to read. But I was actually keeping an eye on Trudi. I thought she was on a razor's edge, and I wasn't sure how things were going to fall. She was under a lot of stress—her pregnancy, having to keep an eye on me, not to mention the day-to-day surviving in this crazy world. Even a superwoman would bow under that weight. But it was the engine noise that had pushed her to the brink. I sighed quietly to myself. Those baddies must have really done a number on her.

Maybe I could calm her down a little. "Catch any more rabbits?" I asked conversationally.

She didn't answer at first. She deliberately opened the oven to check on her biscuits, poking them with a finger before gently shutting it. She slowly turned to face me and leaned against the counter with her arms crossed. "No," she said softly. "I went to see Aaron and Grandpa."

I was surprised. "You mean the same Aaron you see in your dreams?"

She shook her head. "No. The Aaron that's buried under the oak out back. I go see him and Grandpa when I'm upset." She took a deep breath and let it out slowly. "It calms me down."

"Oh," I said softly.

She turned back to her oven, opened the door, and again touched one of the biscuits. She felt another and finally put her whole hand on it. "Shit," she whispered. "Not now."

Standing, she turned on each of the stovetop burners, but none of them lit.

"Dammit!" She bowed her head and rubbed her temples. "God dammit, why today?" She slammed her fist down on the counter, accidentally catching one of the plates she'd set out and flipping it to the floor. It shattered with a loud crash.

Sammy immediately retreated to his bed, watching her with concern.

Trudi looked down at the shattered plate, her shoulders slumping in defeat. "Screw it!" She strode past me, headed for her bedroom. "You're on your own tonight."

"What's wrong?" I asked, putting my book aside and standing as she walked by me.

She stopped and turned to glare at me with tears in her eyes.

"We're out of fucking propane." She trudged on to her room.

I shrugged. "So we go get some. I'll help." I thought it might earn me some trust points.

Trudi did an abrupt U-turn and walked right up to me. She stepped into my space—her face inches from mine and her pregnant middle pushing into my stomach. I tried to step back but came up short, trapped between her and the table. "Mister Dreal," she said through clenched teeth. "I don't need your damn knight-in-shining armor routine. I've gotten propane before, all by myself. No male assistance required."

I held up my hands. "I was just trying to help."

"To hell you were. So just keep your damn mouth shut. Your focus is delivering my babies. Nothing more, nothing less."

She held my gaze a moment more before stomping to her room—Sammy right on her heels. She slammed the door and locked it behind her.

I stared after her. There was no denying it. Trudi was starting to crack. That couldn't be good for getting my book back, nor would it be good for her.

I sighed and turned away, heading in search of a broom. As much as I hated being stuck here, I really didn't want to see Trudi self-destruct.

It would be ugly.

And sadly, there was nothing I could do about it.

* * *

The next morning, a gentle touch awoke me. Trudi stood beside my bed, shadowed by the dim light coming from outside my bedroom door. I was pretty sure the sun wasn't even up yet.

I blinked at her, struggling to get my brain to work. "What...?" I croaked. "What's going on?"

"Sorry to wake you. I'm gonna get propane."

"Okay," I said as I sat up. Suddenly remembering our conversation from the previous evening, I grew a little apprehensive. *Was she going to give me another lecture?*

"Did you..." she paused. She sounded almost embarrassed.

I rubbed my eyes. "Did I what?"

"Did you mean what you said about coming with me?" she asked cautiously. "I know I said I didn't need your help, but after thinking about it, having someone with me would be safer. You know, just in case." She paused. "I *am* pretty close to term."

Surprised, I glanced over at her. "Yeah. I'll help." I threw back the covers and turned on the lantern beside my bed.

Trudi's gaze drifted down my shirtless chest, but her eyes widened in surprise when she realized I was only wearing my boxers. She quickly turned away. "Then we need to leave soon." She gestured toward the end of the bed. "I think those will fit you." Without another word, she left for the kitchen.

I took stock of the flannel shirt, jeans, and new camo jacket she had placed there. They were a definite improvement from what I had been wearing. The jeans were an odd style, but prisoners couldn't be choosers. I quickly dressed.

She served me a breakfast of applesauce and a power bar. While a significant step down from her usual home-cooked meals, it did the job.

She was quiet the whole time we ate. She seemed preoccupied, likely planning out what we were doing today. On top of that, she was in a bad mood. I wasn't looking forward to this.

Today, Trudi wore bib overalls and a flannel shirt, topped off with an oversized camo jacket. While the jacket was loose across her shoulders, her pregnancy bulge required a little extra room. A plain black ball cap was pulled low, with her hair sticking out the back in a short, messy ponytail.

Wendy wouldn't have been caught dead in clothes like that. She favored dresses, nice blouses, and snug jeans. She had always been so put together.

Trudi, on the other hand, was Miss Practicality. She wore whatever made sense and made no bones about it. And yet, in your own way, she always dressed nice. I couldn't explain it. Today, she almost looked cute—in a country-girl-going-hunting sort of way.

Trudi's gaze flicked up from her bowl, catching me watching her. I glanced away, embarrassed she had caught me. I had Wendy, after all. I shouldn't have been looking.

After breakfast, we stepped out on the porch to put on our boots. Trudi had brought her shotgun, but I was shocked when she handed me my handgun. Not my special one, but the one I thought of as my working gun. I checked it, and it was loaded. "You're giving me a loaded gun?" I asked in surprise.

Her eyes met mine. "If you were gonna kill me, I'd already be dead."

"I could change my mind." I joked.

But Trudi didn't smile. She stepped close. So close I could

pick out the individual freckles on her nose. Her deep blue eyes seemed so sad. "Then do it before we go get this fuckin' propane. It will save me a trip."

As her gaze held mine, I couldn't help but wonder if she was brave being out here all alone or just plain crazy. I suspected a little of both.

Trudi hefted the shotgun and motioned me to follow.

It was a cold, wet, and dreary day. Wisps of fog would lazily drift by. Not ideal weather to be out searching for stuff.

"What's got you so pissed off this morning?" I asked as she walked toward the detached garage behind the house. Sammy was on our heels. He, at least, was excited.

"I'm not pissed off," she stated.

"Well, you're sure not Miss Sunshine."

She spun to face me. "You're getting on my nerves. I'm dreading this trip, okay? I just know something is gonna go wrong."

"A dream?"

She shook her head.

"The baddies?"

She sighed. "I don't know. Just a feeling."

"Is that why you asked me to come with you?"

She stopped and glared at me for a moment, then continued toward the garage. "You're being an asshole."

"And you're being a bitch."

She snorted. "At least we understand each other."

"Would you rather I carried the shotgun, and you take my handgun? Your..." I looked down at her stomach... "... babies might get in the way."

She glared at me.

I shrugged. "I'm just saying…"

She huffed. "Mister Dreal, I'm a terrible shot, so I need something where accuracy is not a requirement. So I'll keep my shotgun, thank you." She started to turn away but paused. "By the way, if something comes up, stay behind me. If I shoot you, I want it to be on purpose."

I watched her stalk off toward the garage. *This was not going to be a fun trip.*

She stopped in front of the garage door and tried to squat down while balancing the shotgun. But her advanced pregnancy wasn't helping. I touched her shoulder and lifted it for her. She gave me the strangest expression of relief mixed with anger before entering.

Inside sat a faded red, three-quarter-ton pickup with raised suspension and oversized tires. On the back, a bumper sticker said *SCRATCH AN ITCH*. It had to be connected to the back scratcher in my bedroom.

The truck was high. I doubted it had been street-legal, not that it mattered anymore. I wondered if Trudi could get in it.

But she didn't even slow down. She went to the driver's side, managed to get a leg up, and hauled herself right in. She turned her gaze toward me, daring me to say something.

I wondered why she drove this monster. I was sure there were plenty of trucks or cars still out there. Take one out of the showroom. But when she fired up the engine, with its distinctive diesel throb, I understood. This was a work truck and could go off-road. That would be a huge advantage if you came across a blocked road.

Or a baddie you wanted to get away from.

I waited in the garage while she eased the truck out so I

could close the door behind her. As I waited, I noticed a short coil of garden hose shoved in the corner. It looked unused and out of place compared to the other odds and ends in the garage. I wondered what she had used it for.

With difficulty, I climbed into the passenger seat. Sammy sat between us, his tail in constant motion. He must be happy to be going. He didn't even growl at me.

"Is this your grandpa's truck?" I asked.

"Yeah, he took us everywhere in it." She pulled out, and we bumped slowly down the gravel driveway.

"Why the bumper sticker?"

She glanced over at me. She had the barest smile, but I could tell it was filled with pride. "He was a backscratcher dealer and sold them to the local stores. He even converted the barn into a workshop to make them, but finally figured out he could buy them cheaper from China. He started the whole, 'Scratch an itch. Visit Hopegrove City' campaign. Even got the city council to sponsor him." She sighed wistfully. "It didn't pan out, although he certainly enjoyed trying." She pointed to the glove box. "He was gonna try to do slingshots and made a few demos, but the county took a dim view of them. Said they were lethal weapons."

I turned the latch on the glove box, and it burst open, spilling out old condiment packs, plastic spoons, and two wooden slingshots still in plastic bags.

I took one out and unfolded the thick rubber bands attached to the fork. I smiled, remembering my boyhood days when my best friend Lee and I each had made one. We got pretty damn good with them. Both of us were fiercely competitive, so we would line up cans on a fence and do a shoot-off. Lee was a year older and would usually kick my butt. But I kept practicing. One day, I beat him, knocking off all the cans with no misses. I did it again the next day. After that, Lee preferred playing basketball, something he could always beat me at.

"Nice," I said, stretching out the rubber band and giving it a test pull.

Trudi glanced over at me with an unguarded smile, warm from talking about her grandpa. It struck me that the smile softened her features and made her almost... attractive.

Almost.

Nothing like my Wendy. The thought of my wife killed my joy. I put everything back in the glove box.

She turned right when we reached the paved road in front of her house.

"Where are we going?" I asked.

The smile on her face evaporated, and she was all business again. "The truck needs fuel. That's first. The old Freedmont farm is a few miles away. Their house burned down, but the fire didn't touch the barn. There's a gravity-fed tank that they used for their tractors. We'll fill up there."

I nodded, impressed. "You weren't lying when you said you knew this area."

"Grandpa made me work on their farm one summer. They were nice people." She paused. "From what I can tell, they burned to death while sitting at their kitchen table."

That kind of killed the conversation.

The road was mostly free of abandoned cars and debris. I thought that strange since I'd encountered abandoned autos and trucks on every road I traveled. But here, they were on the side. I finally realized someone had cleared this stretch of road.

As we drove, Trudi would frequently scan the overcast sky. I finally had to ask. "Are you concerned about the weather?"

She shook her head. "No." She slowed to maneuver around a fallen tree branch. "Drones. They shouldn't be flying today, but you never know with the baddies."

I frowned. "Who are these guys?"

Trudi shifted her grip on the steering wheel but did not answer. I let it go. But we both knew we'd eventually have to talk about them.

A short while later, she turned onto a gravel driveway marked with a mailbox and two red reflectors. Big block letters spelled out Freedmont on one side. She pushed the shotgun toward me. "I'm not expecting trouble, but be ready just in case."

We drove up the driveway, past the burned-out shell of a house, and around to a large wooden barn in the back. She pulled up in front of its sliding door and put the truck in park. Digging a key from her pocket, she held it out to me. "Open the door, and I'll drive inside. Then you can close it behind me."

The door was hung on rollers and slid to the right, with a latch on the left. I took the shotgun and reached for the truck's door handle, but Trudi suddenly grabbed my arm. "Wait." She pointed toward the door's latch. "The padlock is gone. I know I put it on the last time I was here."

Sure enough, the latch that would have held a lock was empty. I scanned the ground around the door, and while muddy, I didn't see any tracks. "How long since you were here last?"

She shrugged. "A month or so."

That seemed like a lot of fuel when there was no place to go. "You drive that much?"

She shook her head and continued to stare at the barn's door. "It's how I recharge everything. They'd notice solar panels or a generator."

I frowned, remembering her concern over the baddies. "Are we in danger?"

She didn't even glance my way. "Later," she said. "You open the door, and I'll cover you. Be ready to run back to the truck if anything comes out."

She turned off the engine and slid out, dropping the truck key in her pocket and telling Sammy to stay put.

I got out and cautiously stepped to the door. I grabbed the handle and glanced at Trudi. She stood to the side, feet planted and shotgun raised. She nodded.

I pulled the door back and stepped out of the way, but nothing came out. I poked my head around the corner.

The faint scent of fuel, oil, and hay drifted through the door. A tractor, a couple of plows, and some hay bales were stored to one side, with another door opposite us. I guess this was so a tractor could drive in, refuel, and drive straight out the back. But it was the raised horizontal drum sitting to one side that attracted my eye. It had to be the fuel tank.

Trudi drove the truck into the barn, and I shut the door behind her. I did leave it open a few inches so we could check outside before leaving.

Trudi climbed out and went straight to the drum. She tapped on the tank, going up and down, finally stopping and putting a finger where the sound changed. She then looked at the back of the tank and frowned. "Something's not right." She stepped away and stuck her hands in her back pockets. "I marked the fuel level the last time I was here. I wanted to see how much I was using." She put her finger on the tank to mark the current level. "This is where it is now, which is higher than my last two marks."

"Could you have marked it wrong?" I asked.

Trudi shook her head. "Once maybe, but not twice."

She stepped across the barn to several shelves and grabbed a glass jar full of nuts and bolts. Dumping out the contents, she came back and bled a little of the fuel into the jar. The liquid smelled of diesel and had a red tint, but part of it was a clear liquid that settled to the bottom. Water.

Our eyes met. There was no evidence the roof had leaked, and the floor was bone dry. That meant the water had been deliberately added—likely to disable any vehicle that used it.

And make them a sitting duck.

Trudi whispered in disbelief. "They've found me."

"The baddies?"

She nodded distractedly, her thoughts a thousand miles away. "They must have followed me."

"It might not be you. They could have set the trap for anyone. You did say they were forcing people to join them."

She shrugged. "Doesn't matter. Either way, they must be watching this place. We better get out of here."

I didn't argue.

We headed back toward the truck but hadn't taken two steps when Sammy looked out the cab's back window and gave a woof. Trudi froze in place. The hairs on the back of my neck stood up.

"What is it?" I asked softly, knowing this couldn't be good.

She waved me off, putting a single finger to her lips to indicate silence.

The post-Judgement world was a much quieter place, so any odd sound jumped out at you. As I listened, I could barely make out a faint buzz, which grew gradually louder. My first thought was an insect, but that didn't seem right. As it grew closer, I realized what it was.

A quadcopter drone.

CHAPTER NINE

I RUSHED TO THE door and carefully peeked out. A black quadcopter flew at rooftop level, following the driveway and slowly inching forward like a stalking beast. The sleek craft was large, maybe two feet at its widest, and still distant, just coming up the drive. There was no telling where the operator was.

Trudi had mentioned drones earlier, but I had dismissed her concern as not possible. The lack of GPS and the rainy weather should have grounded any drones. But the sound outside indicated that someone had found a way around those constraints.

But what concerned me more was that Trudi had been looking for them. She must know more than she was telling me.

I stepped away from the door and turned back toward Trudi. Sweat beaded on her forehead, and her fingers were white where they clutched the shotgun. Her eyes kept darting toward the door. No question about it—she was scared.

She dug in her pocket for her keys. "They must have had someone watching or rigged up an alarm." She pointed to the door on the opposite side. "We can drive out the back. I know a tractor path that will take us directly back to the road." She started toward the truck.

I reluctantly followed. "What about waiting them out?" I asked.

She shot me a withering glance. "They likely already have someone on the way. We have to leave now." Her grip tightened on her shotgun. "I won't risk being taken by them again."

I looked toward the sound of the drone. Something about this just didn't feel right. Drones could move fast, yet this one was barely moving. Plus, they made no attempt to hide that they had tampered with the fuel or that the lock was missing from the door. It was like they wanted us to know they were watching. I frowned, realization hitting me. They wanted us to run.

"Wait." I caught her arm.

Trudi wheeled to glare at me defiantly and shook off my hand. For a moment, I thought she might punch me.

I didn't flinch. "I think they're trying to drive us into a trap."

"Then outrunning them—"

I cut her off and pointed toward the back door. "Trudi, when was the last time you drove that tractor path?"

"I don't know," she said in irritation. "Two years ago, maybe."

"Then they could have done something to it." I waved my hands in frustration. "I don't know, nails, a trench. Hell, it could be a landmine for all we know."

Trudi frowned. She looked toward the approaching drone and then back to me. "Then what the hell would you suggest, Mister Dreal? Ask them to tea?"

I glanced toward the door. I honestly wasn't sure. We could try to drive by it, but that would just invite them to follow us. That drone was big and likely had a sizable range, so I didn't think it would have trouble keeping up. No, the drone had to be taken down. *But how?* It needed to appear the drone failed or crashed due to the weather. That meant using the shotgun was out of the question—they'd hear it. I sighed. It had to be silent but still lethal. My eyes widened. The slingshot! But could I do it? There's a big difference between cans on a fence and a moving drone. I thought for a moment. There was only one way to find out.

I turned back to Trudi. "What if I shoot it down?"

She gaped at me in horror. "You can't. It's too risky. A shotgun blast will echo through the trees for miles. If they aren't already on their way, that will definitely bring them."

I shrugged. "Then I'll use a slingshot."

Trudi blinked at me in disbelief. "You've got to be kidding. That would be difficult using a rifle, but with a slingshot?"

"I admit, it'll be difficult. But I used to be pretty good." *I hoped I still was.*

I trotted to the truck and dug out a slingshot. Sammy shifted in his seat nervously, picking up on Trudi's agitation. I gave the slingshot an experimental pull and release. It felt right.

"I'm gonna try it. Just three shots. If I can't hit it, we'll do it your way. No argument."

She looked skeptical and shook her head. "I don't—"

I interrupted her. "Listen. We've got to run no matter what. The only difference is that if I hit the drone, they won't be able to follow us."

She pursed her lips. "You're not listening. This could put

my babies at risk. If they figure out it's us, there will be retribution."

I shook my head. "They won't. I can do this."

I ran over to the pile of parts Trudi had emptied on the ground and picked out three steel nuts about the width of my finger. I grinned. These would do nicely.

I stepped toward the door. "Just three shots," I called. "No more. Then we leave."

She glared at me in irritation. "Arrogant asshole," she mumbled under her breath. She pulled herself into the driver's seat and closed the truck's door.

Counting on the misty rain and dark interior to keep me hidden, I peered through the barn door's narrow opening and loaded my first nut. I pulled the rubber bands back, the sound of their stretching loud to my ears. Holding my breath, I took aim, leading it just a little—then released.

The shot veered wide to the right, and I sagged in disappointment.

"Come on," Trudi called from the truck cab. "Let's just go before they get too close."

I took out another nut and sighted carefully—

And missed again.

Damn.

I took out my last nut and loaded it.

The drone may have spotted my shadow in the doorway—it dropped slightly and headed directly for me. It was only about fifty feet away and closing fast.

I pulled the rubber bands back, stretching it until my arm trembled with the effort. I held my breath, sighted carefully...

Suddenly, the shot felt wrong, and I could almost feel a gentle nudge wanting me to move further to the left.

I didn't have time to think about it. I shifted my aim until it felt right, then smoothly released the shot.

There was a ping, followed by a loud screech. The drone flipped, its propellers suddenly sounding like a swarm of angry hornets. It quickly lost altitude, tumbling end over end while careening to one side. It fell to the ground with a satisfying crunch. Giving one last buzz, it went silent and did not move.

I stuck the slingshot in my pocket. "Let's go!"

Trudi started the truck, and I ran to the other door, shoving it to the side. She immediately started forward, and I climbed in while she was still moving. As she drove, I glanced back and thankfully saw no more drones.

"Is there a less obvious road for us to take? Something they won't expect."

She nodded. "Already on it." She diverted to a barely visible path, leading us in the opposite direction from the main one. After bouncing over several ruts and an overflowing ditch, we emerged onto the road again.

We drove for a bit before she finally broke the silence. "Why didn't you listen to me? What you did was too risky. They might not know it was us, but it might make them look harder."

Her response pissed me off. "They knew someone was at the barn and were gonna ambush them. I gave us an opportunity to escape without them identifying you."

Trudi glared at me. She grabbed Sammy and stomped on the brakes. The truck skidded to a stop, throwing me against the dash. She turned to glare at me. "You were being an asshole and so focused on impressing me with your trick shooting that you wouldn't listen to my concerns. Well, Mister Dreal, it didn't work. You may have put my babies at risk, and I won't stand for it. Heaven help you if you did."

She gave Sammy a reassuring pat and went back to driving.

I wasn't letting this drop. "We had no time to make a safe call. It may have been risky, but shooting it down was the only option to keep you and your babies safe."

"Keep us safe? So says the man who wants to commit suicide. I don't think you're qualified, so why don't you let me make those calls? I could have easily lost the drone in the woods."

God, this ungrateful woman pissed me off. I stabbed a finger in her direction. "I told you. It's not suicide—it's to join Wendy! And besides, my plan worked."

She glared at me. "Okay, it worked for now. But the jury is still out. If they show up on my doorstep, you're gonna be the first one I shoot."

We drove in silence while we both fumed. I crossed my arms and looked out the window.

However, Sammy'd had enough. He leaned over and licked Trudi's face, slapping me with his wagging tail, then turned and did the same with me. I tried to push him away, but it only made him more persistent. He finally decided he had shared enough slobber and settled back into the seat. He seemed quite pleased with himself.

At least Sammy was happy with me. Sometimes, between the three of us, I wondered who was the most intelligent.

After a fallen tree made us backtrack, I was finally calm enough to hopefully get some answers from Trudi.

"These guys. The baddies. Why are they after you?"

She shifted in her seat and tightened her grip on the wheel. "Let's talk about that later." She pointed out the window. "There's another farm about five miles east of here. The old Everston's place. We'll try there next."

I frowned. "Trudi, you can't keep avoiding my question. Why are you hiding from them?"

She stayed focused on the road and did not answer.

I sighed. "I need to know—"

"*Please!*" she interrupted. She tried to squeeze the life out of the steering wheel. "Let's talk about it later." She glanced over at me, her blue eyes pleading. "We need to focus on this first."

I looked away. "All right. But I can't help if you keep me in the dark."

She didn't reply, and I thought the subject was closed, but she finally added, "Tonight. I promise."

* * *

I knew we had arrived at the Everston farm when Trudi unexpectedly stomped on the brake and whipped into a driveway hidden by tall yellow grass and marked with only a single red reflector.

I had to use the truck's grab handle to steady myself as we bumped along the rough drive. After going through a thick stand of pine trees, we came to a faded red metal barn. The rundown building was covered in rust spots, with an ancient tractor beneath the attached carport. In the distance behind it, I could see a small farmhouse with the same faded metal roof.

Trudi pulled in front of the barn's roll-up door, secured with a simple padlock. She hopped out of the truck and reached behind the seat for a set of large bolt cutters.

"I can help," I offered as I joined her.

She gave me a disinterested frown and made a show of cleanly snipping off the padlock and raising the door.

I frowned. *Why is she going out of her way to prove I'm not needed? I should have just stayed at the house.*

Inside, we found the diesel tank, and after confirming the fuel was good, Trudi filled the truck and two five-gallon containers. After our earlier trouble, it went surprisingly well.

She drove us over to the farmhouse so we could check for propane. The structure must have been in bad shape even before the disaster, so I was skeptical. But I kept my opinions to myself. No use in having her jump down my throat again.

We left Sammy in the truck and went inside to see if anything was left. No bodies were inside, which was consistent with what I had observed in other places. For some reason, the crazies wanted to run into the open and attack any kind of tower or official-looking building. That's usually where they died.

In the pantry, we found the rats had gotten to most of everything. But in the basement, we found an untouched food locker with several jars of homemade preserves and a flour tin. While Trudi was dealing with the food, I scouted out a gun locker with a rifle and ammo. Since Trudi had the only shotgun, I thought they might be useful.

After loading our findings into the truck, we went around the side of the house and located their propane tank. It was a large stand-alone job about twenty feet from the house. Like the rest of the farm, it appeared old, with several patches of deep red rust and worn fittings. The cutoff valve and connecting hoses were corroded. To me, it looked like a safety hazard.

Trudi pulled the truck beside it and took out a toolbox, several hoses, and three smaller spare tanks. Before Trudi could shut the door, Sammy managed to slip out of the cab and started sniffing around, his tail wagging in delight.

"Keep watch," she ordered as she bent down to turn off the feed valve. "And don't let Sammy run off."

I sighed in disappointment. Trying to become her White Knight had completely backfired. Instead, I had ended up pissing her off. This lady had some serious trust issues.

Trudi tried turning off the cutoff valve, but it didn't budge. She used several different positions and grips, but it refused to move.

The sky darkened, and the rain switched from a drizzle to a steady rain.

I pulled up my hood. "You're going to get soaked out here," I said. "Come back to the truck, and we'll wait for it to pass."

She didn't even look up. "Then go wait in the truck. I don't need a supervisor."

She gave up on turning it by hand and pulled out a big wrench. She put it on the valve.

"Need me to help?" I asked.

She just rolled her eyes. "I got this. It doesn't require a big, strong man."

She pushed against the wrench, but the stubborn valve refused to budge. She drew a deep breath and tried again, straining with everything she had. "Move, dammit," she muttered.

Sammy had been sniffing around us when his head suddenly came up. He growled. A rabbit darted out of a bush, and Sammy shot after it.

"Sammy!" Trudi called. Unexpectedly, the valve gave a loud snap and cracked, emitting a sharp hiss that stank of rotten eggs and chilled the air. Trudi's wrench slipped, but her momentum carried her forward. She put out a hand to steady herself.

Which landed directly on the broken fitting.

She immediately jerked her hand back. "*Shit!*" she spat. She stepped back, cradling her hand.

"What's wrong?"

"I burnt my damn hand. The propane's under pressure and comes out freezing cold." She cradled the injured limb. "Dammit, it hurts." She had tears in her eyes.

I stepped closer. "Let me see."

"No!" She pulled her hand away. "Go get Sammy, and I'll see if they have any bandages." She hurried inside.

The stubborn dog wanted nothing to do with me. I chased him, cursing every step of the way, but he finally circled back to the house. I found him sitting in front of the house's back door, panting and giving me an impatient "Open the door, dummy" expression.

He darted inside, shoving the door the rest of the way open and getting everything wet as he shook off the rain. He gave me a dirty look before going to sit beside his mistress.

Trudi sat in front of a window at a dusty kitchen table— discolored condiment jars lined up against the sill. She was cursing under her breath and trying to wrap her hand with a strip of medical gauze, only it wasn't going well using just her left hand.

I frowned. This was not the most sanitary place to work. The previous occupant's cleaning habits had been questionable even before the Judgement, and the table looked like an infection waiting to happen. Whether she wanted it or not, she needed help.

Remembering some cheap whiskey I'd spotted in the cabinet, I retrieved it along with a dish towel that wasn't covered in dust. I put the whisky on the table and draped the towel over my arm.

"I can't drink that," she spat.

"I know. It's for me."

She frowned when I poured it over my hands and dried them with the dishtowel. I then held out my open hand to her.

"Let me do it."

"Screw you." She looked up at me through angry tears.

I suppressed the urge to snap back at her. She was hurting and probably embarrassed. Now was not the time.

I took a deep breath and let it out slowly. "I remember someone telling me that 911 didn't work anymore and if a wound became infected, the injured person would die." I paused. "So... please let me bandage your hand."

She gave me a look that would have killed a lesser mortal, her blue eyes blazing in anger. I glared right back and kept my hand extended. "Please," I said.

She sighed and handed me the roll of gauze. Then she held out her hand so I could reach it.

I undid her sloppy dressing and examined her wound more closely. It was blistering, and I could see she had already applied some petroleum jelly to it.

I nodded. "Good idea. We'll need to get you some antibiotic

ointment on the way back." Being careful not to touch anything, I carefully wrapped the gauze around it. She sucked in a breath one time and grimaced but said nothing. When I was done, I secured it with a piece of medical tape.

"Taken anything for pain?" I asked, letting her have her hand back.

She cradled the injured limb against her chest and shook her head. "They only had ibuprofen. I can't take that."

"What about acetaminophen?"

She looked away. "If I had some."

I nodded. "Let's see if we can find it on the way back."

I stood and tried to lighten the situation. "See, that wasn't so bad." I smiled. "If I had one, I'd give you a lollipop for being a good girl."

Her eyes suddenly became moist. She quickly stood and turned away, wiping at them. "Damn hormones," she muttered.

I followed her outside, with Sammy right with us.

Trudi sighed as she inspected the damaged tank. It wasn't hissing anymore, and the sulfur smell was very faint.

"I'm sure all the propane has leaked out," she said sadly. "So we might as well go." She shot me an embarrassed glance. "Would you mind putting my stuff in the truck while I get Sammy in the cab?"

"Sure."

I did as she asked and was doing my last check for any tools I might have missed when I heard cursing like I'd never heard before.

I turned around to find Trudi trying to get in the truck with one hand, pregnant, and a very bad attitude.

Plus, she was trying to get in on the driver's side.

Sammy was sitting in the middle, looking over his shoulder at me like I should do something.

I sighed and stepped over to her. "There is no way in hell I'm letting you drive."

She wheeled on me. "And I'm not giving you the key." She grimaced and pulled her hand closer to her chest.

"Afraid I'm going to drive off."

"You could."

"Not without my book. But if you give it to me, I promise I'll be out of your hair in two seconds flat."

"You know, I can't do that."

"Sure you could. Then I would be out of your life, and you'd be free to drive your truck into a tree any time you wanted."

"I'm not giving you the book. And you're not driving my truck."

I crossed my arms. "You're being stupid."

"I'm not!" she screamed. "I should have shot your ass."

"It's not too late. I'd almost pay to see a one-handed, super-sized pregnant lady do it."

Her face turned bright red, and she was about to hit me with her right hand, but realized that wasn't a good idea.

I held up my hands in surrender. "Trudi. Use your damn head. It was difficult for you to drive around all the obstacles using two hands. How are you gonna do it with one?"

"I've been driving a truck since I was knee-high to a duck. I can navigate these roads with my eyes closed."

"Okay. So navigate. Just tell me where to go."

"I'll tell you where to go, all right."

"Yeah, yeah, yeah. I'm not trying to win a popularity

contest." I leaned forward. "I'm trying to get you, your babies, and Sammy home in one piece."

We glared at each other for several seconds. Sammy whined, and Trudi glanced his way before turning back to me. She reluctantly stepped away and went around to the passenger side. I opened the door for her and gave her a boost to get in.

I got in the driver's side and held out my hand. "Key?"

She started to reach into her pocket with her damaged right hand, then realized that wouldn't work. She switched to her left but found she couldn't get across her middle. She finally leaned back, utterly frustrated. "It's in my fuckin' *pants* pocket."

I threw my hands up. "You've got to be kidding. You mean I have to stick my hand in a pregnant woman's pants?"

"Oh, grow up."

I reached around Sammy.

She looked panicked. "Don't get any funny ideas. I know how you guys think. And for the record, you're not my type."

I just looked at her. "And bitchy pregnant ladies aren't my type either."

I put my hand in her pants pocket and pulled out the keys. Looking up into her face, she was almost white. I had to wonder what had happened to her.

I put them in the ignition. "That wasn't so bad, was it?"

"You groped me."

"I do not grope pregnant ladies." I sighed and started the engine. "Do you have any acetaminophen back at your house?"

She shook her head. "I took all mine. It was on my list to get today."

I put the truck in gear and eased us back onto the dirt road. "Then we'll stop at the next house and see what they have."

"That's too risky."

I rolled my eyes in her direction. "Really? A crazy pregnant woman with a short temper and violent mood swings is sitting beside me with a loaded shotgun." I paused. "Now that's risky."

Sammy barked and wagged his tail.

"See, even Sammy agrees with me."

She looked at me and tried to give me an angry scowl. But for the barest instant—her eyes twinkled.

I counted that as a major victory.

CHAPTER
TEN

ONCE I GOT BACK on the paved road, Trudi suggested we go to the house. Despite her protests, I went in the opposite direction.

"There's nothing out that way," she growled.

"Well, I know there's nothing the way we came, so we'll go exploring."

She settled back in her seat. "You're wasting your time."

"Okay, if we don't find something within a few miles, we'll do it your way."

That seemed to mollify her, so she just frowned out her window and ignored me.

After driving for about fifteen minutes, I was beginning to think Trudi was right. We encountered only the occasional burned-out car, hills, and a never-ending supply of pine trees. I was about to turn back when the trees gave way to a faded yellow sign for Bizher Auto Service. An ugly block building, painted the same faded yellow, squatted just off the road with two ancient gas pumps standing guard out front. Undisturbed patches of tall yellow grass decorated the cracked parking lot's pavement, and several junk cars sat in the open off to one side. While rundown, it appeared untouched. I thought it might be worth checking out.

I pulled in beside two ancient gas pumps and looked around for any sign we were being watched.

"Why are you stopping?" Trudi asked. "It's just a garage. There's nothing here."

Not seeing anything, I glanced at her. "Have you been here before?"

Trudi shook her head. "No, Grandpa said old man Bizher was a shyster."

"Then we won't know if it has anything until we go inside."

She frowned dismissively. "Whatever." She looked out her window. "I'll wait here."

I bit down on any retort and got out. Sammy decided I was the better deal and jumped out behind me.

The interior was dusty but surprisingly untouched. It had primarily been a mechanic's shop, so they hadn't sold a lot of other stuff. But it wasn't totally bare. On the wall behind the counter, I found some little convenience packs hanging from pegs. Right between the condoms and motion sickness pills, I spotted the acetaminophen. I grabbed all of them and then got a couple of bottled waters from a dark self-serve refrigerator beside the door.

Sammy sniffed around and scratched at a cabinet. To my surprise, I found an unopened box of dog treats inside. As I dug out a treat for Sammy, I realized I was a little hungry, too.

I scanned the room for some kind of snack when my eyes fell

on a coffee pot at the back of the room. Beside the pot sat four sealed cups of instant ramen noodles.

In college, I'd frequently eat a bowl for dinner, but once I married, Wendy forbade me to touch the stuff. I sighed. A bowl would certainly hit the spot about now—as it would for my pregnant companion. Too bad I didn't have a way to heat water. But as I looked at the glass coffee carafe sitting on its burner, I got an idea.

I went to the shop area and searched the drawers until I found a propane soldering torch. With a bit of finagling, I managed to heat the water using the torch and the coffee carafe and make two bowls of steaming instant noodles. I don't know if this would calm Trudi down, but it would do wonders for my stomach.

When I got back to the truck, Trudi was staring out the passenger window. I couldn't see her face, but she had an air of tired resignation. She didn't even look my way when I opened the door or when Sammy jumped inside. But once I got in my seat, I heard her sniff, and she wheeled toward me. Her eyes widened when she saw the ramen. "Food?" she asked incredulously.

I held out a cup. "Do you need help? I've also got some pills."

She shook her head and carefully reached for her bowl. She leaned back and propped it on her belly. She stared at it while I shut the door and settled in. I pulled a doggie biscuit from my pocket for Sammy and opened a painkillers packet for her.

Trudi gulped them down dry. "Thank you," she said softly.

We ate in silence. Trudi tore into hers like it was a Thanksgiving feast. I thought she was going to lick the styrofoam cup.

"Want another? I can fix it for you."

She looked forlornly into her cup. "No, I'm good," she said softly.

But I sensed something was bothering her. "What's wrong?"

"Nothing."

"It's got to be something. If it's the propane, we can find more."

She shook her head. "You don't understand. I screwed up. I've made that fitting change several times since the disaster. But today, I messed it up!"

"So." I shrugged. "Accidents happen."

She held up her hand and shook it. "What am I supposed to do with this? I can't do shit now!"

She sat back, and a lone tear started down her cheek. "And I gotta pee." It was like the ultimate insult. She gave a deep sigh and wiped the tear in irritation. "Is there a restroom inside?"

"Yeah."

"Spiders in it?"

"I'll check for you."

She nodded.

I helped her out, and with Sammy supervising, led her to the restroom. I did clear out the spiders.

When she came out, she seemed a little more composed. I set another bowl of ramen down on the checkout counter and offered her a bag of popcorn that wasn't too stale, but she shook her head.

She leaned over the counter to eat her noodles.

"When I was clearing out the bugs," I said, taking a bite of the popcorn. "I saw a propane tank through the window. I'm going to see if it has any left in it."

She set her spoon down. "I know why you're being nice. I wish you wouldn't do it. It makes it harder to hold you here."

I shrugged. "Listen. I'm not going to lie. If I treated you like a bitch, I'd still be chained in my bedroom. But being nice means there is a chance you will give me my book back early. I have no idea if my plan will pan out, but if it doesn't, at least my stay is a little more tolerable."

She gazed up at me uncertainly but finally returned to her noodles. "Thanks," she mumbled.

The word was music to my ears. I smiled to myself. I might have moved the needle just a bit, and I'd take what I could get.

* * *

It was dark by the time we made it back to the house and got the new tanks connected. Trudi tried to help at first, but after hurting herself twice, I shooed her to the house. She wasn't happy about it but grudgingly accepted.

When I finally came back inside, Trudi was sitting at the table nursing a cup of tea. A roll of bandages and antibiotic salve sat in front of her. A second cup sat at my usual place, along with a plate containing…

"A ham and cheese sandwich?" I asked.

"I'm not helpless," she shot back.

"Didn't say you were." I glanced at her hand. "How's it doing?"

"Hurts."

I opened my mouth to ask if she'd taken more pain relievers, but she answered my question for me.

"And yes, Mother, I've taken my pills."

I raised an eyebrow. "I'm not your mother."

"Thank God."

I just shook my head and sat down to eat.

She took a sip of her tea. "Everything connected okay?" she asked.

I nodded. "Everything went fine."

We didn't say anything for a bit. I finished my sandwich as we listened to the house settle. Sammy sat between us, head going from one to the other like he was watching a tennis match. I could sense Trudi wanted to say something, but at the same time, really didn't want to.

When I finished, she finally spoke. "I need your help."

I looked at her and took a sip of my tea.

Her bright blue eyes met mine and did not flinch. "I need to change the bandage on my hand. I accidentally got it wet."

I set my cup down and didn't immediately answer. I nearly asked if it was worth getting my book back but decided it would only piss her off, and she'd try to do it herself.

She took my delay as a refusal and sagged. "Never mind, I'll do it."

She started to get up, but I raised my hand. "I'll re-wrap it." I met her eyes. "I'm not that much of an asshole."

"I'm not giving you your book."

"I thought about asking, but I didn't think you would. You'd spend the night in pain if it might help your babies."

She leaned back and rubbed her belly. "You know I wouldn't make you stay if it wasn't for them."

Her eyes were locked with mine, pleading for under-standing. The sad thing was, I did understand. She was not doing this out of malice but to protect what she held dear. And not for the first time, I admired her pure grit. I wished I could have known her before the disaster.

I looked away, refusing to acknowledge her plea. I had my own problems and needed my book back. I had a promise to keep.

Taking my plate to the kitchen, I washed my hands and pulled my chair up beside her. I picked up the roll of gauze. "Wrap it the same as last time?"

"Yeah. When you get the old one off, I'll put some antibiotic on it."

I removed the old gauze carefully. Trudi held her hand at the wrist like she was preventing it from jerking away. I grimaced when the final wrap came off. Her first two fingers and her palm were one big blister. Her hand was also dirty, likely from working on the fitting.

"We should wash it," I stated.

She shook her head and reached for a disinfectant. "I'll just use this."

"No, it needs to be washed."

Her bright eyes searched mine. "All right. But I better use the water I boil for drinking. There's a jug of it beside the sink, but there isn't that much left. You'll have to draw more."

I met her gaze. "No problem. I'll draw some and boil it for later."

She looked away. "Thanks."

I brought a towel and a bowl of water for Trudi to wash her hand while I went outside and filled the bucket from a manual pump. It was at least forty years old and squeaked loud enough to wake the dead. I had seen water faucets inside, so it couldn't have been the well that fed the house. A short distance away, I spotted another squat structure about as big as a doghouse. That must be where the newer well was. It likely went much deeper than this surface well. With just a little electricity, Trudi wouldn't have to pump water again. The stirrings of an idea began to form. But that would have to be for later.

I put the water on to boil and went back to the table, where Trudi had just finished washing and applying fresh ointment to her hand.

I could feel her eyes on me as I concentrated on applying the bandage with the least amount of pain possible. It was almost like a pressure. I looked up, but her eyes quickly flicked away.

I needed to do something to fill the silence. "How's the babies?" I asked.

The question surprised her. "They've been kicking a lot today. In fact, they're doing it now. Want to feel?"

"Maybe later." She frowned in disappointment, so I thought I should explain. "Like you, I'm trying not to get too close. I'll be leaving when I get my book, and as you already know, I won't be coming back."

"Yeah," she answered softly.

We were silent again.

Trudi shifted in her seat. "Did you have family other than your wife and brother? Parents, maybe?"

I nodded. "Mom and Dad lived in Richmond in the same house I was raised in. It was too big for them, but Dad said it would cost more to sell it than it was worth." I sighed. "They died in the Judgement. I miss them almost as much as Wendy." I glanced up. "What about you? You had a brother. Aaron?"

She nodded.

"What was he like?"

She regarded me with her deep blue eyes, gauging what to tell me.

I returned to the wrapping. "Listen, you don't have to talk about it. But you made me tell you about my wife."

Trudi remained silent as I finished off the bandage with a clip. When I looked up, her gaze met mine, and she began to speak.

"Mom died when we were born, so Aaron and I have always been close. But we couldn't have been more different. I was always the quiet one, with only a few carefully chosen friends." She smiled wistfully. "Aaron, however, never met a stranger and had a string of girlfriends since middle school." Her smile faltered. "Like me, whatever made me immune to the craziness did the same for him. In fact, he saved my life."

She looked away, deep in thought.

"How so?" I asked gently.

She glanced at me tentatively. "When the disaster started, I was sitting in a little breakfast joint, finishing my pancakes and getting miffed at my friend Emily for not showing up. I had texted her several times with no response, and was about to try one last time, when all the phones in the restaurant went off with an emergency warning, telling all students to shelter in place. I was wondering what I should do when I looked out the window and saw a woman walking down the middle of the street, screaming at the cars going by and stabbing at them with a knife. A police car came roaring down the street with lights blazing." Trudi swallowed. "He didn't even slow down. He just plowed right into her and kept on going.

"I stood to go help when a man in a business suit ran in and announced for us not to worry. He was gonna make the voices stop. He ran through a swinging door into the back. When the screaming started in the kitchen, I ran.

"Aaron and I were sharing an apartment, and I couldn't think of anywhere else to go, so I headed in that direction.

"Outside, there was mass confusion. People were ranting about the voices and the need to make them stop. Standing on a corner, I spotted Emily, not moving, just staring into the distance. I went to her and asked her if she was okay. She turned to me and said she had to knock down the tower. That the voices were demanding it. I tried to stop her, but she punched me. As she ran away, a guy with a knife looked in my direction, grinned, and ran toward me. I fled."

Trudi gave a shaky breath and lifted her cup to drink but found it empty. She stared at it, puzzled, before putting it back down.

"The guy with the knife caught me and kept demanding I stop the voices. He raised the knife, and I thought I was gonna die. Out of nowhere, Aaron appeared and body-slammed him to the ground. He pulled me into a delivery van that was idling in the street and we managed to make it out of town. That's when they started blowing up stuff. We took shelter in the basement of an abandoned house and stayed there until it stopped. When we emerged, everyone was dead.

"We decided we needed to find out about Grandpa, so we made our way here. With all the wrecked cars and destruction, it took us three days." She looked down. "But Grandpa wasn't immune like we were. We found him hanging from the oak tree out back. Thankfully, he had released Sammy, so he was okay.

"Since we had everything we needed here, we stayed. Aaron

figured out how to use a wrecker to push or pull all the cars off the road so we could get supplies easier. That's why it's clear."

She paused, continuing to stare at the table.

"But something happened, didn't it?" I asked.

She nodded. Her good hand moved to protectively rest on her tummy. "I guess it was about a month after the disaster when we were out gathering supplies. The baddies caught us coming out of a department store. They claimed it was theirs and demanded compensation for trespassing." She glanced up at me and back down at the table. Her eyes were strangely devoid of emotion. "They shot Aaron, but I got him in the truck and got away. I buried him under the oak tree beside Grandpa."

I tried to keep my expression neutral. Trudi had just lied or omitted some crucial information. Call it a hunch, but something wasn't right. While I believed the baddies had killed Aaron, there was much more to this than she was telling me.

I wondered if I should call her out on it, but she didn't give me a chance.

"I'm headed to bed." She stood and pushed her chair under the table. "I'm exhausted, and my hand is killing me. Turn off the light when you're done." She went to her room and shut the door behind her.

Listening to make sure Trudi was still getting ready for bed, I went to the kitchen and began searching. She spent a lot of time there, so it was one of the areas I hadn't thoroughly searched. I quietly checked all the cabinets, even pulling out the drawers and looking behind them. When that came up empty, I checked the walk-in pantry. But all I found were shelves of neatly stacked food and paper towels.

I closed the pantry door and sighed in frustration. *Where in the hell did she hide it?*

"You won't find it in here," said Trudi, matter-of-factly from directly behind me.

I jumped and wheeled to face her. Trudi stepped around me wearing a long flannel gown and thick socks. She didn't seem concerned that I was hunting for my book. She put a glass in the dish bucket. Sammy sat in the doorway, looking at me like I was stupid. And maybe I was. But I needed to find that book.

She moved closer and looked up at me. Normally, her hair was pulled back with a clip. But now it was loose, forming a curly halo around her face. I couldn't help but think how young she looked.

She sighed. "You can search for it all you want, but you won't find it. I know you'll look for it anyway, so don't sneak around. I'm not stupid."

I wasn't sure what to say.

She searched my eyes. "Thank you for helping me today. I'm not sure what I would have done without you. I had decided I was gonna dislike you, but you're making that damn hard. I know you're not a baddie, but you're not what I expected either."

I sighed. "And you're definitely not what I expected."

The corner of her mouth flickered upward for just a moment. "Better to keep you on your toes."

I opened my mouth to reply, but Sammy gave a soft woof and turned toward the front of the house. Trudi gasped, and we both held our breath. Listening.

It was the dull whine of a drone.

Trudi froze, her face pale. I lunged for the lantern on the

counter and flicked it off, plunging the room into darkness. I turned for the kitchen window shade but collided with Trudi in the dark and stumbled, knocking her off balance. I managed to grab her, and together, we toppled over. I pulled her close and twisted, landing on my side to cushion her fall. She immediately buried her face in my shoulder and shivered.

Sammy sniffed us and lay down with us.

The drone got louder, and I heard it just outside the windows. It paused at the kitchen window above us, but I couldn't see it over the counter. The pitch of its whine shifted like it was moving for a better position to see. It no doubt had some kind of low-light vision, so it could likely see in. Not finding what it wanted, its buzz moved on around the house, looking in each window it passed. Finally, not finding anything, it moved away, the sound fading into the distance.

Trudi shook in my arms, a warm human lump beside me. It had been a long time since I had held someone. My dead wife had been the last, and that was well over eight months ago. I hadn't realized how much I missed being touched by another human.

And as Trudi's tremors subsided. She didn't immediately move away. And so we lay there for several minutes. Just sharing warmth. One human to another.

It was Sammy who broke the spell. He got up in the dark, his nails clacking on the hardwood floor, and lapped water from his bowl.

Trudi moved away from me, and I was surprised that I was reluctant to let her go.

"I've got to pee," she said as she slowly got to her feet. She flicked the lantern on low. I stood with her.

She looked down, embarrassed. "I'm sorry I grabbed you like that. I..." She swallowed. "That thing scares me."

"Was it the baddies?" I asked.

She sighed. "Probably. But we got the lights turned off in time, so I don't think they saw anything. They were probably just checking to make sure I hadn't come back here."

I nodded. "You never did tell me why you're hiding from them."

She looked up, her eyes reflecting the lamplight. "If I tell you, you'll hate me."

I shook my head. "I don't see how. They raped you. I don't think you can top that."

She stared at me a moment. "I can."

She turned away and walked toward her bedroom. At the door, she turned, giving me the saddest expression I'd seen from her. "I killed their second in command."

She went inside her room and firmly shut the door.

CHAPTER
ELEVEN

I DREAMED OF GERI AGAIN.

After Trudi went to her room, I called it a night and went to bed. I was dead tired, so I passed out almost immediately.

Until the dream.

I was sitting on the side of my bed in Trudi's house, trying to twist the ends of two electrical wires together. For some reason, I was desperate to make the connection, but when I brought them together, they would spark loudly and jump apart. After several tries, I finally grew frustrated and threw them at the door. Suddenly, Geri was standing there and caught them.

"Hey bro," he said and tossed them back to me. "Lose something?"

Before me stood a cleaned-up version of Geri, just as he had at Mom's last Christmas dinner. Fashion was never Geri's forte—he preferred contemporary nerd. But in the dream, he wore a nice sports shirt and jeans, his hair was combed, and he'd recently shaved. I could even smell his cologne. He looked good. *Maybe a little too good.*

"Why are you invading my dreams?" I asked. I knew I was dreaming again. It felt strangely similar to the last one he'd been in—it just seemed so *real*.

He laughed and threw himself down on my bed, propping up on my pillow and leaning back with his hands behind his head. "What makes you think this is a dream?"

I frowned. "Because you're dead." Even to my dream self, it seemed weird that he was talking to me.

He rolled his eyes. "Just because I'm dead doesn't mean I can't talk to you."

I couldn't help but smile. "If you were a ghost, you'd be in some girl's locker room trying to catch a peek."

He thought for a moment and nodded. "Yeah, I can see that. If there were any locker rooms left." He sighed. "But unfortunately, I'm not a ghost."

"Then what are you?"

He leaned forward, grinning. "I'm a memory. And the only reason I'm here is because of you."

The hairs on my neck stood up, and I stared at him in disbelief. Something about this conversation felt really off.

Geri shot forward and put a hand on my arm. I could feel the gentle pressure of his grip. "Now, don't go getting excited. You'll break the spell. I've got a lot of things to tell you."

"Like where to find my book?" I asked warily.

He shook his head. "Nope, that's not my department. I don't care if a bat-shit crazy woman is forcing you to shack up with her." He sighed. "Watch out for her, bro. She's not just carrying babies. She's got a crap load of personal baggage."

"I'm not shacked up—"

He waved a dismissive hand. "Like Mr. Waiting-to-die

would even consider cheating on his dead wife. Not that Wendy would care at this point."

I grew angry. "Don't you *dare* talk about her that way!"

Geri held up his hands in surrender. "All right. I'm sorry I brought it up. It's not even why I'm here."

"And that reason is?"

He grinned and sat up. "There's some important information I need to pass on. You could call it Geri's last wish."

I cocked my head to the side. "You are Geri."

He paused. "Not really. I dug up this image because it seemed the best way to deliver the message. But if you'd rather, there are other images I could take." Suddenly, Mom was sitting on the bed in Geri's place, wearing her favorite yellow sundress. Then it switched to Dad in his Go Tigers sweatshirt. And finally, back to Geri. "I just took this form because you wouldn't react so emotionally to it."

"Is that why you're not Wendy?"

He smiled and pointed at me in acknowledgment. "Give the guy a cigar. You'd be all crying, apologizing, and trying to commit suicide and stuff. Then I'd never be able to tell you anything."

"So, what are you?"

He sighed. "I'm what was in the injection that Geri gave you. He programmed me to save you from the Norns. I'm what you might call an anti-Norn. But time is running out—"

I jerked awake. Trudi was standing over me, holding a flashlight. "Are you all right?" she asked. "It sounded like you were having a conversation. You scared me."

I suddenly began to shake. *What just happened?*

Trudi sat down beside me and placed her good hand on my arm. Her touch was warm and surprisingly reassuring.

I put my head in my hands. "It was a dream. Geri was talking to me."

She nodded in understanding. "Aaron started appearing in mine a few weeks after he died. I thought they were just dreams for a while. But he always talked to me and told me things." She paused. "True things."

I frowned. "You mean like see into the future?"

She shook her head. "No, more like where the rabbit trails were or where to find undamaged supplies." She looked away. "Or if there were baddies close by."

I paused, unnerved by what she was telling me. "Geri said he was a memory."

She shrugged. "I don't know what they are. Aaron explained he wasn't really my brother or his spirit, but something different."

I didn't know what to say.

Trudi stood. "I honestly didn't think too much about the dreams. But a few weeks ago, Aaron told me when a certain person was camped nearby."

She hesitated, considering whether to say more. She finally turned back to me.

"And he wasn't a baddie."

* * *

I had lain in bed thinking about Geri, my dreams, and the Norns. I wasn't convinced that my dreams weren't the product of my abused psyche and that Trudi wasn't messing with me about Aaron. But after mulling it over, I eventually decided it didn't matter. I was going to meet Wendy, so I just needed to impress the hell out of Trudi so I could get my book back. As I drifted off to sleep, the beginning of an idea came to me.

I spent the next day trying to help Trudi while I thought about my idea. I did some reconnaissance around the farm and checked out the workshop. By evening, I was sure I could make it work.

The next morning, I got up early and checked the weather. It was looking to be one of those warm late fall days where Mother Nature teases you before slamming you with winter. Perfect for what I had planned.

My housemate wasn't up yet, so I fixed some powdered eggs and toasted some leftover bread. I even opened one of the jars of homemade preserves we had found.

She must have smelled the coffee because Trudi stumbled in just as I was putting the food on the table. She plopped down and stared at her plate, still groggy. If she had been a cartoon character, little bubbles would be floating around her head. It was cute in a strange way.

"How's the hand?" I asked as I sat down.

"Better, but still hurts. Didn't sleep a wink."

I smiled. "I can see that."

She gave me a dirty look. She spooned a large bite into her mouth and made a face as she chewed. "If it wasn't for the babies, I wouldn't eat this shit." She glanced up suddenly in concern. "Not that your cooking is bad. It's just what you had to work with. I'm tired of canned stuff and would love some fresh fruit or veggies."

I nodded. "I know." I took a sip of my coffee.

When she was done, she shoved her plate aside and picked up her coffee. It was time, so I made my request.

"I want to borrow the truck."

She stiffened and carefully set her cup down. "If you want to leave, then leave. But don't take my truck."

"I'm not leaving. I've got an idea that might make it easier on you."

"And why would you do that?"

"Because I'm trying to get on your good side."

She snorted. "I don't have a good side." She took a sip of her coffee. "And I'm not giving you your book."

"Didn't expect you to."

I waited. I knew she would ask. I just had to be patient.

She shifted in her chair and took another sip of her coffee before finally asking. "Aren't you gonna tell me what this great thing is that would help me?"

I gave her a knowing smile. "Water."

She waved toward the back. "I have a manual pump. It gives me what I need."

"Look," I said. "It's a shallow surface well. It's old, and the water quality is likely not that great. But you have another well already connected to the house. All it needs is electricity."

Trudi shook her head. "I don't dare use a generator. The baddies would home in on the sound."

I leaned back in my chair. "There is another solution. The row of pine trees just beyond the barn is thick enough to hide a couple of solar panels and still get sun most of the day. They wouldn't find them unless they searched."

Trudi gazed at me over the rim of the cup, thinking.

I pressed on. "If I can find a few, I can bring them here and have enough to run your pump."

She sat up. "You can do that?"

I nodded. "I used to be an electrical engineer. I haven't worked with solar panels since college, but I should be able to figure it out."

She thought for a moment. "I want to come with you."

"It might be safer if you don't."

"Not a chance. I go where my truck goes." A slow smile spread across her face, her eyes holding a mischievous glint. "I'll be ready to go in two minutes." She quickly slipped into her room.

I frowned. *What was up with that smile?* I got a bad feeling Trudi had her own agenda.

* * *

While Trudi dressed, I loaded some tools and old blankets into the truck bed and drove around to pick her up.

As I waited for her to come out, I closed my eyes and let the sun warm my face. Today reminded me of football weather. Wendy and I had gone to the same university, so attending the homecoming game was mandatory. I remembered tailgating with friends, having chili, and eating way too spicy chicken wings, then washing it down with some beer (only one because I had to drive). I remembered Wendy laughing at some friend's joke and getting soda up her nose. Those were such good times. God, I missed that woman.

The door slammed, and Sammy galloped out, leaping into the truck and assuming his seat in the middle. He gave me that "let's get going" look. I chuckled and turned as Trudi walked up behind me. My eyes widened. This was not the woman I was used to seeing.

Trudi was wearing a pink sweater and a brightly patterned maternity dress—her hair was neatly brushed and pulled back in a clip on one side. A larger coat was draped over her arm, and she held a small picnic basket in her good hand. She looked great. Her pregnancy bulge just added to her natural beauty.

But at the thought, my mind flashed to Wendy hanging in the garage, and guilt crushed my soul. She was waiting for me, my one true love. I needed to join her. I pushed my guilt aside and prayed that my wife understood this was all to get my book back.

"You look great," I said. "Where's the party?"

Trudi actually blushed, a delightful glow touching her cheeks. She tried to keep her face neutral but was struggling. "No party, but I thought a picnic might be nice while we get your panels." She held up her basket. "I brought sandwiches and a drink."

I gave her a mock frown. "Sounds like you're trying to get on my good side."

Leave it to me to sour the mood.

Her mouth turned down. "Mister Dreal, it's sandwiches. The babies might get hungry, and eating in front of you would be rude. Don't read too much into it."

She stepped around me and pulled herself into the truck using her good hand.

Well, there went the day.

* * *

With the baddies out there, we decided to stay away from town. Instead, we headed toward what had been a small, affluent community near a ski resort. I was sure at least one of the houses had solar panels as a backup.

The going was slow. We had to be alert for fallen trees and wrecked or burned-out cars, not to mention stopping while a black bear ambled across the road.

The road we used took us by several small mountains. We had been traveling for about an hour when I saw a sign for an orchard pointing up one of them. The sign promised a great view, and I was considering going up to scout out the surrounding area, maybe even spot some panels, when Trudi spoke up.

"Let's go up there," she said, excitedly pointing to the sign. "Grandpa brought us here every year, and they always had delicious apples. There might still be a few left."

I regarded her skeptically.

"Please," she begged. "I won't take long." She was almost bouncing in her seat.

Her excitement was infectious. I tried to suppress my smile and look stern. "I don't know."

She batted her eyes playfully at me. "If they have apples, I'll make you a pie."

I couldn't help but grin. "And if I won't."

Her face lit up with mischief. "Then this crazy pregnant lady is gonna push your ass out and drive herself."

"Well," I chuckled. "Since you put it like that, I guess we can detour for a little bit."

She patted my arm. "Good choice."

I turned in the entrance.

The orchard road was long and steep, but we eventually emerged onto a fairly level mountaintop with rows and rows of apple trees. A tall open shed rose above the surrounding yellow grass, with a country store and a sandwich shop on either side. The crazies must have missed the place because nothing had been touched. Strangely, the lack of destruction made the place even more lonely, like it hadn't been worth the effort.

To Trudi's delight, some apples were still on the trees despite most of the leaves having turned. At Trudi's direction, I pulled around back to the restrooms and the kind of apples she preferred. My eyes lit up when I spotted solar panels on the store's roof. I smiled. Maybe this was going to be easier than I thought.

Sammy was out as soon as I opened the door, tail wagging and excitedly sniffing around. Trudi had to pee, so I did a quick spider check in the restroom and then left to check out the panels. They looked to be in good condition, so I started searching for a ladder to reach them.

As I searched, I noticed a cell tower toward the edge of the orchard, which had also survived untouched. I frowned. Two parallel ruts marred the unbroken grass on that side—someone had driven up to the tower not too long ago. It couldn't have been more than two weeks. I could only hope it wasn't one of the baddies scavenging parts. I looked around, suddenly feeling very exposed. There was only one road up the mountain, so we needed to hurry along. I didn't want to get trapped.

I went searching for Trudi but didn't find her in the restroom. I paused outside it, wondering where she was, when I heard her call me from somewhere among the rows of trees.

I didn't see her, so I walked in that direction. About mid-way down the row, I spotted her pink sweater and stopped, not believing what I was seeing.

Trudi was up in an apple tree, barefoot and pregnant, and in a dress, no less. She was violating so many common sense rules I didn't know where to start. Her boots sat beside a stack of bushel baskets she must have gotten from the store. On top of that, she was high enough that her ankles were at eye level.

"What the hell do you think you're doing?" I spat as I approached.

I guess she hadn't been able to manage a basket while climbing, so she was using her injured hand to hold the hem of her skirt, forming a makeshift pouch for them.

She reached for another apple. "These things are worth gold. I told you I've been craving fruit." She looked down at me and grinned. "I've already eaten one." She plucked off her target and took a big bite. "And I might eat another."

I frowned. "Should you be up there as pregnant as you are? You could hurt the babies, or more likely, break your damn neck."

"I won't fall," she said, easing further out on the limb and making my heart catch. "I learned to climb with a broken arm when I was eight."

It just confirmed my suspicion that Trudi must have had an active childhood. She quickly took a couple more bites and tossed away the core. Her cheeks were so full she looked like a chipmunk.

"Trudi…"

She interrupted. "Here, let me hand these to you, and you can put them in the basket."

"I don't think…"

"And don't bruise them. I want these to last for a few days. I might be able to preserve some."

Her dress was only knee length, but with her holding the hem, she was showing a good bit of attractive thigh. I tried hard not to stare, but my eyes seemed to be irresistibly pulled toward them.

When she squatted on her limb to hold out an apple, her legs naturally widened to accommodate her bulging middle, revealing all of her toned, smooth legs.

And her panties were white.

I couldn't take my eyes away. Inside of me, I felt a stirring. Something I hadn't felt since that morning when Wendy and I were in bed—

"Mister Dreal," Trudi said teasingly. She tapped me on the head. "My eyes are up here."

My head slowly rotated up, and I gazed up at her in horror—my face going red hot. I turned away so quickly I made Trudi drop the apple she was holding out.

"Hey! What's the big deal? It's gonna be bruised now."

My body trembled, my chest tight, and my breath came in gasps. *Why was I acting like this?* She was eight months pregnant, for God's sake. *Am I a pervert?* I wanted to run. I wanted to get away from her. I felt my eyes grow damp. I wanted my Wendy.

I strode away, almost running, my emotions swirling. "I'll go get some more baskets," I said without looking back.

"Mister Dreal?" Trudi called after me in confusion. "Are you all right? I was only joking."

I didn't pause, desperate to get away. I heard Trudi mumble something to herself.

I was so deep in my need to get away that I didn't notice the approaching sound. When it finally broke into my consciousness, I skidded to a stop and listened. My eyes shot to the orchard road. While still out of sight, I could hear a vehicle approaching.

And we were out in the open where anyone could see us.

CHAPTER TWELVE

I IMMEDIATELY SPRINTED back to Trudi. She was still squatting on her limb, trying to figure out how to get down while juggling everything and not using her injured hand.

"We have company," I shouted, running up to her. "You need to climb down. Now!"

Her expression went hard. She flicked her skirt, and the apples went flying. "Help me," she ordered.

Before I was ready, she held out her arms and fell forward, trusting I would catch her. Her arms went around my neck, grasping tight. With no other place to grab and trying to be careful of the babies, I caught her waist and carefully let her slide down my body until she was on the ground. She paused for the barest moment and looked up at me, our arms around each other. After three long heartbeats, she stepped back.

The trees provided little cover, and Trudi's clothes stood out more than a hunter's blaze orange vest. I immediately grabbed the baskets and pulled her into the row of trees.

I quickly set the baskets out in a row and stripped off my camo jacket. I then pulled Trudi down with me behind the baskets and used the jacket to cover us.

She squirmed. "I have to be on my side."

She changed position and lay facing me, pulling up her feet to get under the jacket. I tried to keep a little distance between us, but the jacket wasn't that large.

Trudi sighed in irritation. She grabbed my arm and pulled it toward her, but I resisted.

"Now is not the time," she stated flatly. "I can't help that I'm a woman, but we both need to get under this coat. The worst that could happen is I kiss you, and that is not gonna happen today."

I swallowed. *Wendy, please forgive me.*

I allowed her to pull me closer, her face just inches from mine. I was so close I could smell the coconut from her shampoo and see the flecks of gray in her blue eyes. I swallowed and quickly looked through the gaps between the baskets, which gave a good view of the orchard's buildings.

Without a moment to spare, a shiny black SUV drove by the store, leaving a trail of dust and heading for the cell tower. Luckily, Trudi's truck was parked by the restrooms and not visible from where they drove. And even if they saw it, they would likely assume it had been abandoned.

"Do you know who they are?" I whispered.

Trudi shifted to see better, and I could feel her every curve move. I swallowed. This was going to be hard.

She shook her head. "Not yet."

The SUV followed the trail I'd spotted up to the cell tower. It parked, and four young men got out. The last one was a tall guy wearing a cowboy hat and a western-style shirt and jeans. I couldn't tell for sure, but I thought he had on a gun belt and holster. He looked like something from a 1950s western.

Trudi began to tremble. "It's the baddies," she whispered.

Suddenly, her head whipped around. "Where's Sammy?"

I blinked at her. "I don't know. I haven't seen him since he jumped out of the truck."

She tried to see him through the gaps between the baskets. "I've got to get him."

"That's not a good idea. Sammy's not wearing a collar, so they'll likely think he's a stray and just ignore him. But if they see you, there's no telling what they'll do."

She rolled to face me. "I have to look for him. He's the only family I have left." She moved to get up. "I have to."

I clamped a hand on her arm, preventing her from moving.

She stiffened. "Let go of me, Mister Dreal." There was fire in her eyes.

But I didn't back down. "Sammy's probably safer running free than with us. Which is why we have to be quiet and wait them out."

She stared at me a moment and then sighed. "I guess you're right."

Alarm bells went off in my head. There was no way Trudi was giving up that easily.

She suddenly reached around me and pulled my gun from the back of my pants—shoving its business end under my chin. "Let go of me, Mister Dreal. I want you to help me deliver my babies, but I will kill you if you don't let me go."

I searched her eyes, and I could tell she wasn't lying. But maybe I just didn't care. "All right. Shoot me. Let the baddies know where we are. Put your babies at risk. But if you fire that gun, they *will* come, and you won't be able to kill all four of them. And when they shoot you, and you die, so do your babies. As for me, I'll just have to explain to Wendy why some crazy-ass pregnant lady shot me. Either way, I come out ahead."

She searched my eyes, knowing I was right. Her arm trembled with the effort, but she lowered the gun. "If anything happens to Sammy, I'll shoot your ass."

She kept my gun.

They were too far away to hear, but they talked among themselves and pointed to various things on the tower. From their body language, I could tell Cowboy was their leader.

"Do you know them?" I asked.

"Two of them. The one in the cowboy hat is Zane." I felt her shiver. "He's the leader. The one in the blue shirt's name is something with a C. Charlie, or Cory, or..." she trailed off, thinking. "*Carson.* His name is Carson. He's one of Zane's captains. The other two, I don't know."

We silently watched them. After talking a little longer, the one Trudi called Carson broke away from the others and headed toward the store. He also seemed to be interested in the solar panels on the roof. Trudi and I watched him warily, worried he might find the truck.

Unexpectedly, we heard a baying howl. Carson looked over at a group of trees. "What the hell?" we could barely hear him say.

Trudi and I shifted to see the source of the sound. But it wasn't Sammy. This dog was a smaller breed—white with brown spots. *A beagle, maybe?* And it was not happy with Carson approaching. It continued to howl.

The man slowly pulled his gun from where it was tucked into the back of his pants and aimed it at the beagle. Trudi gasped, and I felt her tense.

Suddenly, an angry growl came from the trees in a deep voice that both Trudi and I recognized. Sammy stepped out. He paced back and forth, barking angrily. The man paused, glancing at Sammy.

Trudi gasped and tried to bring up her gun. But I grabbed it, and we struggled. "No," I said through clinched teeth. "You'll get us all killed. Sammy included."

"Please!" she whispered. "I have to."

But I didn't let up. Trudi gave a sob as I forced the gun to the ground between us.

The beagle howled once more and then tore toward Sammy. The man took aim at the retreating dog but lowered his gun when the pair reached the trees and sped out of sight.

Zane called to Carson, motioning him back to the truck. The man reluctantly put his gun away and went to join them.

After he rejoined the group, an argument broke out between one of those Trudi didn't know and Zane. The young man kept motioning at the cell tower, but Zane just looked at him and didn't move. Suddenly, Zane's gun was in his hand and pointed at the guy's face. Everyone in the group froze.

Zane said something and motioned to their SUV. The young man dropped his eyes and nodded. They all climbed back into the SUV and left.

Trudi and I watched and waited in case they returned, but they didn't reappear. I breathed a sigh of relief.

"You can let go now," said Trudi, a note of impatience in her voice. I still had her hand pinned to the ground.

"Sorry." I released her, and standing, threw off the jacket.

She took my offered hand to stand, but when she came up, she used her momentum to pull up close until our faces were inches apart. "Mister Dreal, if you grab me like that again, I will shoot you." She paused, her eyes boring into mine before finally letting go. She nodded toward her baskets. "Now, pick us some apples while I search for Sammy."

Her attitude pissed me off. "Only if you say please. I'm a prisoner, not a slave."

"You're an asshole."

"And you're a bitch."

We glared at each other.

She rolled her eyes. "Would you *please* pick some apples while I search for Sammy? That way, we can get out of here faster."

"Do I get some pie?"

"Don't push it."

She stepped away but turned back to face me. "I'm really pissed at you, but I have to admit, your quick thinking kept us safe." She paused. "Thanks." Her eyes searched mine. "And yes, I will make you your very own apple pie."

She then continued on into the orchard, calling for Sammy.

I smiled. Maybe, just maybe, there was hope I could get her to trust me after all.

* * *

I picked five bushels of apples and loaded them into the truck. Since the baddies had already scoped the place, I thought it best to leave the store's solar panels. I was sure there were others nearby.

Around noon, Trudi gave up on trying to get Sammy. She saw him several times, but he and that mysterious beagle would always take off. She didn't understand it. Sammy usually came when she called him.

She finally took a break, and we sat on the pickup's tailgate to eat our lunch. We were just finishing when Sammy showed up. And he brought a guest.

The beagle was thin, skittish, and female. No wonder Sammy liked her. I threw her some scraps of my sandwich, and she quickly wolfed them down, but five feet was as close as she would come. Any closer, and she would back away.

Trudi had brought some food and water for Sammy, so she laid part of it out for our guest and tried to coax her into the truck. The beagle wasn't going for it. She ate what was offered but kept her distance, and when everything was gone, she just walked away.

Sammy barked at her, but she looked back once before trotting off into the trees.

I hated to leave the beagle out there by herself, but then again, she'd been surviving just fine without us. Since I was afraid to stay much longer, we packed and left.

The next day, Trudi turned into an apple-peeling demon and started canning apple jelly, apple slices, apple butter—even two pies.

Since I wasn't allowed in the kitchen, Trudi let me take her truck and resume my search for solar panels. As I drove, I kept thinking about the beagle we had left at the orchard. The thought of her being alone on that mountain top bothered me. I was never a big fan of dogs, so I was puzzled why I felt that way. I guess it was because I identified with her. She probably had belonged to the orchard's owners and stayed, hoping that one day they would come home. I knew what that kind of longing felt like. The wanting to rejoin with someone you deeply loved.

When I passed close to the mountaintop orchard, I detoured and turned onto its drive to search for the beagle one more time. I called, put out food, and waited, watching the rows and rows of trees and hoping she would appear. But I couldn't find her. It was like she wasn't there anymore. Disappointed, I left some food just in case and continued my search for solar panels. I couldn't help but wonder if seeing another dog had given her the courage to move on. It was a comforting thought, and I wished her the best. Thank God I still had my reunion with Wendy to look forward to.

I did find some solar panels on top of a veterinarian's office, of all places. It was completely untouched. The crazies' logic baffled me sometimes. While they seemed to hate human medical facilities, they were okay with the ones for animals. It just seemed so weird.

Over the next week, I got them installed. They were low to the ground and concealed by some pine trees, so you wouldn't notice them unless you knew where to look. I had found plenty of panels, so even just a few hours of sunlight would give Trudi all she needed.

After that, I scavenged some batteries and concealed everything. The pump was more of a challenge than I thought, but I finally got it working. I was almost disappointed when I had everything connected and working. I had surprisingly enjoyed the work.

Trudi jumped for joy when water flowed from the faucets. She acted like it was Christmas. She danced around and made me watch as she flushed the toilet. I actually got a kiss on the cheek.

Things were going better than planned, and not just with the pump. My plan to gain Trudi's trust was working. She didn't feel the need to keep an eye on me anymore, which meant I could search for my book. I still felt guilty, leading her to believe I was on board with her baby delivery plan. But she was the one who had taken my book, so I felt justified. Once I had it, I was out of there.

A couple of days later, while cleaning up after lunch, Trudi asked if I could stay out of the house until dinnertime. She said it was a surprise. I was curious, thinking it might be related to my book. But when I later snuck a peek, all she was doing was cooking, so I left her alone and continued my search.

It was almost dark when Trudi called me to wash up. To my surprise, I found a fresh dress shirt, a bowl of clean water, and a towel on the porch. A note accompanying them asked if I could clean up on the porch before joining her at the table. *What was going on?* Intrigued, I did as she asked.

When I entered the house, I was welcomed by the sound of soft music and the wonderful smell of food and spices. When I went to the kitchen table, it was laid with fresh rolls, beef with gravy, mashed potatoes, and a real honest-to-god pound cake. Two tall, slender table candles provided the light, and of all things, a bottle of champagne sat to the side.

But what surprised me more was Trudi herself. She was not the frumpy pregnant lady I had seen over the last few days. Not by a long shot. This evening, she wore an elegant black gown and had put up her hair in a loose bun. Silver earrings dangled from her ears, and a silver necklace sparkled in the candlelight, calling attention to just a hint of cleavage. She had applied makeup, which highlighted her eyes and lips. She was every bit the young woman going out for a date.

She sat waiting at the table, looking nervous. For a moment, I was afraid she was trying to seduce me. But when I noticed five other places set at the table, each with a folded name card on the plate, I realized this had a different purpose.

"Wow," I said, carefully easing into my place at the table. "Everything looks great." I leaned towards her. "And you look beautiful."

Trudi's eyes twinkled in the reflected candlelight, pleased at the compliment. She gave me an embarrassed smile and relaxed a little. "Thanks," she said.

"What's the occasion?"

"Two things, really. One is to thank you for getting the water running. You have no idea how much I missed that."

I gave a deep, appreciative nod. "Don't mention it. I hope it helps you out." I almost added *after I'm gone,* but decided that probably wasn't a good thing to do right then.

"What's the second thing?" I asked.

She smiled. "To celebrate Aaron's birthday." She paused. "And my own."

I blinked at her in confusion. "Your birthday?"

She nodded. "I turn twenty-one today." She glanced at the other places at the table, and her smile faded. "I had a group of friends I hung out with—just a bunch of goofy girls. Since I was the youngest, we decided that on my birthday, we would have a night out on the town. You know, dress up, first legal drinks, dancing…" She paused and sighed deeply—I could see her eyes begin to shimmer. She blinked, refusing to let the tears come further. "But… things didn't work out that way. So this little party is for them as much as it is for me. I included Aaron because…" She shrugged, "…I just couldn't leave him out."

I nodded in understanding.

She took a deep breath. "So, first things first." She got up, opened the champagne, and poured each of us a glass, being sure to include those at the empty places. I stood with her as she raised her glass in salute. "Emily, Misty, Kiko, Beth, and of course, you too, Aaron. This is for you. Wherever you are, I wish you the best. And girls, and you too, bro…" she fought for control, "I miss you like hell." We drank and sat back down.

Trudi was subdued as she served us, and I thought this might be yet another opportunity to earn some trust points. So I asked about her friends. At first, she was reluctant to talk about them, but with a little prodding, it was a flood. She told me all about them, and then about how her mother died in childbirth, her father dying in the military, and how her grandfather raised her and Aaron. That led to stories of her and her brother, which I found quite funny.

Then, I talked about Geri's adventures, my childhood experiences, and my early dating disasters. Which, of course, led to me telling her about Wendy. How we met at a cosplay event—her dressed as a ninja princess and me a mecha pilot. Our first date—a Mexican place where she hated the food, but pretended it was great. Where I proposed at a mountain overlook as the sky put on a beautiful sunset.

Before I knew it, two hours had passed. It was the most fun I'd had since...

I immediately felt guilty. *What would Wendy think of me laughing like this?* She was waiting for me.

"Sorry," I said, trying to hide my guilt. "I didn't mean to ramble."

"It's all right," she said. "I enjoyed listening." She paused. "I can tell you loved her a lot."

"She was my everything." I looked off into the distance. "But I'll be with her soon."

The smile that had been on Trudi's face for most of the evening turned sad. An awkward silence descended upon us.

Her eyes went up. "The cake. We've got to have some cake."

She went to the kitchen and returned with two dessert plates, a knife, and a box of birthday candles. She took out three candles and placed them on the cake. "I don't have enough for twenty-one," she said apologetically, "so I'm putting two on this side and one on the other." Then she lit them. She was surprised when I broke into a really, really bad rendition of *Happy Birthday*. She grinned through the whole thing.

I leaned forward. "Now blow out your candles and make a wish."

She took a big breath and quickly blew them out. Then she looked at me expectantly. "Mister Dreal, would you please grant me my wish?"

I blinked in puzzlement. "And what is that?"

"Would you dance with me?"

I was paralyzed. *Dance with her?*

Wendy leaped to mind. She and I had danced a few times. The slow ones. "I..."

But my book. I needed to get Trudi to trust me.

I swallowed and rose, holding out my hand to her. "Be warned, your toes may be at risk. I don't dance all that well."

She smiled. "Neither do I. Just remember, I'm working with a whale-sized handicap."

We walked further into the open den to a clear spot between the TV and the sofa. A slow ballad was playing, so I took her hand and pulled her closer. We gently eased into the rhythm.

I glanced down to make some smartass comment when I caught her looking up at me. Her eyes caught the soft light and sparkled with a combination of mischief and delight—a simply perfect frozen instant. For the first time since we'd met, she looked happy and almost seemed to glow. At that moment, I wondered how someone with so much determination, so much pain, and so much courage—could be so beautiful. Despite how things were between us, I wanted to remember this moment. I was going to miss her when I left.

But as always happens with frozen moments, reality shatters them.

Sammy, who had been snoozing for most of the evening, suddenly leaped up and turned toward the front door. He gave a soft woof. Trudi froze and pushed away from me. She dove for her laptop, shutting it off and plunging us into silence. We each held our breath.

A moment later, I could make out the faint growl of an engine. Then another joined it, and finally, a third. And they were getting closer.

"I was afraid this would happen," she whispered. There was pain and resignation in her voice.

The engines grew louder. The loudest they had since I

arrived. Trudi quickly extinguished the candles and snapped off the lanterns. I retrieved my rifle while Trudi got her shotgun. Once we were done, we sat back down at the table, and Trudi turned off the last lantern, plunging us into darkness.

We sat listening to the engines get louder. I was pretty sure they didn't even have mufflers on them.

I felt Trudi's hand on my arm. In the dark, she was only a shadow. "I appreciate everything you've done," she said, sadness in her voice. "You have no idea. But they're gonna do something, and I need you to sit with me." Her voice caught. "You *cannot* go out there."

I heard the riders yell and hoop in delight. The engines roared, and I instantly knew what they had come to do. *My panels!*

I leaped to my feet, but Trudi grabbed my arm and squeezed it so hard it hurt. "Please," she begged. "Don't."

I sighed and sat back down. It's not like it mattered. I wasn't invested in this place. I would be leaving soon, and the panels were Trudi's gift. Yet, my hand curled into a fist.

Then why did I feel so angry?

They roared past the house, heading to where I had set up the panels. I jerked at the rapid blasts of an automatic rifle, the dull impact of the bullets, and then the loud smashing of something with a bat or hammer. It lasted only about five minutes, and then they roared away, whooping in victory. I could make out one saying, "*Take that bitch!*"

Trudi laid her head on my arm. "Thank you," she whispered. I felt her tears wet my shirt.

I sat in the darkness, listening as the violence of their

engines receded—my face expressionless and hard. *What the hell had I gotten myself into?*

What the hell had Trudi done to them?

CHAPTER THIRTEEN

THE NEXT MORNING, I was up at first light. Dreading what I would find, I quickly dressed, grabbed my rifle, and headed out back. Sammy decided he needed a little morning relief and went with me.

The air was cold as I walked to the panel's hidden location—my breath fogged, and the ground crunched under my feet. When I saw the damage, I stopped and shook my head in disbelief. Someone had taken a baseball bat and beat the shit out of one, and two lines of bullet holes ran through the rest. But it was the single word spray painted over them that infuriated me. A simple scrawled "NO" in blood red.

I didn't need this. I was simply trying to get Trudi to trust me enough to return my book. Maybe leave her something for when I was gone. But this? This was not just destructive—it was cruel.

I looked up at the sky, trying to calm my frustration. This was not my fight. I should just leave. Even without my book, surely Wendy would understand.

Sammy sniffed around the edges, then cocked his leg and

relieved himself on one of the broken supports. I shook my head. "You too, Sammy?"

He came over, tail wagging like he'd just done something freaking fantastic.

I couldn't help but give him a pat.

"Just let it go," I heard Trudi behind me.

I didn't say anything—just stood staring at the wreckage of my labor.

"Please," she added after a moment.

I turned to see her huddled in her oversized pink coat, which did nothing to hide her size. Her pregnancy had to be reaching the end. I didn't think she could get much bigger.

I breathed in deeply and exhaled slowly, my breath looking like steam in the chilly air.

"You knew they were going to do this." It was a statement, not a question.

"I thought they might do something, but I didn't dream they would go this far."

"Who are these people, and why are they so pissed at you? If you didn't have my book, I would be out of here so fast it would make your head spin."

"I'll explain." She pulled her coat tighter. "Can we go inside first? I'm freezing."

I waved her on inside but froze when I heard a faint buzzing in the distance. *Drone.* I didn't even hesitate. I raised my rifle while turning and took aim at the offending target. It was quite distant, and there was no way I'd hit it, but I was so angry that I just didn't care.

I aimed until it felt right and squeezed off a shot. To my surprise, the drone immediately dropped.

I lowered the rifle in shock. I'd hit it—just like with the slingshot. I felt the hairs on the back of my neck stand up. That should not have been possible. Yet, I knew exactly where to aim. *Something was different with me.*

"You shouldn't have done that," Trudi said softly.

"And they shouldn't have wrecked my panels."

"I thought you gave them to me."

I rolled my eyes. "You know what I mean."

"Still, you've shot down two of their drones now."

"It was a lucky shot."

"I'm not sure I believe that, but it wasn't what I was talking about. They're gonna do something else."

I frowned at her. "Then we'll need to be ready. Let's go inside, and you can enlighten me on why they're such assholes."

Trudi turned away without another word. But as we walked, I was so angry with her. *Damn her!* She was drawing me into her problems. I didn't need this. All I wanted was my book.

We went inside, and Trudi served us some cold cereal and instant milk. I thought it tasted like crap, but Trudi had no reservations about it. She dug out every morsel, tipped the bowl up to drain it, and then poured another bowl. She noticed me watching, then shrugged. "The babies are hungry."

We didn't talk while we ate. But when she had drained her bowl for the second time, I addressed the elephant in the room. "Tell me all about the baddies." I let my spoon clatter into my bowl. "And don't tell me you don't want to talk about it."

"I got to pee." And she started to rise.

I grabbed her hand and glared at her. "Then tell me quick. I won't be put off again. You know what's going on here, and I don't."

She sighed and sat back down. Her bright blue eyes held both sadness—and fear. "Talking about this is hard for me. It always brings on bad dreams." She looked away. "So forgive me if I skip over certain... things."

I nodded in understanding.

"The important thing to know is that they *did* capture us, and they *did* shoot Aaron. But what you don't know is that after he was shot, I made a break for it. In the process of escaping, I grabbed the gun from Zane's second-in-command—Brody was his name—and I..." Her voice dropped to a whisper. "Shot him."

She sighed. "I thought I had escaped from them. I holed up here for weeks, afraid to go beyond the water pump or the garage. That's also why I keep the lights low and blacked out the windows. Aaron and I had stockpiled a lot of stuff, but a couple of months ago, I was getting low on food and had to go scavenging. They must have spotted me because the night visits started a few days later. Just an engine on the road late at night or a drone flying past." She looked at me sadly. "I think it's his punishment. The *not knowing* if today will be the day that they don't just ride by... and they come for me."

"Do they know about the babies?"

She shrugged. "I'm not sure. But it's obvious they've been watching me closer than I thought. My greatest fear is that they will try to take them away from me."

I sat back, considering her. "Why didn't you just leave?"

She rubbed her forehead. "When the harassment started, I was too far along to consider moving." She paused and searched my face. It was like she was saving the best for last. "Please don't think I'm crazy for saying this. But the dream

Aaron told me my best hope of living was to stay right here until the babies were born."

I thought back to my dreams with Geri and the way I had shot those drones down.

Were the Norns helping us?

* * *

I lay in my bed thinking about my conversation with Trudi earlier that day. It was no wonder she freaked out when she heard their engines. As if killing her brother and raping her wasn't enough, they were tormenting her. The psychological toll of their drive-bys was huge. And she had still stayed. I couldn't decide if she was exceedingly brave or just plain stupid.

I turned on my side and pulled the covers up. What was I going to do? What *could* I do? With their numbers, there was no way I could go up against them. It was a shame I didn't have my book. I could have just gone to Wendy's favorite place, waited until her special day, and then joined her.

My eyes flew open. *What day is it?* I didn't have my phone, so I quickly counted the days since I arrived. I sighed in relief when I realized it had only been about fifteen days.

That meant I only had a little over two weeks until I had to have my book back and still make it to Wendy's place in time. The book worried me. What if I couldn't find it?

"Then you're screwed. And you'll greatly disappoint Wendy."

I sat up to find Geri sitting on the end of my bed and grinning. I flopped back down. "Go away. You're just a dream."

He sighed. "Unfortunately, I'm not just a dream. It's like saying a car is a fast wagon." He tapped the side of his head. "There's a lot going on under the hood."

I sat back up and carefully considered him. With a growing dread, I asked, "What are you?"

He thought for a moment. "I guess the closest technical term would be an avatar based on your memories."

I grimaced. "You make it sound like you're something out of a bad science fiction movie. Some kind of evil AI possessing my subconscious."

He chuckled. "I guess, in a way, I am. Not the evil part, though."

I studied him, getting an inkling of alarm in my head. "What do you mean?"

"That's what I've been trying to tell you. Geri injected you with not only something to help you survive, but also a series of messages." He glanced over at me. "The first was to explain what happened."

My eyes narrowed. "Go on."

He stood and started pacing. "As you know, Geri was involved in some deep research refining tiny robots, smaller than a bacterium. His team named them *Norns*."

"Isn't that from Norse mythology?"

Geri nodded. "The deities responsible for the destiny of all creatures."

I frowned. "The Norse considered them more powerful than the gods. Isn't it a little arrogant to name them after something so powerful?"

He shrugged. "I would have to agree."

I let it go. "So Geri was working on nanobots. We've had those for years, but they have serious limitations and were only used in a few specialty niches."

Geri nodded. "Exactly. Your brother's team found a way to

use them successfully as sensors and network nodes. Each individual node was not that smart, but once they were networked together, they could do all sorts of things. The team's big breakthrough was to crack the neural interface problem. No implants required, just having the Norns organize and stimulate the right neurons in the brain. They were self-replicating, too. Just one Norn could quickly replicate to connect a person's entire brain to the network." Geri smiled, radiating pride. "It was designed to be the ultimate interface. You would be able to chat with a friend by just thinking about it. Access the Internet. Even be warned of imminent dangers." He paused. "It would have made us gods."

I frowned. "But something went wrong."

Geri's shoulders slumped as he nodded. He sat back down on the bed. "There were problems. When we tested it on animals..." he looked away, "... let's just say they developed behavioral issues. We thought it might be an intelligence thing, so we allowed a few volunteers to try it. They complained of hallucinations, and we had to immediately remove them. We finally figured out the problem wasn't the Norns." He tapped the side of his head. "It was us. Our brains couldn't handle the flood of data. So we stopped all tests until we could figure out a way to filter it."

I nodded. "So far, so good. But something must have happened."

He sighed. "Remember those animal tests? We immediately stopped when we saw the results and returned all the animals. But rumors started on social media that we were torturing them. So on February 2nd..." He looked at me sadly. "... That's right, Groundhog Day, some activists broke into the facility.

The animals were gone, but they assumed we were hiding them and broke into the restricted areas."

Geri took a deep breath and let it out slowly. "They released the prototype Norns. And as they were programmed to do, they started spreading. It only took a few minutes for the people to begin behaving irrationally."

I gasped. "The hallucinations. The crazies. It came from them."

He nodded. "Geri happened to be in an isolation chamber working on a retardant to slow down the Norns and hopefully give the brain a chance to adapt. Only the retardant had a major flaw—it would only work on young adult brains, late twenties at most. Brains more mature than that didn't have enough neuro-plasticity." Geri looked at me levelly. "That's why he gave it to you. You were in the target age range."

"But how is it that some survived without the retardant?"

Geri sighed. "It appears a tiny percentage of highly intelligent young people had brains malleable enough to adapt. But of those I can detect, none are older than twenty-five." He paused. "Which means you're one of the oldest people left in the world."

That was a disturbing thought. But I had one burning question I had to ask. "Why didn't my brother use it on himself?"

Geri looked away. "He did, but he was too old. It bought him a few extra hours to get to you. But his brain couldn't handle it."

I mulled that over. "Will the survivors die in a few years as their brains mature?"

He shrugged. "The research is inconclusive, but Geri believed that those with adapted brains would live a normal lifespan."

"What about me?"

"You have not completed your transformation because your brain has been fighting the adaptation. Your depression is likely coming from that."

I sat straighter. "I'm not depressed."

Geri sighed. "Yes, you are. You're suicidal."

I shot back, my anger rising. "Only because my reason for living is gone."

He shook his head sadly but did not answer.

I shrugged. "It doesn't matter. I just want to be with Wendy. I feel so lost without her, and the pain of living is unbearable. She needs me."

Geri paused. "As does Trudi."

"No!" I yelled. "I won't do it!"

"But—"

"*I want my Wendy!*"

I jerked awake, my heart pounding. Trudi was leaning over me, touching my arm. I blinked up at her, completely disoriented. The room had the barest hint of light from the approaching dawn.

"You were yelling in your sleep again, and I couldn't wake you."

I sat up and put my head in my hands. The wisps of the dream circled in my head.

She sat down beside me. I could feel the warmth of her body in the chilly air. "You sounded angry," she added.

"I was!" I said with a little more anger than I meant to. "It was my stupid brother. I would be dead now if it wasn't for him. I would be with my Wendy." I rubbed my face—my emotions almost overwhelming me. But I refused to cry in front of Trudi.

She touched my shoulder. "In my dreams, Aaron makes me angry sometimes. What did your brother say?"

"He told me a bunch of nonsense about him working on what caused everyone to go crazy." I added more softly, "And that I'm depressed."

She slipped an arm around my back and pulled me into a brief hug. "Aren't we all?"

CHAPTER FOURTEEN

AGITATED BECAUSE OF my dream, I couldn't settle down. I was up early, brought in water, and did a few other chores, but nothing settled my mind. I finally told Trudi I was going for a walk. I think she was relieved. As I headed for the door, Sammy thought I needed company and followed me out.

The weather had decided to warm again, so it was a pleasant stroll. I walked along a path that meandered beside a field and made a right turn into a patch of trees. I hadn't explored much beyond that, but I was pretty sure it led to a neighbor's house. Sammy stayed right on my heels like he was protecting me.

But the walk didn't calm me. Regardless of what Geri had said, I *would* join Wendy. I had to. I just needed to figure out how to get my phone and book.

I sighed. I was sadly coming to the conclusion that just being nice wasn't working. Trudi was not about to give me anything voluntarily. No, I needed something she wanted so badly that she'd give up a piece of her leverage. That way, I could at least get part of my stuff back. Probably not my book, but maybe my phone.

Beside me, Sammy halted and gave his characteristic woof. I froze, thinking the baddies had snuck up on me. But when I looked in the direction he was facing, I was surprised to see in the distance the little beagle we had befriended a few days ago. Although it would have been quite a trek, she must have followed our scent. I was relieved to see she was all right.

Sammy gave another soft woof. I put a hand on his back and told him to stay. I didn't want to face Trudi's wrath if he ran off.

Unfortunately, I didn't have any food to coax her, so I gently called her, trying to get her to come closer.

After a moment of watching us, the beagle turned and was quickly lost in the woods. Sammy whined and looked up at me but did not follow. I guess he was missing his own kind—dogs were social animals, just like humans.

The beagle running away soured my walk, so I headed back, ending up in the workshop. I let myself in and tried to motivate myself to work on my latest creation. I had dubbed it Push Back One.

I had conceived of it in my anger over the destroyed solar panels. It was just a simple anti-drone measure. It transmitted radio noise on a spread of frequencies and should jam any signals for several miles around. But getting motivated to work on it was hard. I tinkered with it a little bit but finally gave up. What was the point? Something like this would only piss off the baddies and make it tougher for Trudi. I would be gone soon anyway.

I finally gave up and headed toward the house. It was unusually warm for November, but judging from the line of clouds in the distance, that would likely change. I imagined that much colder temperatures would be coming in the next few weeks, probably with lots of ice and snow.

I smiled, remembering how Wendy and I would cuddle under a blanket in the dead of winter with mugs of hot chocolate. But sometimes, she would break out the ice cream. She claimed it gave us an excuse to cuddle closer. She liked strawberry, while I preferred rocky road. I sighed. The days of ice cream were long gone.

I froze in place, not ten paces from the back door. Trudi had said she was craving ice cream. I glanced over at the propane tank attached to the house. There were refrigerators that ran off propane. I smiled. I knew exactly what to offer her.

I went inside the house, where she sat at the table, looking through one of her medical books. She wore an old sweatshirt and baggy jogging pants today. And of course, her pink slippers.

"Trudi?" I asked. "Can we talk for a minute?"

She eyed me guardedly. "I guess."

I sat down across from her. "I want to make a bargain."

"I won't give you your book back," she shot back.

"I know." I licked my lips nervously. "How would you like some ice cream?"

She frowned. "Are you gonna pop down to the store? I heard they're having a buy one, get one free special?"

I shook my head. "Seriously. What I would do is install a

refrigerator freezer, make some ice, and then make the ice cream in a churn."

She cocked her head to the side. "How…? Wait, you mean a propane one? I had thought about it, but I wasn't sure I could get one by myself or connect it up."

I nodded. "Just think how good some homemade ice cream would taste right now."

She glared at me. "You are evil."

"Also, a refrigerator would certainly come in handy with the babies. You could use it to keep milk cool. Not to mention, food would last longer."

She rubbed her forehead. "You're not being fair. I've been craving ice cream so bad it hurts." She sighed heavily. "You can't have the book. What else would you want?"

This was it! I jumped on it. "My phone. You would still have my book for leverage, and I could see my pictures of Wendy."

She considered me.

I held out my hand. "How about it? Do we have a deal?"

She looked at my hand in displeasure. "You're taking advantage of a pregnant woman."

I just grinned at her.

She stared up at the ceiling and then back at me. "You are Satan. If you can install a fridge and make ice cream, I'll manage to find your phone."

I nodded. "I can do it. Deal?"

She closed her eyes for a moment, her face a mask of concentration. When she opened them, the corner of her mouth curled up ever so slightly. "Chocolate?"

"Of course."

She slipped her smaller hand into my bigger one and gripped it tightly. "Deal."

* * *

Over the next five days, I worked on locating and installing a propane refrigerator-freezer. It wouldn't have taken that long if I hadn't been trying to conceal it from the baddies—doing outside work at night and using my now-completed Push Back One to block aerial spying. I even got us walkie-talkies so I could tell her when to turn it on. Trudi also contributed by pulling out an old ice cream churn from her attic.

On the sixth day, I decided tonight was the night. Since this was for my phone, I wanted to do everything I could to make Trudi think this was the best ice cream she'd ever had. My culinary skills weren't the best, so I decided to go for a showy presentation. Well, as showy as I could get in this broken world.

That morning, I convinced Trudi to let me fix dinner, and she agreed I could have the kitchen all afternoon. She probably suspected I was attempting the ice cream, but she kept quiet and played along. I did ask her to wear a dress for dinner, which made her give me a wary frown.

I worked in the kitchen getting everything ready, and when I had it just right, I went to Trudi's bedroom door and knocked. "Mademoiselle, your table awaits," I said in a fake French accent.

Trudi opened the door hesitantly and gave me a surprised once over. I had changed into my best clothes and donned a sports jacket I found in the attic. With a white towel draped over my arm, I stood erect and did my best to have a stoic expression.

I bowed formally. "Good evening, Mademoiselle. This way, s'il vous plaît." I turned and led her to the dining room, where I held her chair for her and placed her linen napkin in her lap. "Your dinner will be served shortly."

She watched in shock, unsure what to make of it. But there was a faint smile on her lips, which I took as encouragement.

I went to the kitchen and returned a moment later with a plate of spaghetti.

Her eyes widened. "You found sauce?" she asked in surprise as I set it before her.

"Oui, Mademoiselle. Courtesy of a house not too far away. I assure you it is the finest that can be found. It even still had the label on the jar."

She chuckled and took a bite. "It's good."

"Thank you, Mademoiselle. I will pass your compliments on to the chef."

Trudi just seemed to notice that only one place had been set. "Where's yours?"

That was deliberate on my part. I didn't want her to think I was treating this as a date. I wouldn't dream of cheating on Wendy that way, and it might have angered Trudi for trying to get close to her.

"Thanks for your concern," I said, bowing. "But the staff has already eaten. Tonight is Mademoiselle's special treat."

As she ate, she made some more comments about the food and really seemed to enjoy it. When she was done, I whisked away her plate, saying dessert would be served shortly.

I went to the kitchen and returned a moment later with my

creation. With a dramatic flare, I placed in front of her a bowl of homemade chocolate ice cream with a cherry on top.

Trudi gasped. She gazed up at me in amazement. "Wow," she said. She took a bite, and from her expression, it was utter bliss. "It's wonderful," she breathed. "I just can't believe it."

That was the last word she spoke until she had consumed the whole bowl. She looked up from her empty bowl with an expression of utter satisfaction. Her contentment was so genuine it warmed my heart and made this whole exercise worthwhile. And she was so pretty when she smiled.

I jerked myself out of those thoughts. "Was everything to Mademoiselle's satisfaction?" I asked.

She nodded. "You have no idea."

I wanted my phone but didn't want to ruin the moment either, so I helped her with her chair, intending to walk her back to her room.

But when she stood, she turned to face me—stepping close and looking into my eyes. "You have far exceeded my expectations, Mister Dreal." She paused, tilting her head as she regarded me. "Thank you." She rose on her tiptoes and gave me a soft kiss on the cheek.

She stepped back and gazed up at me for the barest moment, then seemed to catch herself and fumbled in her dress pocket. Taking my hand, she placed something small and square into it.

I was afraid to move. Afraid to look. *Was it really my phone?*

She smiled. "Go ahead. You can turn it on. I charged it for you."

I couldn't hesitate any longer. I hit the power button, and a moment later, my phone's background picture popped up. It was Wendy just before we were married. I ran a finger down the edge of my phone, wishing I could actually touch her. *Soon, my love. Soon.*

I looked up and caught Trudi gazing at me sadly, but she glanced away. She placed a hand on my arm. "That ice cream tired me out. I'm headed to bed."

Then she shuffled slowly toward her bedroom, her previous enjoyment gone.

I stood there, confused and feeling a strange disappointment. I had gotten my phone back, and I was slowly getting Trudi to trust me. The kiss proved it. I was accomplishing what I set out to do. But why did it leave me with such a hollow feeling?

And why did I feel so guilty?

I turned to clean up my mess when Sammy suddenly scrambled to his feet and gave a soft woof. Trudi, almost in her room, froze. She slowly turned to look at me.

Oh God, please no.

Trudi strode across the room, killing all the lights. I dashed to my room for my rifle, but when I turned around, Trudi blocked the door.

She was nothing but shadow, the only light coming from a tiny nightlight beside my bed. But I could tell her shotgun was pointed at me. "Sit on your bed and put down the rifle."

"Why...?"

"Shhh!" she whispered. "Please, just do it." She was almost begging.

Confused, I did as she asked. We listened closely as engines approached the house. Just like they had the other night, they roared to the back and then shut off. I heard male voices and gruff laughter, followed by the rattle of chains and scraping against the back of the house. Then, with the roar of an engine and a loud clang, the whole house shook.

I jumped up, but Trudi motioned for me to sit back down. "I swear I will shoot you if you try to get past me. You go out there, and you're as good as dead. It's what they're hoping for. So if you're that stupid, I might as well do it myself."

Trudi paused. "Besides," she said, bitterness creeping into her voice. "Getting killed right now might mess up your wife's plans to take you with her."

Her tone both angered and confused me. *Why did she say that?* She'd known my plans from the start—we talked about it all the time. It was like she resented me for wanting to join Wendy. But that made no sense. It was not like Trudi at all. The pregnancy must be affecting her mind.

I opened my mouth to protest but paused as the shouting resumed and their engines roared back to life. Then, accompanied by yells and gunshots, they tore past the house, the sound of their engines fading into the night.

After waiting at least fifteen minutes, Trudi lowered her weapon and turned away. She dropped into a chair at the table and put her face in her hands.

I grabbed a lantern and, with rifle in hand, made my way outside. I immediately saw what they had done. My grip tightened on my weapon.

The propane tank was gone.

They'd ripped it from the house.

Trudi was right behind me. She covered her mouth in disbelief. "Oh, shit," she whispered.

I stared at it. My anger burned. All I had wanted was to give

Trudi a little ice cream. Make her feel good about me and maybe get my book back. Up to this point, all I cared about was joining Wendy. But this? This was totally uncalled for. While Trudi didn't deserve it, they were also threatening the one person who knew where my book was. They were *interfering*. Their harassment of Trudi had just crossed over into my fucking business.

I looked into Trudi's eyes, and she gasped. I knew she saw the storm that was coming.

This had become personal.

CHAPTER
FIFTEEN

THE NEXT MORNING, after breakfast, I told Trudi I was going hunting. I grabbed my rifle and headed for the door, but I hadn't taken two steps before she jumped in front of me.

"You haven't mentioned wanting to go before," she said suspiciously. "What are you hunting for?"

"Dignity."

Her eyes went wide. "I won't let you."

I glared at her. "You can't stop me."

"I have your book," she shot back.

"Yeah, I know, which is why I have to do this. But if you'd give it to me, I could be out of this mess."

Her face grew pained. "You know why." She unconsciously placed a hand on her belly.

"Yeah, unfortunately, I do sort of understand, but I'm being drawn into something I don't want, and I need to see who my enemy is." I sighed. "Which is why I'm not planning on dying today."

"You're angry."

"Damn right I am." I gritted my teeth. "You have no idea. Someone is harassing the one person who knows where my book is, so I have to keep you safe to get it back."

She chuckled. I couldn't believe it. "You know, your logic is a little screwed up. You want to keep me from dying so you can commit suicide."

"It's not suicide," I spat. "It's to be with Wendy."

Her eyes searched mine again. "Are you sure?"

I shrugged. "What else could it be?"

She crossed her arms. "I can't let you take my truck."

"I wasn't going to. Too obvious."

She stared into my eyes a moment longer and stepped aside. She began gathering the dishes from the table. "Please be careful, Eyrian. I... we need you."

I snorted. "Yeah." I went outside, striding with purpose toward the woods at the very back of the little farm. When I was halfway across the yard, the realization hit. I froze in place and looked back at the house.

She'd called me by my first name.

* * *

I walked an old path headed in what I thought was the general direction of the baddies. The sky was a dull gray, and the breeze had a nip to it, much cooler than it had been the day before. It perfectly matched my stewing anger.

I found this trail a little over a week ago while searching for my book in the woods. Trudi said the local kids used it to race their ATVs. I was hoping that by sticking to the trail, I could avoid the eyes of whoever was watching Trudi's house. I was convinced they had a hidden camera somewhere on her property. It's the only way they could have known about the refrigerator. All the more reason to keep a low profile and not alert them that I was up to something. I needed more information about these baddies. And since Trudi wouldn't give it to me, I'd just have to go searching for it.

As I walked, I kept going over Trudi's explanation for why they were tormenting her. I couldn't shake the feeling she wasn't telling me everything. The punishment theory was definitely possible, but it seemed they would just kill her or take her prisoner rather than allow her to live separately. And why go to all the trouble of harassing one lone pregnant woman? It just wasn't adding up. Which was another reason to do this alone. I needed to know the unvarnished truth before someone got seriously hurt.

I walked for about two hours, checking a few houses and barns as I went. It was at the fourth one that I found what I was looking for—an ATV in decent shape. My theory had been that if the kids used the trail for racing, then there had to be an ATV somewhere close. This one was camo-painted and had four wheels, which was even better. It only took a little fuel and a jump from the battery I carried to get it started.

Since the garage had provided transportation, I explored the house's interior, hoping they had something else I could use. Initially, I was disappointed. Animals had gotten into most of the stuff through a doggie door. But surprisingly, behind a locked basement door, I hit the jackpot.

The owners must have been part of a militia or a survivalist group. Not only did I find the high-powered binoculars I needed, but I also found two drones, a bulletproof jacket, boxes of freeze-dried food, and enough guns and ammo to take over a small country. They even had flashbang grenades.

I would have to return and do an inventory, but not today. Today was a reconnaissance mission only. I loaded the binoculars, a spare gas can, and some of the preserved food into the ATV and once more hit the trail.

A short while later, I came across an old electric transmission line and decided to follow it, thinking it might be an easier route. However, I quickly began to regret that decision. Each transmission tower had been knocked over, forcing me to weave through their wreckage and costing me time.

I was about to turn around when, to my amazement, I topped a hill and spotted a tower still intact. I slowed my approach, wondering why it had survived. Then I nearly fell into the reason—a wide gully, hidden by the tall yellow grass, was carved across the path. I skidded to a stop only inches from the edge.

I got out to examine my options. I remembered reading about severe floods in this area right before the disaster. I thought this gully must have been created during that storm, and a lack of maintenance had only allowed it to get larger.

While the gully was only about three feet deep, its nearly vertical banks made it impossible for the ATV to cross. My only options were to backtrack or to proceed on foot.

The tower beyond it was easily a hundred feet tall and constructed of dull gray steel supports. For a moment, I considered climbing it to get a better view of the area. There were even ladder rungs built into one of the legs, practically inviting me.

But the corpse hanging from a support was a major red flag. With so many having died during the Judgement, it was not unusual to find bodies in odd places. But this felt different. The corpse was only a month or two old and swung from a rope around its neck. Even from where I stood, I could smell its decay. From the clothes, it had been male. But the real giveaway was his hands tied behind his back. This was no suicide.

It was a warning. The baddies must live close by.

I decided to go ahead on foot and scout the area. I should be able to narrow down their general location and determine how I could approach them without getting caught. Since I was running out of daylight, observations might have to wait until tomorrow.

Concerned with drones patrolling the area, I drove back up the path a bit and hid the ATV under some bushes. I wanted to be sure I had a way to leave quickly if I needed it.

I'd just stepped up to the gully's edge when the breeze teased my ears with the sound of a distant, dull growl. My head came up. *An engine?*

I shut my eyes and held my breath, listening. It was a small engine, but it was definitely coming closer. And fast.

I needed to hide.

I spotted a big cedar tree off to the side and sprinted for it. I just managed to slip behind it when a dirt bike crested the hill, heading in my direction at breakneck speed. A man drove with a woman riding behind—both wore helmets and jackets. From the sound of the engine, he had the throttle wide open. A moment later, a black SUV came into view, hot on their trail. I groaned. It was the exact same color and model that had been at the orchard.

I pulled back behind the tree and readied my rifle. It had to be the baddies chasing someone. My first impulse was to run, but the other trees and bushes close by had lost their leaves. There was no cover aside from the cedar. I was stuck.

The dirt bike zoomed past the tower, but the driver didn't see the gully until it was too late. He braked hard, but the bike skidded into it, hurling the passenger clear while slamming down on top of the driver.

The woman was immediately up. She jerked off her helmet, revealing her dark complexion and bushy brown hair. She scrambled to the bike. "Kyle!" she screamed at him. "Get up!" She heaved the bike off him, but the man didn't move.

The SUV stopped at the gully's edge, and two men with rifles got out, carefully approaching the drop-off. One of the men wore a blue-and-white college letterman jacket. He had really broad shoulders, and I thought he might have been a football player before the Judgement. The other man was leaner and dressed in a brown leather jacket and a black cowboy hat. While not the Zane character I had seen at the orchard, he had to be one of his captains.

The woman knelt protectively over the man and pulled a knife from her belt. She held it out defensively toward the men. Even from where I stood, I could see her hand trembling.

She watched them warily approach. "I'm not going back," she spat.

Black Hat squatted on the gully's edge while the football guy trained his rifle on her.

"Luce," Black Hat said calmly. "It doesn't have to be this way. You're going back whether you want to or not. The only question is how many bruises you'll have. Make it easy on yourself."

Luce glared up at him with absolute hatred. "I am not that bastard's whore. I'll die before I go back."

"All right," he said in that same calm voice. "Zane wanted me to ask you nicely, but he also said we could kill you if you put up a fight." He took off his hat and wiped his forehead on his sleeve. "So I'll ask one more time. Will you please come back with us?"

She pulled her unconscious friend closer. "No way in hell."

The man reseated his hat and stood. He paused for a moment, thinking. He pointed to her friend. "You like Kyle, don't you? That must be the reason you ran. Why you like that wimp, I'll never—"

"He's not a wimp!" she spat. "He's more man than all of you put together."

Black Hat sighed. "Sorry, but I have my orders." He readied his rifle, pointing it at her. "I'll shoot Kyle first and then you." He made a show of taking the safety off and aiming at the man's head.

"On three." He paused, carefully taking aim. "One… two—"

"WAIT!" she screamed.

Black Hat leisurely looked in her direction. "What."

Luce licked her lips. "If I come with you, will you let Kyle go?"

The man thought for a moment. "Sorry, but Zane said I have to shoot him. He stole property."

"I'm not that bastard's property," she spat.

He shrugged. "Doesn't matter. I still have to shoot him."

"Then I will fight you." She stood and raised her knife.

Black Hat thought for a moment. "How about we compromise?"

He quickly re-aimed his rifle and shot the unconscious man in the thigh.

Luce screamed. She dropped her knife and immediately put pressure on her friend's wound.

"There," said Black Hat without a trace of emotion. "I shot him. And if you'll come with us quietly, I won't shoot him again." He paused. "But next time, I'll aim a little better."

Anger boiled inside me. I ached to jump out and take them all on. But I didn't dare. I might get one, but I wasn't sure I could get both. Plus, there was Trudi to consider. I didn't want to cause her any more trouble.

Luce glared up at him, then turned with a softer gaze to her friend. "I'll go," she said with resignation.

Black Hat turned to the football guy and nodded his head in her direction. The man hopped down into the gully.

Luce started to unzip her companion's jacket. "Let me bandage his wound, and you can help me—"

He grabbed her arm and jerked her up.

"What?" She struggled to pull her arm back. "I have to bandage his leg before we move him."

Black Hat's gaze was cold. "Sorry Luce. Kyle's not coming with us."

Luce shook her head. "But..."

Black Hat squatted down again on the gully's edge. "This is the best I can do. If Zane sees him, he'll put one in his head for sure."

Luce looked close to tears. "He might die. Just let me…" She reached toward him.

Black Hat whipped his rifle around and shot into the dirt just inches from Kyle's head.

"No more discussion." He looked toward the football guy. "Bring her."

Without hesitation, the man pushed her toward the gully's edge and shoved her up. Black Hat caught her and helped her stand. Despite her protests, they dragged her to the truck and stuffed her inside the cab. They drove back the way they had come.

I watched the truck go over the hill, shaking in anger. I kept telling myself there was nothing I could do. But I still felt so helpless. I hadn't been able to help that girl. Everything I tried to give Trudi had been destroyed. And I'd let Wendy die. There was no other way to look at it. I was of no use in this new world. I just needed to join my wife and leave all this mess behind.

After making sure they were gone, I headed back to the ATV but stopped when I heard moaning. The guy was still alive. I was no doctor, but he probably had a concussion and could bleed out from his leg wound. I felt terrible, but there was nothing I could do for him. I couldn't get mixed up further in their mess.

I sadly went to my ATV and pulled the branches off of it, but thoughts of the young man wouldn't leave. Wasn't his name Kyle? Luce must have really loved him to sacrifice herself like she did. At least love was alive somewhere in the world.

I looked toward the gully. I didn't dare help him. I didn't know if he was a victim or someone worse than the baddies.

Even if I did take him back to Trudi's, there was no guarantee he wouldn't try to kill us. Cold logic said I should leave him.

I sat down in the driver's seat and reached for the key.

But I couldn't make myself turn it.

Wendy would have helped him. She was the kindest, sweetest person I'd known.

She would be disappointed if I left him.

"Dammit!" I smacked the wheel.

I took a deep breath and let it out slowly.

I drove the ATV back to the gully's edge and jumped down beside him. His pant leg was soaked with blood, and he was trying to sit up. I gently pushed him back down and pulled off his helmet. He had a head of blond hair and glasses that were surprisingly intact but bent against his face. He was barely old enough to vote.

Luce's knife was lying beside him, so I cut off his pant leg and used it, along with his belt, to tightly bandage the wound. Fortunately, the bullet had gone completely through the fleshy part of his thigh, so I thought the lucky bastard might actually survive.

"Can you stand?" I asked. He seemed to have trouble focusing on me but nodded. Working together, I got him out of the gully and onto the ATV behind me. He passed out immediately, but the seat held him in place, so I didn't think he would fall off.

As I retraced my path back home, I wondered what Trudi would think about having an unexpected houseguest. I snorted. Maybe she'd take him prisoner instead of me.

But as I drove away, I felt something I hadn't felt in quite some time. The feeling that I was doing the right thing. I'd told Trudi I was going to hunt for dignity. And by helping this man—

I think I'd found it.

CHAPTER
SIXTEEN

IT WAS DARK WHEN I arrived back at the house. When I got
back in range, I radioed Trudi so she wouldn't freak out when
she heard my ATV. I chose not to mention that I was bringing a
guest, which might also have freaked her out.

Trudi had her back to me when I eased open the back door
and carried the unconscious Kyle in on my back.

"About time…" She turned and stopped dead, her eyes going
wide. I set him down on the table, which was thankfully clear.

Trudi helped me lay him back. "What did you do to him?" she
asked accusingly.

I rolled my eyes. "I didn't do a damn thing. The baddies shot
him and took the woman that was with him."

She touched his forehead and then grabbed his wrist, feeling
for a pulse. "He's in shock." She eyed the bullet wound on his
thigh and my makeshift bandage. "What happened?"

I sighed. "I was in the wrong place." I then told her about
what I had seen.

She gave a tiny shake of her head. "And you brought him here? You're putting all of us in danger."

I looked at him lying on the table, remembering my own internal debate. "Could you have left him to die?"

She gazed at me with those blue eyes. I saw conflict, but then they settled, and she put a hand on her pregnancy bulge. "No," she said. "I couldn't have."

I nodded. "What do I need to do for his wound? Do I need to stitch it up or anything?"

She frowned. "What makes you think I know how to treat a bullet wound?"

"Because you were studying to be an RN. Surely, you've had a first aid course."

Trudi looked at me like she was trying to decide whether to help me. She finally said, "You treat it like a puncture wound. Judging from where it hit his thigh, it missed the major blood vessels. It just needs to be bandaged tightly."

"I'll get…"

She held up a hand. "*You* stay out of my stuff. I'll get bandages."

Trudi came back with a well-stocked first aid kit, and she quickly disinfected the wound.

"Do you know him?" I asked as she began to bandage the wound.

Trudi remained focused on her task. "I didn't see him. He must be new."

"Hmmm. There was…"

Trudi paused and gave me a deadly scowl. "No more."

I guess I'd pushed her too far. I nodded, and she went back to working on Kyle.

When she was done, she pulled me into the kitchen. "You know it's dangerous for him to be here," she whispered. "If they shot him and then don't find his body, they're gonna come looking. And if they find him here, they'll do more than jerk out the propane."

I waved toward the dining room table. "Then what are we supposed to do? We can't send him out like that."

She frowned. "I don't know. I guess we're stuck with him for tonight. But we need him out of here as soon as possible."

"Any suggestions where?"

She thought for a moment. "What about relocating him to one of the other houses close by?"

I shook my head. "He's going to need help with that leg, and they would likely notice us traveling back and forth."

We both grew quiet, thinking.

I rubbed my eyes, the day's activity catching up to me. "Let's sleep on it. Maybe we'll think of something." I glanced in his direction. "Should we handcuff him to make sure he doesn't try to hurt one of us?"

Trudi met my gaze. "I don't have the cuffs anymore. I hated them."

I started to ask why. But I realized it was likely because they had been used on her. I began to appreciate just how far out of her comfort zone she had gone to capture me.

She looked away. "Besides, I gave him something for pain. He will sleep for a while."

"Let's put him in my bed for tonight. I'll sleep on the floor beside him." I paused. "Keep your shotgun with you, just in case."

She nodded. "I always do." She sighed and pointed to the

kitchen. "I left you a plate on the counter. I found an old camping stove, so it's at least more than a sandwich."

"Thanks."

She gazed up at me like she wanted to say more, but instead patted my arm and turned away, heading for her bedroom.

But I had one last question. It had bothered me since the girl, Luce, had been taken.

"Trudi, the girl that they took."

She stopped and looked over her shoulder at me.

I knew the answer before I asked it, but I had to know, "Are they going to... you know... do what they did to you?"

She sighed sadly. "Yeah."

* * *

Kyle awoke once in the night, calling for Luce, but he didn't seem to know where he was. By the time I awoke enough to think, he had passed out again.

The next morning, just as the sun was rising, he woke me. "Mister, I've got to go to the bathroom real bad."

Thankfully, the bucket was still in my room. With a lot of groaning from his injury, I helped him with his business while explaining where he was, what happened after his crash, and who shot him. He was weak, but his eyes were alert. He didn't say much until I got him back in bed and propped up with a couple pillows. Then he asked the question I didn't want to answer.

"Where's Luce? She was with me on the bike." He licked his lips. "What happened to her?"

I forced myself to look him in the eye. "The men that shot you took her. She only went to keep them from killing you."

His shoulders slumped. "She should have let them."

"She knew they were taking her one way or another. Keeping you alive was the best deal she could get."

He tried to get up. "I have to go get her." But his breath caught, and his hand went to his leg.

I shrugged. "I'm not going to try to keep you here. But I don't think it wise to go anywhere in your condition."

He glared up at me. "Do you have any idea what they are going to do to her?" he spat.

I frowned. "Unfortunately, I do. But running off half-cocked isn't going to help anyone. Yourself included." Kyle looked determined, so I thought I would distract him. "What's your name? Mine's Eyrian Dreal. I used to live in Norfolk."

"I'm Kyle Wilston, and my girlfriend's name is Luce Everhart. We're both from Kentucky." He looked down at his hands. "Not that it matters anymore. We didn't meet until a few months ago when a wildfire came through. We just happened to pick the same lake to ride it out on. Luce said it was God looking out for us. I think it was just dumb luck."

The luck comment made me think of the Norns. Was it possible they had arranged for the couple to meet? Before my conversation with Geri, I would have dismissed it. But now? I wasn't so sure.

"Anyway," he continued. "We kind of latched on to one another and headed east, hoping to meet some other people. Luce said she had some relatives in this area and was hoping they had survived." He looked sheepish. "We encountered Zane's bunch a couple of weeks ago. They were the first humans we'd seen since crossing the mountains."

"So they didn't force you to join them?"

Kyle shook his head. "No. At first, they treated us like celebrities, especially that Zane fellow. But I could tell he was really only interested in Luce. Things got ugly when she turned down his offer to warm his bed. We managed to escape, but…" He looked down and swallowed. "You saw. Which is why I've got to get her."

"How many people does the group have? I mean, in total?"

He thought for a minute. "About twenty-four. There's fourteen guys and ten women."

"What about Zane? What's he like?"

Kyle snorted. "He's a narcissistic psycho. Sweet as honey one minute, then a bastard the next. Thinks he's some kind of gunslinger and wears a cowboy hat and boots. He acts like he owns everything."

I heard movement in the kitchen. Trudi must have snuck by while I was helping Kyle.

"Breakfast," she said flatly from outside the door. I glanced up at her and could tell she was wound tight. This must be dredging up some painful memories.

She wore her typical slippers, pink socks, and maternity jumper dress. Sammy was right on her heels, his tail wagging and eyes on the plate she carried. Trudi gave him a glare, and the dog dropped his head and went to his bed.

"I figured you'd want to eat here and let your leg rest," she said to our guest.

His eyes locked on her pregnancy bulge. "You're her, aren't you?" he said softly. He looked up at Trudi in amazement. "Zane talked about you every day."

Trudi froze. She glared at him, lips pursed and face turning red. "Say his name again, and you'll eat buckshot instead of eggs."

She slowly turned her gaze on me, daring me to say anything. I held up my hands in surrender.

My new friend, however, couldn't read the room. "Someone said you're his baby momma. Is it true?"

Trudi threw her plate at him, barely missing his head—the plate shattered against the wall, scattering eggs and sausage across the floor and bed. She stomped off into the kitchen. A moment later, I heard the door slam hard enough to rattle the windows.

I hesitated, wondering if I could leave Kyle unattended. Sammy knew his priorities and went to check out the spilled food on the floor. I grabbed him and pulled him toward the door so he didn't accidentally cut himself or, heaven forbid, chomp down on some glass.

I yelled at the young man as I stepped outside. "Don't think of moving off that bed!"

I grabbed my coat and headed out back, dragging Sammy after me.

Once outside, I let him go. He gave the back door a longing look but finally huffed and trotted off. I followed.

When I rounded the barn, I found Trudi standing with her back to me, arms tense, facing the huge oak. She looked to be shivering in the cold—no coat and still in her slippers.

Sammy eased up beside her and sat, looking up at his mistress with concern. I walked over, took off my coat, and placed it on her shoulders.

It was then I realized she wasn't shivering. She was crying.

It touched me. What was it like carrying the children of the man who took you prisoner? Who murdered your brother? Raped you? Impregnated you with babies that could kill you? I shook my head. No wonder she was a little insane. I would have crumpled under that weight.

I stepped beside her, careful not to glance her way. "I'm looking for a crazy pregnant lady who throws a deadly dinner plate. Know where I can find her?"

Out of the corner of my eye, I saw her wipe her eyes on her sleeve. She sniffed. "You're not funny."

"Wasn't trying to be. I call'm as I see'm."

We stood there for a few moments, saying nothing, as she occasionally wiped her eyes. She finally sighed and pulled the coat tighter around herself.

I rubbed my arms. "You know it's cold out here."

"It's not that bad."

I huffed. "It's because you're wearing my coat."

"Then you're a dumbass for giving it to me."

"Wendy used to tell me that too. The dumbass part."

"Smart lady."

I looked over at her. The cool breeze was gently ruffling her hair, and her eyes were red and puffy.

I sighed. "I thought we agreed we weren't going to lie to each other."

Her head snapped in my direction. "I didn't lie."

"You did by omission."

"I *omit* the location of your book. That doesn't mean I'm lying."

I shook my head. "This is different. This affects not only my safety but yours. I think I need to know."

She looked near tears again. "It's hard to tell it." She paused. "It might affect how you see the babies." She tugged the coat a little tighter. "And what you think of me."

I snorted. "You mean worse than a batshit crazy pregnant lady?" I shook my head. "I don't think you can get worse than that."

She looked up at me. "You sound like an asshole when you try to be funny."

I chuckled. "Then don't laugh."

Despite her best efforts, the corner of her mouth curled up. "You know I hate you." She met my gaze, and for just a moment, I saw the glint of something I didn't think she intended for me to see. A longing. A need. And then, just as quickly, her guard was back up.

I rubbed my arms. "So, are you going to tell me?"

She sighed. "Yes, but not here. Let's get out of the wind." She grabbed my hand and pulled me toward the garage.

"Are we taking the truck somewhere?" I asked.

She shook her head. "No. My back is killing me, and the truck is the only place we can sit down away from our guest."

Inside the garage, Trudi opened the truck's driver's side but had to slide the seat back one more notch before she could sit comfortably. I got in beside her.

"They've grown," I commented.

She rubbed her bulge and gave a half smile. "I know. When I think I can't get any bigger, I do."

"It's soon, isn't it?"

She nodded and looked out the windshield distractedly. "By my reckoning, it could be anytime between now and the next two weeks. If it's longer than three, I'll be in trouble."

We sat in silence for a moment. Then she jumped.

"The little buggers. One of them kicked me." She reached across and grabbed my hand, putting it on her bulge. "They're really active right now. It almost feels like they've started fighting already."

Then I felt it. A little lump that moved, disappeared, and then reappeared. It really was a miracle. I became aware of the warmth of her hand on top of mine, and I couldn't help but look into her clear blue eyes. Gazing into those pools was so very dangerous. I could easily get lost in them. Suck me right in.

But I had Wendy.

I jerked my hand away harder than I meant to, cradling it like it was burned. I could still feel her warmth on my skin. I wasn't sure I wanted it to leave.

I cleared my throat and sat back. "You were going to tell me the truth about what happened."

Trudi stared out her window for at least a full minute before she started. "I didn't tell you the complete story of our capture. The basics were right, so I didn't lie. I really was taken captive, and Aaron was shot. But I left out some things between those two events. I don't like to talk about it. It makes the dreams all that much worse."

She took a deep breath. "On that first day, both of us were captured. Aaron and I were bound with zip-ties, and they drove us to one of those upscale neighborhoods on a lake. Zane had set himself up in the biggest mansion in the area."

Her eyes grew moist, but her face stayed rigid. "We were separated. The men took Aaron off to the mansion next door while Zane and a couple of the women took me inside. They had everything in there. Guns, jewelry, TVs, games, you name it, he had it."

She paused for several heartbeats. "He then explained that he wanted to..." She made air quotes. "'Get to know me,' and as long as I did everything he said, Aaron would be safe."

Looking away, she blinked several times before continuing. "And if I was really nice—in other words, go to bed with him— he would let us go after a week. He gave me the rest of the day to decide. Like I had a choice." She shivered. "He was a creepy bastard, too. I found out later he only wanted me because I looked like his dead girlfriend."

A tear rolled down her cheek. "So I accepted his offer. And I was very, *very* good to him—for *seven fuckin' days.*"

She shook her head. "But we didn't, you know, do it all the time. It was like he needed to prove he was the better man. Toward the end, he started calling me Julie and would beat me for cheating. It was fuckin' bizarre. He also kept referring to Aaron as my boyfriend. I told him Aaron was my brother, but all it did was earn me more..." she paused, "...discipline."

She wiped at her eyes. "I did figure out why he was their leader. Everyone was afraid of him. Not only was he a psychopath with absolutely no fear, he was some kind of martial arts student. I saw him talking to one guy, and he was all chummy with him. Then, the very next second, the guy was on the ground with a broken arm, and Zane's six-shooter shoved up his nose. No one was brave enough to stand against him or leave."

She looked away—her face pained. "So, on the eighth day, I worked up my courage. I asked if he was gonna keep his word and let us go. I think it shocked him that I would even ask. But then he nodded and said we would go see Aaron."

She put her face in her hands. "He made me dress up like a slut, saying I needed to look good for my man. And I did it. Anything to get Aaron free. He grabbed Kendrick, his second in command, plus some girl that would flinch if you talked to her too loud, and then took me to the mansion next door. They had him in this massive garage with three pickup trucks."

Her voice trailed off, and she looked out the window, not speaking. I thought maybe she was done, but she sighed and continued. "Aaron had been beaten. All of his fingers were broken. His eyes and face were all cut and swollen." She gripped the steering wheel tightly. "He was tied to a chair, and when I walked in, he tried to smile, but... he couldn't. Then he whispered my name." She looked at me. "Zane went to him and jerked his head back by his hair. He asked me if this was the man I wanted? This pathetic piece of shit." She took a deep breath. "I yelled at Zane that he was my brother. Then I knelt before Aaron and told him I was sorry. We were leaving. I told Zane to let him go."

She was quiet for a moment. "Then, fast as lightning, Zane pulled his revolver and shot Aaron in the head." Trudi's hands began to tremble. "His blood splattered all over me. I remember looking up at Zane in horror at what he had done. He told me that it was my fault Aaron was dead. If I had chosen correctly, he wouldn't have had to do it." She swallowed. "Zane told Kendrick to clean up the mess and left." She was quiet again. "I'm not sure how much time passed. I was vaguely aware of someone talking, but my brain kept looping. I kept thinking of the Aaron who raced me home after school. The Aaron who taught me to ride a bike. The Aaron that saved me during the madness. When Kenrick touched my arm…"

Trudi gripped the steering wheel so tight I thought she might break it.

"I totally—fuckin'—lost it. I just didn't care anymore."

"I grabbed the gun from his holster and shot him in the stomach and then in the chest. I pointed the gun at the girl and told her if she didn't help me, I would shoot her, too. She helped me get Aaron in one of the trucks. I started that baby, and I peeled rubber as I backed out. I didn't even open the garage door—I just crashed through it.

"I whipped the truck into the street, shifted gears, and was about to punch it when I happened to glance toward the house. Zane was standing in the yard, smiling at me. I remember him yelling, 'I'll be waiting for you to come back, Julie.'" Trudi shook her head. "I tore out of there and came here. I buried Aaron, and I lived in a daze until I realized I hadn't had my period in a long time. At first, I attributed it to stress. But when I started feeling sick, I knew. The bastard had not only killed my brother, but he had knocked me up. When I confirmed it, I came out to sit in this very truck."

She pointed over her shoulder at the garden hose I had noticed the first time I'd been in the garage.

"I rigged up a hose to go from the exhaust into the cab. I was done. There was no point in going on. There was no way I could have babies. I was gonna die in childbirth. Painfully. Going to sleep and never waking up seemed much less painful."

She shifted in her seat. "I remember sitting in this very spot, my hand on the ignition key about ready to turn it, when I thought of the lives I carried. I was killing them, too. They were just as much a victim as I was, and I wasn't even giving them a chance." She took a big breath. "It was at that moment I decided I had to give them that chance. That no matter who their sperm donor—they were *my* babies. Mine and mine alone. And I would move heaven and earth to see them born."

She looked up at me. "And that's everything. Zane left me alone up until recently. I don't think he knows I'm having twins or that I could die in childbirth. But what he does know is that the babies are his, and based upon something he told me, I'm pretty sure he wants them. He might kill me after they're born, but my best guess is that he plans to take them, so I'll have no choice but to follow." She gazed at me with her bright blue eyes. "And he's right."

I frowned. "How can he be sure they're his?"

She stared at me for several seconds before answering. "I hadn't found that special person yet, Mister Dreal. I was a virgin."

My mouth came open, but no words came out. I couldn't believe what she just told me. "I'm sorry," I finally said. "I had no idea." I couldn't help myself. I leaned over and gave her a hug.

"Don't squeeze!" she yelled. "I've got to pee!"

I quickly released her. "Sorry."

She patted my hand. "I need to go in." She opened the door.

I nodded. "Yeah, and I need to check on the patient."

It was then that I heard the ATV start up. We both looked at each other. We ran outside just in time to see Kyle turn the ATV onto the road and speed off.

This was not good.

CHAPTER
SEVENTEEN

OTHER THAN THE ATV, Kyle only took my rifle and some bandages. While I was grateful he hadn't taken more, I still couldn't understand why he had left. It was pointless to think that he could get his girlfriend back. The guy was going to die. I briefly thought about going after him, but that would involve using Trudi's truck and putting myself in danger. Even I wasn't that stupid. He'd made his choice.

Trudi was clearly relieved that he was gone. And after hearing her story, I understood why.

We spent the rest of the morning cleaning up the broken plate and doing a few other chores. But the whole time, Trudi seemed preoccupied. I asked her about it, but she just shrugged it off, saying it was hormones. I wasn't convinced. I put it down to worrying about her coming birth, but I felt I was missing something.

After lunch, she pulled out the birthing books again, insisting we were running out of time. I'd planned to work on restoring the propane, but she said it could wait. So I relented and sat down with her.

We practiced breathing and reviewed things like cutting the cord and keeping the babies warm. But when she flipped to pictures of the different positions twins could be in during labor, I held up a hand to stop her. "Which one of these are you?" I asked.

She considered me. "Why don't you tell me?"

She went to the sofa and lay back on it, then pulled up her shirt to expose her very pregnant belly. "See if you can figure it out."

I went to stand over her. She blushed furiously, but I could see she was determined to do this. The skin on her rounded middle was pale, with faint stretch marks woven across it. In a strange way, she was beautiful—a living miracle. I knew I needed to treat her with respect.

I glanced up at her, watching me. "I'll have to touch you. Is that all right?"

"Yes," she chuckled. "I was kind of expecting it."

"Okay," I said softly. I hesitantly placed a hand on her bulge, and the first thing I noticed was how soft and warm her skin felt. I knew I shouldn't feel that way, but it felt good. *Would Wendy's have felt this way?*

I forced the thoughts away and focused on the babies. I probed her stomach and eventually found the head of the first one pointing downward. But I couldn't feel the second one.

Trudi must have seen my confusion. She took my hand and placed it a little more to the side and a lot higher. I probed a little more but shook my head. "I don't..."

Trudi repositioned my hand. "Right there. Feel it?"

I did as she directed. I could feel something, but I couldn't tell what it was. "I don't feel anything."

She nodded. "That one can be hard to feel." She positioned her hand high on her stomach. "The baby's head is right here, more toward the back."

A realization hit me. "This one's pointing the wrong way."

Trudi nodded. "The baby might turn before birth, but there's a good chance she will present breech. We'll just have to deal with it."

Even I knew this was not good.

I froze. I felt faint—my heart going a thousand miles an hour. My mind snapped back to that morning—walking into my parents' garage finding Wendy hanging from a support, unmoving, lifeless. Despite my best efforts, I hadn't been able to save her. I hadn't been strong enough. Those thoughts kept circling in my brain. Would Trudi be next? Was I going to fail her too?

"*Eyrian.*" Trudi touched my arm, and I jerked, breaking out of my trance.

I rubbed my face, trying to calm down. *What just happened?*

"Are you all right?" she asked in concern. "You were doing so good."

I sat on the couch and buried my face in my hands. "I don't..." I paused and took a deep breath. I was going to say I couldn't do it. It was just too damn hard. But as I calmed down, I realized that wasn't it. Trudi and I had promised no lies. *But did I dare tell her the real reason?*

She sat down beside me, and I reluctantly met her gaze. "Trudi. I'm..." I swallowed. "I'm scared. I know it sounds stupid, since you're the one birthing them. But I don't have a good track record. I couldn't keep Wendy alive. I failed. What if I do the same to you? What if I mess up and you die?"

I expected her to scoff or make fun of me. Even call me an asshole. But she didn't. Instead, she laid a hand on my arm. "Thank you," she said softly. "You're the only person in the world who cares whether I live or die." Her eyes searched mine. "That one thing tells me you'll do fine."

We sat for a moment in silence, then she patted my leg. "Hey, I got an idea. What if we do a practice run?"

I glanced over at her. "And just how are we going to do that?"

She strode purposely out of the room and returned a few minutes later with two towels, a pillowcase, and two plastic baby dolls. I watched in puzzlement as she stuffed the folded towels and dolls into the pillowcase. She then lay back on the couch with the stuffed pillowcase on her tummy. "Ta-da!"

I frowned. "You've got to be kidding."

"You got a better idea?"

I sighed. "Okay."

She laid back. "Now, I've been having the urge to push, but I haven't started yet. Am I dilated enough?"

"Is this where I have to stick my fingers up your... you know?"

She glared at me. "Duh."

I glanced at the pillowcase but made no move toward her. "Yeah, you're ready."

"Are the babies in position?"

I glanced at the pillowcase, becoming increasingly uncomfortable. "Yeah."

She sighed. "Mister Dreal. You'll need to feel the babies to know."

I glanced at her and then reluctantly probed the lumps in the pillowcase. "One baby's head is down, but the other is head up."

"Right. Oh! Here comes a contraction." Trudi squeezed the pillowcase. "Which one is coming first?"

"The one with the head down."

"I'm pushing hard. Here comes the first one." Trudi pushed out one of the dolls. I put it up on her chest.

"Do I try to turn the second baby?" I had seen that done in one of the videos.

"No time. Can you tell which part is coming first?"

I looked inside the pillowcase. "It's butt."

"Help get its legs free."

Trudi had folded the legs up, so I pulled out one and then the other. The doll fell out. I placed it on Trudi's chest with the other one.

"Now, the placentas."

She squeezed out one towel and then the other. "You've got to wait until they separate. You don't want to pull on them, or I'll bleed to death."

I set the towels aside. "What's to keep a placenta from coming out before the second baby is delivered?"

Trudi cradled both dolls in her arms like they were real. "That would be bad. It's called a pre-mature separation, and I could bleed to death before the second baby is born. But those don't usually happen." She rolled to her side and sat up. "See, that wasn't so bad."

I stared at her in disbelief. "There's a big difference between squeezing dolls out of a pillowcase and squeezing them out of…" I felt my face turn hot, "your…" I waved my hand toward her belly.

"You're right. There will be embryonic fluid and blood, life-size babies, and me probably screaming and calling you every name under the sun." She scratched her chin. "I guess I could use a plastic bag and fill it with some fake blood. I've got red food coloring."

I just blinked at her. "Trudi, you're not getting it. This terrifies me. I could kill all three of you."

Trudi came closer and put a hand on my arm. "Mister Dreal. Before you came along, I was a dead woman walking. With you, I at least have a chance. I'll take whatever improvement in the odds I can get."

She turned away and lay back on the bed. "Now, as my band director used to say, let's try this again, only this time with *feeling.*"

I just stared at her. All I wanted was my book. But she was depending on me.

What the hell was I going to do?

* * *

I was dead asleep when a horrendous scream jerked me awake—the agonized cry of a tormented soul. With my heart pounding, I threw back the covers and grabbed my gun.

A lone solar nightlight illuminated the hall as I stepped quickly, yet silently, to Trudi's door. I tried the knob, and finding it unlocked, I opened it to peek inside. Trudi sat on the side of the bed, head in her hands, her shoulders trembling.

I eased inside. She jerked when I sat down beside her.

"Are you all right?" I asked.

She kept her face hidden in her hands. "It was the dream again." Her voice was gravely but held no emotion. "I get one every time I think about what happened. As if Zane didn't punish me enough, he now does it in my sleep."

I got up and went to the kitchen, returning a moment later with a glass of water. She took a sip and carefully set it aside. She was still shaking, but not as bad. "Thanks, but I can't drink too much. It'll make me have to pee."

"I'm sorry I made you tell me. I had no idea."

She shrugged. "Not your fault."

We sat in silence for a moment.

"Can I get you anything?" I asked.

"No," she took a ragged breath. "I just need to let my heart calm down a bit. I'll try to go back to sleep in a minute."

I felt she wanted to say more, but she didn't. Instead, she grabbed a tissue from her bedside table and dabbed at her nose.

I stood. "Okay. I'll go back to bed then."

She nodded.

I turned to leave, but she quickly grabbed my hand. "Eyrian," she gazed up at me with pleading eyes. "Would you sleep beside me? I don't mean for sex or anything. I..." she looked away. "...I just need someone to be with me. The dream was really bad this time." Her cheeks were wet. "At least until the tremors pass."

This was the bitch that took me prisoner at gunpoint. Stole my book. Stood in the way of joining Wendy. I would be well within my rights to tell her, *No way in hell!*

But I felt I owed it to her. I triggered this revisit of her pain when I made her tell me her secret.

I sighed. Sometimes, being human meant—you just had to be human.

"Sure," I said.

Her eyes widened, and then she looked away. "T-thank you."

I went to the bed's other side and slid under the covers, lying on my back.

She turned off the light and lay down with her back to me. I felt her shifting around, trying to get comfortable. When she quit moving, I still felt her trembling.

Lord, help me. I turned toward her and snuggled up to her back, putting my arm around her and drawing her close. She stiffened at first, but when I made no further moves, she relaxed into my embrace. I had to admit it felt good to me, too. The smell of her hair, the warmth of her body, the beat of her heart—it all felt good. For the first time in a long time, I felt content.

After a few minutes, her tremors settled, and then I heard her sniff and wipe a tear.

"Damn hormones."

It didn't take much longer for exhaustion to overtake her, and she settled into a gentle slumber. I decided to wait a couple minutes longer and then return to my own bed. It would save us the embarrassment of waking up together. I didn't want to make things worse between us.

As I stared into the dark, guilt twisted my guts. Here I was, lying beside a woman who was not my wife. And it felt good. It made me feel like I was betraying Wendy. How was I going to explain this to her when we finally met?

On top of that, I was pretty sure Trudi had started to develop feelings for me. I had encouraged those to get my book back. But now, I realized just what an impact it might have when I abandoned her. She would be all alone and might die when her time came. I had to wonder if I was any better than the baddies?

Trudi mumbled something in her sleep and stirred, but

quickly settled, snuggling further into my embrace. She grabbed my arm and wrapped her arms around it, pinning it to her chest.

Then there were the practice sessions. I really didn't want to be involved. What was the point? I would be gone as soon as I located my book. But she was trying so hard to show me what to do. I snorted. Just something else to feel guilty about.

I had to admit, the pillowcase thing was great improvising. She even included the extra towels for the placentas and squeezed them out in the proper order.

I smiled. I could see her leaning back on the sofa, the pillowcase on her stomach, and talking me through the sequence. She had been so cute.

Unexpectedly, the memory shifted, filling out my vision and becoming more than real. Trudi was now lying in a hospital bed and wearing a medical gown. Her face was slick with sweat as she panted and groaned in pain.

"You have to help me," she gasped. "The babies are coming, and something's wrong."

I reached to help, but found I was holding my book in my right hand and my phone in the left. I stared at them, wondering how I got them. A dark shadow drew my eye, and I looked down at my feet. A deep blackness covered the floor, sucking in any light that touched it. I knew that if I set my book and phone down, they would disappear into that emptiness. Forever. I didn't dare do that. I had to have them.

"Help me, please!" Trudi called. She reached for me, groaning in pain. "We're gonna die."

I shook my head. I couldn't. I wouldn't put down my book. I had to get away.

In panic, I turned. But—

Wendy stood in my way. She was wearing her wedding dress and held a bouquet in front of her. She looked gorgeous, and my heart leaped in with joy at seeing her. "My love," I whispered. "I've missed you."

Wendy stepped toward me. I frowned, noticing that the flowers in the bouquet were wilted and dried up.

"Help me!" Trudi screamed in agony.

I glanced at the book and phone in my hands, unsure of what to do. I finally looked up at my bride.

"What do I do?" I asked.

She smiled. Her lips were blood red, and her eyes seemed to peer into my soul. Placing a hand on either side of my head, she drew me down to her. Her touch was deadly cold, and I shivered. She kissed my forehead.

"My love," she said softly.

"*You will know what to do.*"

I jerked and opened my eyes. Dim light filtered in from the room's open door. Trudi's bedroom. I must have slept through the night.

I lay on my side with Trudi turned toward me, her face mere inches from mine—her hair mussed and face relaxed in slumber. Strands of her hair caught the light and swayed gently as she breathed.

As I watched her sleep, Trudi shifted and then opened her eyes. It was strange to see her blue eyes gazing at me instead of Wendy's brown. But it felt right, too. If I was perfectly honest, in that moment, Trudi was beautiful.

I watched her eyes flick up and down as she realized how close we were and how we had slept.

"Good morning," she said softly.

I felt I needed to explain. "I didn't mean to sleep here all night, but I was tired and—"

She interrupted. "I'm glad. It felt good."

I sighed. "Yeah."

We gazed at each other a moment longer. "I've got to pee."

I chuckled. "You certainly know how to kill a moment."

"Yeah, tell it to the twins." But Trudi didn't move. She lay there, her eyes searching my face. Almost like she was trying to memorize my every feature.

She finally rose and put on her robe and slippers. As I watched her walk to the bathroom, I realized that sleeping beside her had felt too good, too intimate. And I longed to do it again.

There lay the danger.

I knew if I stayed much longer, I might not want to leave.

CHAPTER
EIGHTEEN

———————————

I WIPED THE EXCESS shaving cream from my face and stared at my reflection in the bathroom mirror. My eyes were once more drawn to my forehead, which looked the same as it always had. Yet, I could almost feel where Wendy had pressed her lips against me. The dream had been so real.

Its symbolism was all too obvious. Pick Trudi or Wendy. I sighed and looked into the eyes of the man in the mirror. The dream had been a reminder of my promise. A promise I *had* to keep.

In my head, I counted the days, confirming what I already knew. I had to find my book, and soon. If I waited much longer, I might not locate Wendy's special place in time. I couldn't count on Trudi telling me where it was. So, I needed to find my book and soon.

I sighed. There was another reason I couldn't afford to stay much longer. I was getting too comfortable with Trudi. Last night in bed had felt good. Hell, just being around her felt good. I was starting to like her. She could be such a bitch at times, and then others—a true friend. The longer I stayed, the harder it would be to leave.

"Breakfast is ready," I heard Trudi call from the kitchen.

I grabbed my shirt and watched my reflection while I slipped it on. I needed to step up my game and find that book. I'd make one last try to impress her. If that didn't work, I might have to consider leaving without it.

I had a promise to keep.

Breakfast was unusually quiet—a strange tension between us. Trudi barely said a word, but I'd catch her glancing my way when she thought I wasn't looking. Likewise, my mind was filled with thoughts of leaving, and anything I could say or do that might soften the impact. Sammy sensed our discomfort and cowered in his bed.

When we'd finished, I finally broke the silence. "I was wondering if you needed anything for the birth."

"Already got everything," she quickly answered.

"Everything?"

"Yeap."

I frowned. "What about something around the house? I could—"

"Nope. I don't need anything. The manual pump is fine, and I'll manage on the small camping stove."

"Then what about—"

Trudi suddenly stood. "Mister Dreal!" she was pleading. "I don't need anything. Why don't you go out to the shop for a while? I've got some things I need to do today, and I don't need you getting in the way."

I blinked at her. She was back to calling me mister. Maybe sharing a bed had worked on her more than I thought.

"All right." I took my plate to the kitchen, leaving Trudi to sit at the table. If there was nothing I could do for her, then I would spend the day searching for my book. It had to be someplace I'd missed.

I grabbed my gun and headed for the back door.

"Wait," Trudi called after me.

I looked back.

Her eyes locked with mine, and she held my gaze for five long heartbeats. "Can you come back before dark? I need to talk something over with you."

"Okay, do you want to talk now?" I asked. "I don't have anything special planned."

"No, it will keep." She forced a weak smile. "We'll do it later this evening."

This is so unlike Trudi. "Any hints?"

She shook her head and turned away. "No. It won't take long."

I hesitated, watching her walk away and wondering what she needed to talk about? Probably to clarify that us sleeping together didn't mean anything.

I continued on to the workshop.

I was on board with that.

* * *

It was right before dark when I made it back to the house. I had searched everywhere. I was convinced it had to be close by, but I could not find any trace—not a hidden compartment, not a spot in the loft, not even a hole in the ground. It was like she had made it vanish. I was at my wit's end.

When I walked in, the house was deadly quiet. Too quiet. I

didn't even hear the ticking of the clock. It was like the house was holding its breath.

Sammy met me at the door, his tail drooping. He turned and led me inside. I was afraid something had happened to Trudi while I was gone, but I found her sitting at the kitchen table staring at a cold cup of tea. Sammy sat faithfully beside her. He looked up at me as if begging me to help his mistress.

Oddly, a box wrapped in festive Happy Birthday paper and tied up with a bright red ribbon sat in the middle of the table. I wondered if maybe it was the birthday of one of her deceased relatives.

"Trudi?" I asked cautiously.

She slowly raised her head and looked at me. Her eyes were red and swollen. *Had she been crying?*

"Hey," she said softly.

"Are you all right?"

She looked back down at her tea. "Yeah. I'm okay." She pointed to my chair. "Eyrian. Can you sit with me a moment?"

"Sure." I sat down and nervously leaned back in my chair.

Trudi turned her deep blue eyes on me. She seemed so sad. "Eyrian," she said softly. "I can't do this anymore."

I frowned in puzzlement. "What? I don't understand."

Trudi pushed the gift-wrapped box over to me. I glanced at it and then back to her.

"Open it," she said. "It's for you. Sorry about the paper. It's all I had."

I didn't know what was going on, but I did as she requested—carefully undoing the ribbon and removing the paper.

Trudi sat silent, watching.

When I finally opened the box, I was shocked to see it was a leather-bound book titled *The Paladin's Last Command* in big gold letters.

It was Wendy's book.

I stared at it. It was what I wanted. What I craved. I ran a finger across the cover.

"Why?" I asked.

Trudi shook her head. "Because I took it from you. I have been using it to force you to do something you don't want to do." She looked at me. "You're a really nice guy and don't deserve what I've been doing. The guilt has been crushing me." She took a deep breath and let it out slowly. "Plus, with the baddies now lurking at my door, I can't stand the thought of them hurting you to get to me." She looked down. "It's better if I let you go. I may be bat shit crazy, but Zane is just evil."

"What about the babies?" I asked.

Trudi looked away. "I'll figure it out. Women have delivered by themselves before. I'm sure I won't be the last."

I picked up my book. I couldn't believe I had it back. But strangely, I felt no victory. Only loss.

But I had a promise to keep.

"Is it okay if I leave tomorrow morning?" I asked.

"Leave whenever you want." Trudi stood and headed to her bedroom. "Dinner is on you. I was gonna fix something special..." she paused at the door, "... but I just don't feel like it."

She went inside and softly shut her door.

That night, I didn't sleep well. Thoughts of Trudi kept churning through my mind. I couldn't believe she had given me my book back. All on her own. I had expected her to be mad about it. Maybe even shed a tear or two. But her total collapse came as a shock. She had seemed so defeated. It was like giving me my book had utterly destroyed her. I thought of sharing a bed and comforting her. It must have pushed her over the edge. I guess I severely underestimated how much she agonized over forcing me to stay.

But what bothered me more was my own reaction. I had defeated my captor and gotten back what I wanted. I even still had time to find Wendy's special place. I had *won!* I should be ecstatic.

Only I wasn't.

All I felt was sad.

When the first hint of light entered the room, I got up, dressed, and made my final preparations. There was no point in delaying. I needed to get away for both our sakes.

I wanted to tell Trudi goodbye and thought perhaps we could have one last breakfast together. I messed around, waiting for her to get up—but she didn't come out. After waiting past her usual time, I gently knocked on her door and asked if she wanted anything. She didn't answer at first. But after a moment, I heard a definite "No" from the other side.

I fixed some oatmeal for myself, but after the first bite, it seemed to lose all its taste. I pushed it away and just sipped my coffee.

After waiting as long as I could, I grabbed my backpack and took one last look around. I thought about telling Trudi goodbye but decided not to say anything. I could only assume she was done with me and just wanted me out.

I headed for the woods out back, thinking I would try that old trail again. Maybe I could find another ATV. The day was colder than it had been, with high clouds that cast a gray pallor over the area. It fit my mood. I trudged along, looking at the ground, and tried to think of Wendy. But thoughts of Trudi kept intruding, and I felt so—

Alone.

I just stepped inside the woods when a growing sense of unease hit me. I stopped dead in my tracks, glancing around and trying to pinpoint the source. A frigid breeze tugged at my jacket, carrying the hint of a faint sound.

Engines.

Not one, not two, but at least three of them. And they were closing fast.

I immediately dropped my pack on the path, grabbed my gun, and ran toward the garage. The noise came closer and finally stopped just as I reached the workshop. I peeked around it to see three black SUVs stop in Trudi's driveway. The doors opened, and several men spilled out, each armed with a rifle. Not hunting rifles, but military assault rifles.

Shit! My little handgun stood no chance against them.

They crashed through Trudi's back door, leaving it a splintered mess, and piled inside. Two men remained on guard outside, their weapons held at the ready.

From inside the house, I could hear shouting and Sammy furiously barking. I studied the guards, trying to plot a path to get to the house, when the men strode out, dragging a struggling and cursing Trudi between two of them. She was wearing only her robe and gown with her hands zip-tied in front of her pregnancy bulge. They hustled her over to the rear SUV.

A lone man stepped out, towering over Trudi. He wore a white cowboy hat with a gun on his hip.

I groaned. Zane.

I tightened my grip on my gun, desperately wanting to shoot all of them. But I knew if I tried, I'd be dead the moment I stepped out.

She glared up at him with absolute hatred. He smiled down at her and gently touched her cheek. Trudi didn't flinch but instead tried to bite him. He got his hand back in time and chuckled. "So vicious. I've missed that."

He backhanded her.

Her head rocked, and she staggered. She would have fallen had the men not been holding her. Once she had regained her feet, she raised her head and glared at him defiantly.

A loud growl came from inside the house, and all eyes turned in that direction. Sammy launched out the back door, dragging a broken leash behind him. He bowled down a man standing in his way before turning and glaring at Zane.

The world seemed to slow.

Zane smirked and calmly drew his pistol.

Sammy surged toward him, teeth bared and snarling.

Trudi's eyes went wide in shock. "NO SAMMY!" she screamed.

The dog launched himself at Zane, leaping high into the air and going for the man's throat.

But Zane already had his gun up.

He shot Sammy point-blank. The sound of the gunshot echoed loudly off the trees, and a silence settled over us.

Sammy jerked and fell, landing with a sickening thud in an unmoving heap.

Trudi screamed. "NO!"

She lunged toward her friend and managed to break free.

She knelt beside Sammy, burying her face in his neck and sobbing in great, painful heaves.

Zane holstered his weapon, his face wearing a self-satisfied smirk. "Now that was fun!" He pointed to his men, who pulled a distraught Trudi to her feet and directed her toward the truck. She didn't protest—all fight was gone.

The SUVs pulled out in a line and sped away.

When I was sure they were gone, I walked cautiously over to where Sammy lay sprawled. The wind was still, like the earth itself had lost the will to move. It made each step over the gravel sound like crunching bones.

I stared down at Trudi's one last friend. I shook my head. Why did Zane have to kill him? There were so few of the animals we humans had cared for. Depended on. And then we treat them like this.

When I'd first met him, Sammy had tried to be friendly, but on that first night, I'd upset him by hurting Trudi. He'd made his stance clear several times that his mistress was his number one concern. You couldn't help but admire someone so devoted. At the end, he had even started to tolerate me. I blinked, surprised at my wet eyes. I looked away and waited for my emotions to settle.

I couldn't leave him like that. I eased by the broken door and went inside to find something to wrap him in. It was the least I could do for the fallen hero.

I gasped as I entered the kitchen and stared in disbelief. The place had been ransacked. Trudi's cabinets were open, and her dishes smashed. The table lay in pieces, and her furniture was broken. When I looked in her bedroom, someone had taken a knife to the mattress. Strangely, the nursery was untouched, and I wondered if they had noticed there were two beds.

As I was checking my old room, I spotted the quilt Trudi had been so particular about lying on the floor. For some reason, it seemed just the right thing for Sammy.

Grabbing the quilt, I took it outside and carefully wrapped him in it. Taking him to the workshop, I laid him on some hay in the corner. It was where he always liked to take a nap while I worked.

I paused for a moment out of respect. As I looked sadly at the bundle that had once been Trudi's closest friend, her protector, it hit me—she had no one now. She'd lost her grandfather to the craziness, Aaron to the baddies, and now Sammy. Plus, with me leaving...

Trudi was now truly alone.

She had no friends. No allies.

No one.

After saying one last goodbye to Sammy, I left and headed toward the woods where I had left my backpack. It had started raining while I was inside—a cold, damp rain that settled into my bones. I pulled my coat closer around me. My jacket was waterproof, so I wasn't too worried. I pulled up my hood and settled in for the slog.

Shouldn't you go after her? whispered a small voice in my mind.

I shook my head. *Hell, no.* Sure, she'd treated me nice, but I was nothing more than a tool to save her babies. She had captured me and forced me to stay with her. You can be a prisoner without bars around you.

Like Trudi was a prisoner of her body.

I shook my head again. Nope, not going to do it. Knowing her, she'll just escape them. She's probably the most intelligent woman I've ever encountered. I'm sure she'll figure it out. There's no way I'm going back now. It's not my fight. I've got my book, and as soon as I find Wendy's special place, I can be with my wife.

Unbidden, memories of Trudi came to mind. Her wicked smile when she beat me at cards, or her blunt assessment of my bad smell, or her exasperation when I didn't understand her teachings.

The time we danced.

How good her hair smelled when I held her close.

My legs stopped moving, and I just stood there. Of its own accord, my gaze shifted toward the west. I could feel her presence in that direction. It was like a light that I couldn't see. It had to be the Norns doing it, filtering that information into my brain. But I *knew* Trudi was in that direction.

Zane will kill her after the babies are born.

Water ran down into my face as I stared off into the distance. The only sound was the rain hitting my jacket's hood and its pitter-patter against the ground. I could almost see them forcing her to do things. Hitting her. Ripping her babies from her body.

I've got my book. I'm free!

Then why did it feel so wrong?

Damn the bitch! Damn her to hell! I leaned my head back and screamed at the sky. *God, how I hated the bitch.*

I had tried to get her to trust me so I could get my book back.

I was kind to her. I talked nice. I did things for her. Even tried to do things that pleased her. And I'd finally gotten her to give it to me. But dammit—

I fell into my own trap.

Yes, I got her to let me into her heart.

But damn her...

She'd also snuck into mine.

CHAPTER NINETEEN

AS I OBSERVED the baddie enclave from my rooftop perch, I contemplated my foolhardy plan to rescue Trudi. I was determined to try no matter what, but the odds were definitely stacked against me.

The rain from earlier had stopped, but it had left the air with a chill dampness that I felt in my bones. I shivered and tried to sink further into my coat. Lying on the cold roof wasn't helping.

After deciding to go after Trudi, I had used the truck to make a mad dash to the arsenal of weapons I had uncovered. I was one person going up against two dozen, so I needed every advantage I could get. After loading what I needed, I rushed back to finish a piece of technology that was my fallback. I wasn't sure it would work, so I only planned to use it if I had to.

It was evening by the time I finished my preparations and drove to where the baddies had established their enclave. Expecting sentries, I had left Trudi's truck a few blocks away and approached cautiously on foot. I moved from house to house, alert for any guards. Surprisingly, there were none—unless you counted the raccoon that nearly gave me a heart attack. They must have thought no one was stupid enough to bother them.

I guess they hadn't met me.

At the end of a cul-de-sac, they had turned three upscale houses into a sort of compound. Six-foot high chain-link fencing surrounded the houses, leaving only one gate at the entrance to the cul-de-sac. As I studied the fencing, I couldn't help but wonder if it was to keep bad things out—or hold their own people in.

Five stands of work lights illuminated the exterior of all three houses, making their yards as bright as day. Surprisingly, only the central house's interior was lit. I assumed that was the one attached to their generator. Finding it was key to my plan.

Music pounded from inside the central house, loud enough to clearly make out the words. I wasn't impressed with their selection—the throb of death metal grated on my nerves. Thankfully, it would cover any noise I might make.

The two men guarding the gate worried me. They were hunched around a propane heater with rifles slung across their shoulders. They appeared to be chatting, but from their frequent glances toward the main house, I thought they were expecting someone.

I took one last look around. It was time to make my move.

I climbed down the ladder I'd found in a neighbor's backyard, grabbed my backpack, and crept closer to the gate, using a house for cover.

I fingered the stun gun in my pocket and plotted ways to get the guards—but I kept coming up short. I guess I would have to circle around the perimeter, searching for some weakness in the fence.

A young man came out of the house carrying a drone with a VR headset pushed up on his head. He briefly chatted with the guards and joined them just outside the gate. After talking a little longer, he lowered his headset and launched the drone, unfortunately, in my direction.

I quickly backed away and scanned the backyard for someplace to hide. I spotted an open tool shed, and just as the drone rounded the corner, I managed to make it inside. I was greeted by a hiss as Mr. Raccoon showed his displeasure at being interrupted. I slowly reached for my stun gun in case he attacked me, but Mr. Raccoon only regarded me with disdain and went back to licking the candy wrapper he held in his paws.

He looked up as the drone came closer, while I tried to ease further into the darkness. The drone flicked on a small spotlight and shined it inside. That was too much for Mr. Raccoon. He dropped to all fours and quickly darted out. The drone's light fixed on the raccoon long enough to ensure it was leaving, then snapped off. It flew on, continuing its patrol.

I breathed a sigh of relief. I carefully crept out and watched the drone continue around the nearby houses. Once finished, it flew toward the chain link fence, I assumed, to run the perimeter. I was lucky I hadn't tried that route.

I shook my head. The gate was going to be my best bet, but I'd need a distraction to get through it. I had already spotted an empty house with a large plate glass window on the opposite side of the cul-de-sac. I thought I could use that. I moved to where I had a clear view of the guards and my target house. I pulled out my trusty slingshot and took aim at the window. I was going to have to hit it pretty hard for any effect, and I was hoping it would be loud enough to attract their attention.

I took careful aim, pulled hard, and let it fly. It hit with a loud pop but did not shatter it. The men jumped at the sound, scanning the area for the source. I reloaded and shot again, only this time, the window shattered, and a chunk fell inward.

The guards zeroed in on the sound and peered into the darkness. I was hoping they would go investigate, but they didn't. One of them called the drone pilot over and pointed in the sound's direction. Sure enough, in a few minutes, the drone appeared over the top of the houses. I debated trying to shoot the drone down, but I didn't think I should press my luck. So, I chose a more technical solution.

I dropped my backpack and pulled out Push Back One. I had added a directional antenna, and I was hoping it could disable the drone from this distance. I waited until it was almost to the broken window before I aimed and pressed the switch. The drone wobbled and then sank to the ground. The pilot jerked off his headset and had a terse conversation with the two guards. Then, all three of them walked to where the drone had landed.

With the guards preoccupied, I darted out. It took five long, exposed seconds to reach the gate. I quietly lifted the latch and slipped inside, making a beeline for the dimly lit side of the house.

Once in the backyard, I was in relative darkness since the house blocked the work lights out front. I paused a moment to lean against the back wall while my breathing slowed and my eyes adjusted to the darkness.

I scanned the area, searching for my target. The muffled

throb of an engine in the back corner of the lot led me to what I was looking for. The generator was big and placed well away from the house in its own metal housing. It had obviously been permanently installed prior to the Judgement. This explained why the baddies had chosen this particular house. I scanned further and found its fuel source—a standalone propane tank just beyond the generator.

I crept over to the generator and took out my special piece of technology, attaching it to the generator's housing. This was the part I wasn't sure about. I had never built anything like this before and hadn't been able to do an extensive test. Hopefully, I wouldn't have to use it. But if I did, we were going to find out just how good of an engineer I actually was.

Knowing I could be discovered at any time, I went to the fuel tank. My original thinking was to blow it up, but I was afraid it would set the houses on fire, and then I would have a much bigger problem. Instead, I opted to disable it.

With a bit of searching, I found the tank's main cutoff. I removed the screw that held the turn handle to the valve so it would come off. I quickly turned the valve off and threw the handle into the darkness, leaving just the valve stem. That would only slow them down, but it would buy me the time I needed.

I ran to hide in some bushes next to the house with a clear view of the patio and the sliding glass door that led into the house. I was only behind the bush for a few seconds before the generator sputtered, and all the lights went out.

Darkness enveloped me, and my ears rang from the sudden absence of music. I heard groans and curses come from inside, as well as some banging around. As expected, I heard the patio door open, and several people with flashlights exited and headed toward the generator.

After waiting until no one else came out, I stood and turned on my own flashlight. I walked toward the house as if I owned it. I stepped onto the patio and went through the sliding door. I promptly ran smack into a young woman coming out. She gasped.

I grabbed her by the throat, firmly but not too hard, and shone the light in her face, blinding her so she couldn't see who I was. "Aren't you supposed to be with the pregnant chick?" I growled, hopefully hiding my voice.

"Bobbie?" she asked, confused. "You know it's not my turn. Hayley's downstairs with her." She squinted, trying to see through the glare. "I don't even know why we're watching her. It's not like she can run off, and we sure don't know how to deliver a fucking baby."

Someone turned our way with a flashlight. I shoved her toward the door and strode further into the house. Thankfully, most everyone had gone outside, so it only took a few false turns to find the stairs leading down. I turned off my light and went down slowly, feeling my way. It got lighter near the bottom.

The source of the illumination was a small battery-powered nightlight that was plugged into the wall socket. It must have come on when the power died. The room was still dark, but I could tell it was laid out like a rec room, with thick carpet and plush couches. At the far end was an open door with light flickering from inside.

I moved closer and peered in. A dim lamp illuminated the room. A young brown-haired woman, barely out of her teens and with a faded bruise on her cheek, sat in a chair with one leg under her. She was intently focused on her phone and would flick her screen periodically. I couldn't figure out what she was doing since the internet had long since gone down, but then I noticed the shimmer of tears in her eyes and realized she was looking at pictures.

But the person I was really interested in was on the bed, lying on her side. Her hands and feet were zip-tied. I just knew she was alive, but confirming it with my eyes was an intense relief.

I shined my light in the girl's face. "Hayley! Get your ass upstairs," I ordered. "I'm supposed to watch her until the lights come back on."

The girl flinched at my voice. She had the frightened expression of someone who was expecting to be abused.

"Move!" I shouted.

The girl leaped from her chair and ran up the stairs.

I reached into my coat pocket and pulled out my knife, freeing Trudi's feet and hands.

I gently tugged on her shoulder. "Hey—"

She rolled and came off the bed, moving faster than I thought possible for a pregnant woman. She slugged me right in the jaw, and I staggered back.

I shined the light into my face. "Trudi, dammit. It's me!"

Trudi froze mid-punch. Her eyes got big. "Eyrian? You... you came?" She shot forward and wrapped her arms around me, burying her face in my chest. "I thought I was all alone."

I returned the hug. "I thought I was supposed to help you deliver those babies."

"Yeah," her voice was muffled by my shirt. "But this is above and beyond." She looked up at me. "You know he's gonna kill you."

I shook my head. "Not going to happen. Let's focus on getting out of here."

A huge smile spread across her face, and she nodded.

I grabbed her hand and pulled her through the basement. At the base of the stairs, I paused and took out my special device from my backpack. It was a simple PVC tube with a button on the end. It looked more like a toy than something dangerous.

I turned to Trudi. "They'll be focused on me, so hold this for me. When I tell you to, press the button on the end and immediately close your eyes."

She nodded. "What's it do?"

"Hopefully, we won't need it." I grinned. "But if you press that button, all hell is going to break loose."

She gave me a wicked smile.

I pulled out my handgun, and we went slowly up the stairs. At the top, I turned off my flashlight and silently stepped out into the room. To my surprise, the room was dark and quiet. I got a very bad feeling.

The lights suddenly came on. I blinked in the blinding glare to find us surrounded by three men with rifles and one other man holding a long-nosed revolver. That one was frowning.

"Going somewhere?" he asked.

It was Zane.

CHAPTER
TWENTY

I LOOKED AROUND the room. Behind the men, the other members of this little tribe hung back. From most of their expressions, they were afraid. But I didn't think it was because of Trudi or me. They were afraid they would get pulled into the fight. There would be no help there. They had been abused too much.

Standing among them, holding himself up with a pair of crutches, was Kyle Wilston. The bandage on his leg looked new, but he was barely staying upright. I was surprised they'd let him live. I wondered what price he'd paid for that. Likely the information that led to Trudi's capture.

Beside him stood Luce, the girl who had been running away with him. Her outfit was very different from the other women in the room. She wore painted-on hot pants and a blouse that was two sizes too tight, which contrasted starkly with her completely bald head. She looked uncomfortable, and I suddenly realized that Kyle hadn't been the only one to pay a price.

Trudi tried to let go of my hand, perhaps to draw Zane's

attention away, but I held on. I gave it a gentle squeeze, and she stopped.

Zane was wearing his cowboy hat, and I couldn't see any reason for it other than vanity. From the glint in his eyes, I was as good as dead to him.

He nodded toward my gun. "Guns aren't allowed in the house. I think you should let us hold that for you. I'd hate to have to arrest you." Zane smiled.

"Let us go," I demanded, trying to express more bravado than I felt.

"I don't think so," Zane said, raising his gun to point at my head. "My seed was sowed, and it's time for the harvest."

"What?"

"My baby," he said with pride. "She's carrying my baby. My firstborn. He'll be this world's new prince."

He didn't know Trudi was having twins.

"Trudi won't live with you," I stated.

He snorted. "She won't *live*, you mean. Once I have my baby, I'll have no need for her. She's been nothing but an incubator." His lips grew into an evil grin. "You should have heard her squeal that first time. I still get excited when I think about it."

Trudi squeezed my hand so hard I felt the joints pop.

Zane thought for a moment. "I did like that squeal. If she wasn't so much trouble, I might consider having another with her."

I cocked my jaw. It took every ounce of my control not to launch myself at him. The thought of this guy forcing Trudi angered me to my core. He was a psychopath and drunk on power. I swore that no matter what happened here today, this guy was going down. But Trudi's safety came first.

"They're not yours!" Trudi spat. "Did you think I didn't take precautions?"

He shook his head. "I've had you watched since you left. There were no other men around since we had our little vacation." He nodded in my direction. "And don't credit your man there. He didn't come along until a few weeks ago." He looked back at me. "Now, hand over your gun, or I'm going to shoot you right here."

Trudi frowned. "It's me you want Zane. Just let him go."

Zane considered her. "If he plays along, I think I'll keep him. It will keep you in line, so we can give my baby a little brother." He grinned. "So what will it be?"

I eyed the men behind him. I was not going to get a better chance.

Giving a defeated sigh, I held out my handgun to him.

Confident in his victory, he leaned forward to take it.

"Trudi," I said, glancing over and locking eyes with her.

"*Now.*"

Her smile was radiant. I heard the button click.

A loud pop came from the backyard as the explosive I left took out the generator. All the lights went out.

Zane shouted, "Don't let them leave!"

I immediately pulled Trudi to me. "Cover your eyes," I whispered.

I pulled out a flashbang and tossed it on the floor. I barely got my own eyes covered before the explosion of light and noise sent the room into chaos. Screams of panic and angry yelling gave us cover to join the crush of bodies trying to flee. I immediately shoved Trudi out the door, pushing aside two other people to do it. I pulled out my flashlight and headed for the gate.

The lone guard pointed his rifle at us. "Stop!" he ordered.

I immediately lobbed another flashbang toward him. "Catch!"

He had just enough time to say, "Shit—" before it detonated, blinding him. I dropped him with my stun gun and pulled Trudi after me.

Once outside the gate, I stopped, grabbed her hand, and slapped the truck keys into it. "The truck is just up that street. I'll hold them off while you—"

"*NO!* They'll know where I'm going. Come with me, and we'll find somewhere to hide."

"There's no time. Find somewhere safe, and I'll meet you there later. I'll know where you are."

She hesitated.

"*Go!*" I shouted. "Do it for the babies."

She gasped, and then her mask of determination fell into place. "Don't you *dare* die on me."

I couldn't help but chuckle. "For once, we agree on something." I could hear a commotion behind me. "Now go!"

She took off, waddling as fast as her pregnancy would allow.

Standing in the middle of the street, I was a sitting duck. But I needed all their attention on me. I pulled out my last flashbang and threw it toward the approaching men. I didn't think they would fall for that again, so I used it as a diversion. Right before the bang went off, I pulled out my last little trick and lit the fuse. The firecrackers went off, and the approaching men dropped to the ground.

I turned and ran f up the street. In the distance, I saw the truck's headlights come on. *Thank God she made it.*

I was tackled from behind, slamming me to the asphalt. My

head smacked hard against the pavement, and the air was driven from my lungs. For the barest moment, I lay dazed, my face aching and the taste of blood in my mouth. Hands grabbed at my arms, but on pure instinct, I fought them off and rolled to my feet to face my attacker. The brute of a man swung at me, and I barely managed to dodge it. But his follow-up punch was dead on, and my world exploded in light and pain.

I staggered. The punches kept coming, but I covered my face and tried to back away. Unexpectedly, a blunt object was shoved hard into my back, and for the next three seconds, I was filled with agony as an electric shock locked every muscle in my body. I collapsed, twitching uncontrollably.

At the scuff of a boot nearby, I managed to get my trembling body to turn over. Zane was standing over me, wearing his irritating smirk. He pulled his revolver and pointed it at my head. "You chose the wrong side, mister."

I closed my eyes, awaiting the shot. It wasn't what I wanted, but at least I was going to see Wendy. I would tell her about how I had gotten Trudi out. I thought my wife would forgive me.

But instead of a shot, I heard the roar of an engine and the squeal of tires as the operator punched it. A vehicle rapidly approached. Zane looked up with an expression of surprise and horror. He took a step back, then another, before the vehicle's crazy operator stood on the brakes, their squeal deafening—

And then the damn truck passed right beside me mere inches from my head.

Was she trying to save me or kill me?

I heard the truck hit something as it came to a stop. I looked up at its taillights, not believing she'd missed me.

Trudi yelled, "Get in!"

I pulled myself up using the truck's tailgate and leaned into the bed. That was good enough for Trudi. I saw the backup lights come on, and she burned rubber in reverse.

The sudden acceleration flipped me over the tailgate, and I landed hard in the truck bed. I lay there dazed as she drove in reverse and then whipped the truck around to point the other way. The tires squealed loudly as she sped away.

A few minutes later, she slowed to a stop, and the sliding door of the rear window shot open. "Eyran, are you all right? Did they shoot you?"

I rolled over so I could look at her. "Where did you learn to drive like that?"

There was just enough light from the taillights to see the corner of her mouth curl up. "I was a tomboy growing up. I learned to drive tractors when I was six and started racing the backroads before I had my license."

I sat up and turned toward her. "Well, I guess I should thank you for saving me. I think."

She shrugged. "I wasn't gonna let you get one up on me."

I couldn't help but chuckle. "True."

She suddenly grew serious. "Now, get your ass up here and drive. I've got a little problem."

Alarmed, I pulled myself out of the truck's bed and opened the driver's door. "Trudi, is everything all right? You're not hurt, are you?"

It was then I noticed the seat was damp. I got a sinking feeling.

Trudi sighed. "My water broke."

CHAPTER
TWENTY-ONE

TRUDI DEMANDED WE go back to the house and grab all the medical supplies and books she'd collected. A simple dash in, dash out. But I vetoed that move, insisting it was too risky.

Whoever said "hell hath no fury" had never been stuck in a pickup with a crazy pregnant woman starting labor and being told "No."

She only calmed down when I pointed out that Zane had been watching her for some time, so it was a sure bet he would use that to either ambush us or track us. It would be better to go directly to somewhere safe that had medical supplies. She grumbled about how long it had taken to find all those things, but grudgingly went along.

She was surprised when I pulled up to a veterinarian's office—the same one I'd collected the solar panels from. I had obviously checked out the inside and noticed all the supplies that the crazies hadn't touched.

At first, she was insulted, saying she was delivering babies, not puppies. But after looking around inside, she began to see the advantages. I think it was the blood pressure cuff and heart monitor that sold her.

"We can make this work," she said, nodding. "She patted me on the shoulder. Good work." Then she made a face. "Of course, everything will need to be cleaned."

I knew who that was going to fall to.

She sighed. "And just in time, my contractions are starting."

I knew from my lessons that Trudi had many hours of labor before the actual birth. So I set her up on a couch in the vet's office with some clean scrubs and a blanket while I went to prepare things. For once, Trudi didn't argue. She was exhausted from being taken prisoner and the late hour. She curled up on her side and was out.

The first thing I did was head to the men's room and examine my wounds. I had a serious scrape on my forehead, I was bleeding in my mouth, and I was going to have a hell of a shiner tomorrow. But as I looked at myself in the mirror, I realized just how close I had come to death. Staring down a gun barrel was a lot more scary than I ever imagined.

I shook it off. I had to pull myself together. Trudi needed me. I just hoped I didn't get too stiff.

And that Zane didn't find us.

I went to the office's break area, with its moldy coffee pot and a long-dead refrigerator, but only found some cat food pouches. While tempting, I wasn't that hard up yet.

Trudi was still asleep, so I left a note and her shotgun and went outside to hide the truck. I didn't want to take the chance that Zane's people might use their drones to find it.

I hid the truck in a nearby garage and stopped at a

convenience store for disinfectant and food. But when I stepped back inside the vet's office, I got a shotgun shoved in my face.

Trudi glared at me. In the dim light of our lantern, I could see a fine sheen of sweat on her forehead and her hair in a sleep-mussed disarray. She lowered her weapon. "You nearly got shot."

I set the groceries down on the desk. "Remind me not to be nice to you again. I was trying to let you sleep."

"I thought you were one of them…" She turned away. "And that you had left me."

I started to give her hell, but realized she was feeling scared and a bit insecure. I decided to provide some reassurance instead. "Give me a little credit," I said jovially. "I may be an idiot, but I'm not a complete asshole. There are two little babies that need to be born first."

She looked up. Her eyes searched mine, looking for some trace of a lie. "You mean it?"

I couldn't help but grin. "I had to hunt you down, rescue you from a psycho cowboy, and have a truck almost drive over me. Hell yeah, I'm serious."

I wasn't prepared for the pregnant lady to launch herself at me. She wrapped her arms around me and buried her face in my jacket. "Thank you," she whispered. Then she flinched. She stepped away and put a hand over her stomach. "They're getting stronger."

I pulled out a power bar and gave it to her. "You need to keep your energy up. Eat something while I get some supplies. This couch is as good as it gets, but I need to clean everything."

I stepped toward the door, but paused and looked back.

Trudi was working her way into the power bar, but she jerked as a contraction hit her. She glanced my way. She put on her best face, but I could tell she was worried.

I was, too.

* * *

I did what I could to prepare. I cleaned the room from head to toe—twice. I stacked gloves, masks, and medical tools on the desk, plus an assortment of towels, blankets, and specimen pans. If I thought it might be useful, I grabbed it. And water. I'd found an unopened box of distilled water in the back. I even found a small propane heater to make Trudi more comfortable.

Then I helped her put on a fetal monitor, and I heard the baby's heartbeats for the first time. We even tried out the portable ultrasound. Trudi had been right all along. There were two babies inside her.

However, my heart sank when I saw one of the twins was head up. We would just have to deal with it as best we could.

I carried, cleaned, and prepped until I couldn't go anymore. I sat down on the floor in the hall with my back to the wall. I was simply exhausted. I looked out the front window and saw the faint beginnings of dawn. Trudi was still a couple of hours away from delivering, but the time drew closer with each contraction.

I leaned my head back against the wall. *What was I going to do?* I guess the best hope was to pray the babies were small enough to fit through Trudi's pelvis. If one of them got stuck. I sighed and refused to think about it.

I went through my mental list of everything that needed to

be done. I began to wish I'd spent more time learning. I snorted. Geri always told me I should have been a doctor.

I smiled as I remembered the day I'd told him I'd chosen a different path.

Geri had looked at me in shock. "You want to be an electrical engineer?"

I remembered the high school senior version of myself nodding. "Our energy systems are changing," I had explained. "With renewables, we'll need an even smarter grid." I smiled with an almost religious fervor. "And with fusion energy coming on, we'll need to integrate that, too. I want to be a part of it."

Geri had just shaken his head. "And here I thought you would go into something challenging, like neurosurgery or nanotechnology. But electrical engineer? It's so stone age."

I smiled. It was a good memory. Geri was a freaking genius. He got his doctorate in medicine *and* nanoengineering. To him, electrical engineering was like playing with a battery and wires.

"Don't cut yourself short, bro." I started at the voice beside me. I looked over, and Geri sat on the floor next to me. I was surprised—yet not.

"Why's that?" I asked. I noticed he looked different from the other times. Blurry. Almost pixelated.

Geri smiled. "You're just as smart—just in a different way." He nodded to himself. "You're a survivor, bro. You have a toughness that most people don't." He pointed across the hall to the room Trudi was in. "She's one, too. You chose well."

I chuckled. "I don't know about choosing her. I think it was the other way around. But I do admit, she's a hell of a woman."

We sat in silence for a moment. Geri glanced over at me. "The twins are boy and girl, you know," he said.

I blinked at him in surprise. "How do you know that? You're this thing in my head, so you should only know what I know."

He shrugged. "The Norns whisper things."

My eyes widened as realization struck. "The hunches."

Geri nodded. "The Norns are feeding you information, but they have now learned to give sips instead of a flood. Just a little bit trickles into your brain."

I nodded. "So, why are you here this time? More great wisdom to impart? If it's to tell me what I should do about this birth, I'd appreciate it."

He shook his head. "Sorry, I'm just an avatar." He sighed. "No, the reason I'm here is to say goodbye."

I frowned. "What do you mean?"

He looked away. "The retardant nanos Geri injected into you were only designed to slow things down. Give your brain a chance to adapt and to pass on a message. But the Norns have been removing them and will soon completely eradicate Geri's nanomachines. At that point, this avatar will cease to exist." He sighed. "But that's all right. They have accomplished their purpose."

Eyrian.

Trudi's voice filtered into my conscious, sounding faint and far away. But I didn't want to leave this dream yet.

Geri nodded toward where Trudi lay. "She's calling you."

My apprehension suddenly overwhelmed me. Geri was leaving. I reached out to grab my brother's arm. "What if I can't do this?" I asked. "What if I kill her?"

Eyrian.

Trudi's voice came again, louder this time. More insistent.

Geri smiled with pride. He ruffled my hair as he had done when I was younger. "I didn't save the life of a loser."

"Eyrian," I jerked awake at Trudi's voice calling me from the other room.

In panic, I momentarily fought with the blanket covering me. *How long had I been out?* I glanced out the window, which showed early morning. I hadn't been asleep that long. Then I noticed the blanket. Trudi must have covered me up.

"What do you need?" I called back. I slowly stood as my butt and back protested my every single move.

"I'm sorry to wake you, I know you're exhausted, but the contractions are getting strong... er." I heard her grunt and do her breathing pattern.

I went to sit beside her. She grabbed my hand like it was her lifeline. When the contraction passed, she asked, "Could you check how dilated I am?"

I made a face. "Is this the part where I have to put my fingers in your..."

Trudi nodded.

I sighed and tried to make light of it. "You realize this is the first time we've been intimate. I had expected a kiss before we got this far."

She blinked at me. "Come here a minute?"

Puzzled, I did as she asked.

"Closer."

I leaned over her. Unexpectedly, she reached up, grabbed me by the shirt, and jerked me down. She put an arm around my neck and drew me in for a kiss.

It stirred up something deep inside me. Wendy came to

mind, but I instead focused on the woman before me. Trudi needed me. Wendy's time would come later.

I gently pulled back, our faces mere inches apart. "Why did you do that?" I asked.

The corner of her mouth curled up. "I can't have you complaining about not getting your kiss."

I couldn't help but chuckle. I gently brushed a strand of hair out of her face. "You're crazy, you know that?"

She nodded. "So I've been..." She grimaced. "Told."

She started her breathing as the contraction hit. They were coming closer together.

I put on gloves and did the check. "If I did it right, you're about seven centimeters. You're definitely in transition."

"You sure it's not more than that? I feel like I need to push."

"You can't yet."

She sighed in resignation.

We went through another half-hour of intense contractions. I could see it wearing her down. After one particularly bad one, tears came to her eyes. She looked over at me, exhausted. "I can't do this anymore." She wiped at her eyes. "I just want it to stop." She grew angry. "And don't give me any platitudes saying I can do it. I'm beyond that!"

I stripped off my gloves and took her hand. I tried to think of something to say that would help, but she was right. A platitude wasn't it. Then I remembered something. "Right after Wendy and I had first started dating, she decided she would run in a marathon for charity. She wasn't all that athletic, but I couldn't talk her out of it. I was in slightly better shape, so I ran with her. Now, I didn't know her that well yet, so I expected to hear a lot of whining, and thought she'd quit well before the finish.

But she didn't. She tripped and skint her knee one time, threw up another, but she kept on and managed to stagger across the finish line. I asked her afterward what made her continue." I paused and looked into Trudi's eyes. "She said she didn't focus on the painful individual steps—just the joy of finishing."

Trudi blinked at me.

I smiled at her. "You're going to be a great mother, *Momma Bear.*"

She searched my eyes and sniffed. "I can't decide whether to hit you or kiss you."

A contraction hit, and Trudi fell into her breathing pattern. But she attacked it with renewed energy. She was still in a lot of pain, but that look of determination was back. I took a wicked pleasure in that.

Momma Bear had returned.

CHAPTER
TWENTY-TWO

——————————————

"CAN I PUSH NOW?" asked Trudi, getting the words out while doing her "*hee-hee, who*" breathing.

"Not until you're at ten centimeters," I said. "You're only at eight."

She groaned. The room was cool, but sweat dampened the hair around her face.

The contraction passed, and her head fell back into the pillow. "I am not doing this again," she said softly. "Any man that even looks at me, I'm gonna cut his parts off." She glared at me. "Including you!"

I took a towel and wiped her face. "You don't have to worry about me. You're not my type."

Her eyes met mine, a touch of anger in them. "I am, too! I saw you looking at my legs."

"And you have fantastic legs." I patted her shoulder. "Want a sip of water?"

She shook her head.

She went through two more contractions without speaking,

only the sound of her breathing. On the third, she gasped as it hit. She grabbed my hand, squeezing it hard. "Can you check me? That one felt different."

I did as she asked and was surprised that the first baby was crowning. "Trudi, I think you can start pushing now."

"About damn time." Another contraction hit her, and she pushed.

When that one passed, she took my hand and pulled me close, looking at me with her crystal blue eyes. "Eyrian, I'm sorry I dragged you into this."

I patted her hand. "Let's talk about this later."

She shook her head. "No, I need to apologize. I interfered with your grief." She gave my hand a squeeze. "But I'm sure as hell glad it was you. Whatever happens, I want you to know I couldn't have gotten this far without you."

She held my gaze. I didn't know what to say.

She had two more contractions, bearing down each time. On the third, her face screwed up in pain. "This... is going to be... a good one."

She pushed, and suddenly, I was holding a slippery handful of baby boy. He wasn't pleased at being out in the world and started crying on his own. I gently wiped his nose and mouth and then set him on his mother's stomach before clamping the cord and cutting it. I quickly wrapped him in a blanket and gave him to Trudi. She looked down at him and smiled. "He's beautiful," she said in awe. She stroked his tiny cheek. Then she said in baby talk, "And you've been a real pain in Mommy's ass."

I sat on my stool and rested for a moment. We should have a few minutes before the next one was born. I was pleased with myself. That hadn't been so hard.

Trudi had a couple mild contractions, and I checked her progress. I tried to show no emotion, but I could see the baby's butt showing. "Baby two is breech," I stated, hopefully with more confidence than I felt.

Trudi gave me a weak smile. "Do it just like we... we..." Trudi suddenly cut off.

I looked up in alarm. She was staring at me, her eyes glassy. She was struggling to keep them open, and her head drooped to one side. "Oh... shit..." she mumbled.

She sagged back against the pillow.

I quickly checked her blood pressure and gaped at the reading. It was down.

Shit!

I checked the remaining baby, and I could see blood. I wasn't sure if it was normal, but I thought one placenta must have separated early. She was bleeding. That baby needed to come out as soon as possible.

I panicked. My heart leaped into my chest. *She's going to die.* I looked at the baby lying on her chest. In this world, he would die without a mother.

What am I going to do?

Then I remembered the stupid pillowcase. How she squeezed out a doll butt first and explained each step. And her smile when I got it right.

I took a deep breath and steeled myself. "Just like we practiced," I said to myself.

I examined how the baby was presenting. "This is called a Frank Breech," I said to myself. "The first step is delivering the legs."

Working as quickly as I dared, I freed one leg and then the

other so the body could come through. Noting the baby was a girl, I rotated her, getting one shoulder out and rotating again to get the second. And now, the hard part. I carefully rotated the baby one last time until she was face down, then placing my fingers just as Trudi had shown me, I managed to get the baby's head free.

A gush of blood came out. I nearly panicked again but focused on what I was doing. Clamp and cut the cord. Wrap the baby and place her on her mother's chest. I pushed on Trudi's stomach while applying pressure to the cords. A moment later, each of the placentas came out. I massaged her stomach, trying to get her uterus to contract, and I was relieved that it was working. Finally, the bleeding slowed, and I prayed it wasn't because she was running out.

I quickly checked her vitals, and thank God she was stable and her heartbeat strong. Next, I checked on the babies, who were sleeping from their ordeal. I breathed a sigh of relief.

Standing by Trudi's head, I gently brushed a strand of sweaty hair away from her eyes. As I looked down at her unconscious face, I prayed she would be okay. I leaned over her, bringing my face close to hers. I could barely feel her breath on my cheek. I couldn't help myself. I gently pressed my lips to hers.

She groaned, and I jerked back, embarrassed at what I had done.

Trudi's eyes slowly opened, staring at me in an unfocused daze. But awareness quickly returned, and in panic, she glanced down at her daughter and son. She sagged in relief.

I placed a hand on her shoulder. "Rest. You lost a lot of blood. One of the placenta separated early."

She blinked up at me and nodded weakly. Her eyes grew wet, and a tear trickled down her cheek. "Thank you," she whispered.

I cupped her face and carefully wiped the dampness with my thumb. "You're welcome. But you really need to get something done about those hormones."

She smiled. "Yeah, I guess I do."

We looked into each other's eyes.

I was so glad this was over.

The room's quiet was broken by the scrape of a boot behind me. I heard a gun being cocked. Trudi looked toward the door and gasped.

"Well, isn't this touching?" The voice sent a chill down my spine.

Zane.

I raised my hands and slowly turned around. Zane was standing in the doorway, his revolver drawn and aimed right at me. But this was not the cocky young man that had threatened me—his hat was gone, his clothes were torn and mud-splattered, while his left leg had a crude splint of boards and cloth ties. He now carried an air of tired desperation.

"Get out!" yelled Trudi. She clutched her babies protectively to her. She carefully moved them to one side and shifted to shield them with her body.

Zane glared at her. "Bitch, that trick with your truck not only messed up my leg, but it made me look weak. Now, everyone thinks I'm pathetic. There were even a few whispers about kicking me out." He grinned. "But you're going to help me fix that. You and your boyfriend are coming with me. When they see your execution, they'll fall back in line."

This was not looking good. Trudi was behind me. If he shot, it might pass through me and hit her or one of the babies. I tried to remember where the shotgun was. I hadn't seen it since I took my nap. I glanced to the corner where I thought I'd left it, but it wasn't there.

He smirked and motioned with his gun. "Now, let's get moving."

When I didn't budge, he screamed at me, "NOW!"

One of the babies whimpered.

"She's just given birth and almost bled out," I said, trying to placate him. "She's too weak to go anywhere. And the babies—"

He cut me off. "Like I give a shit! Now get her up, *now!*"

The babies started crying, and Trudi tried to comfort them. "Shh, my babies. Everything will be all right. Momma Bear is here."

I stiffened. I suddenly knew where the shotgun was.

Trudi leaned around me to face Zane. "We're not going anywhere, you jerk. You've already said you're gonna kill us. Why make it easy for you?"

He glared at her. "Have it your way." He cocked his gun.

I couldn't see her, but I knew that flat, expressionless tone. She had a plan.

"But I will make you a deal," she said. "We'll cooperate *if* you keep the babies safe and care for them. They are yours, after all. That way, I'll at least salvage something from this, and you'll have your children. One of the other women could take care of them."

He nodded in my direction. "What about him?"

She smiled evilly. "I know his secret. Once I tell you, you'll own him. How do you think I got him to stay with me?"

He snorted. "You mean he's a pervert? Really?"

Trudi just smiled.

Zane considered her. He glanced at the babies wrapped in their blankets and then back to me.

He smirked. "All right. You got a deal. But only if you do exactly what I say. One wrong move and both of you die." He glanced at me. "Help her."

I turned slowly so that my back was to him. Trudi's eyes met mine. Her eyes were bright and utterly determined. I think it was at that moment I realized I loved her.

"Eyrian, this sheet is stuck under me." Her eyes held mine for a mere second, and then she looked down at her sheets as she lifted one. I followed her gaze. Laying right beside her, under the sheet, was the shotgun. It had been there during the entire delivery, and I was so focused on her that I didn't even notice.

I looked back up into her blue eyes and blew her a silent kiss. One side of her mouth curled up.

"All right, Trudi," I said. "Lift up." I leaned forward to better block Zane's view and raised the sheet. Trudi shoved the shotgun toward me and, at the same time, knocked over a metal pan, which clattered loudly to the floor.

I grabbed the shotgun and wheeled. Zane was distracted by the pan, giving me enough time to raise my weapon.

His eyes flicked to the shotgun, but he didn't have a chance to react. I fired.

The deafening blast caught Zane in the chest, and he staggered back. His own gun went off, but the shot was wild, going up into the ceiling. I chambered another shell and fired again, once more catching him in the chest. He staggered back into the hall, hit the wall, and slid to the floor. He didn't move.

As I lowered the shotgun, I thought I would at least feel a little remorse for killing another human. But for this one, I didn't.

I thought back to when Trudi and I were having our first discussion—me chained in my room while she sat in the talking chair. She had asked me a strange question. Would I kill to protect someone I cared about? I was now sure of the answer.

I would do *anything* to protect them.

The babies were screaming, and Trudi was trying to comfort them, apologizing in baby talk. She looked up at me and smiled. I wish I'd had a camera to capture that perfect moment. She looked so beautiful.

I turned away so she wouldn't see my face. My joy was only temporary.

I still had a promise to keep.

CHAPTER TWENTY-THREE

_____

I AWOKE TO THE pitter-pat of rain on the window. The clouds obscuring the barely risen sun cast a dull gray pallor across the den. It perfectly matched my mood. I had some unfinished business.

From the other end of the house, I heard a newborn start to fuss. I was surprised I could tell it was Opal. I counted to five before her brother, Silas, joined her complaint. I heard the shuffle of Trudi's slippers and then her gentle whispers as she spoke to them in the way that mothers talk to their babies. She was a good mother. I felt a smile grow on my lips. But it quickly faltered.

Today was the day.

The day I was supposed to join Wendy.

I got up and dressed, then made up the bed, trying to make it look as good as the evening I arrived. I had cleaned the room the day before and removed all my things. Plus, I had boxed up my stuff in the workshop and put it away. All that was left was in my backpack beside the bed. It contained the few things I would need to cross to Wendy's side.

The twins quieted, so I guess Trudi was feeding them. I was going to miss them. I never realized babies could generate so much mess and confusion while being so cute and adorable.

Seven days had passed since the twins had been born. And I had helped Trudi as best I could—she certainly appreciated it. But my heart broke to see her glance longingly at me when she didn't think I was looking. I knew what she wanted, but I was promised to another.

Since I needed Trudi to guide me to Wendy's place, I had delayed leaving to give her time to heal. But today was the day, and I could wait no longer.

I think Trudi was hoping we were settling in together. She'd even hinted that I might want to sleep in her bed—just sleep since she was still healing. But I put her off, continuing to stay in my old room. While I think I hurt her feelings, I had to do it. I had a promise to keep.

The night before, I set the table and made it as festive as possible, claiming it was an early Thanksgiving. I had found some canned turkey and cranberry sauce, and even tried my hand at stuffing and gravy. The stuffing wasn't too bad, but the gravy was awful. Trudi was pleased with my effort and seemed to enjoy the meal. But she was not stupid. She knew something was coming.

When we were done, I made my request. "Can you take me to the place tomorrow?"

She cocked her head in surprise. "What place?"

"Wendy's place. You promised you would show me. It was part of our deal."

Her fork clattered to her plate. Her expression vacillated between hurt, anger, and disbelief. "You're still gonna do it? You're gonna kill yourself after all we've been through?"

I had no desire to argue. "Will you take me there? I've done everything you asked."

She stared at me a moment before pushing away from the table and standing. She turned but stopped and just stood with her back to me. She took a deep breath. "Yes." Her voice was heavy with grief. "I will take you." She wiped at her face. "I keep my word." She went to her bedroom and didn't come back out.

I sighed as I listened to the rain against my window. I wish I could have told her differently. I had hurt her feelings. And I owed her better, but I knew no other way to do it.

I got up and dressed before going to the kitchen to fix breakfast. Trudi must have heard me clanking around because the door to her room opened. "Don't fix me anything," she said softly. "I'm not hungry."

Her door closed with a firm finality.

I sighed. I knew this would be hard on her. But I never promised I would stay. I had done everything we'd agreed. More even. Rescuing her from Zane was a little extra. She had no reason to complain.

I fixed some powdered eggs, but when I took a couple of bites, they didn't suit me. Sammy would have loved to have those eggs. I sometimes wondered if I could have saved him, but I couldn't see how. I sighed. Maybe I will see him when I join Wendy.

I put the eggs in the trash.

I went to the truck and brought in the car seats I'd found. I set them on the table. It wasn't safe for Trudi to hold them during the drive over. And so I sat at the table sipping my coffee while I waited for her to finish getting ready.

I had wondered about the baddies now that Zane was gone. I had checked on them a few days after the twins were born, but to my surprise, they were gone. I had no idea what had happened. They might have disbanded, or they might have simply moved on. In either case, I was glad they would no longer be a problem. Maybe next time, they will choose a better leader.

The door to Trudi's bedroom opened, and she came out carrying the twins. Her expression was flat, and her eyes went first to me and then to the car carriers on the table.

I stood. "Let me hold—"

"I got it," she shot back, irritation in her voice. "I have to learn how to do this on my own."

I licked my lips. "I..."

"Go on outside," she commanded. "I'll be there in a minute. Start the truck warming. I don't want them catching a cold."

She then turned to put the twins in their carriers. I had clearly been dismissed.

I went outside and pulled the truck up close to the door. I left the engine idling and went inside to see if I could help.

Trudi shoved a diaper bag into my arms and carried the twins outside.

I took the opportunity to take one last look around the place. The bedroom where Trudi had chained me. The table we'd played cards at and eaten our dinner. The kitchen she had used to prepare our meals. While our relationship had started a little rocky, it had turned into something I'd never expected.

I sighed. But now I had to go to Wendy. I'd promised. She was the one I loved. I shook my head. But I couldn't understand why I was so sad.

I made it outside just as Trudi was finishing up with the twins. They were fast asleep. She had bundled them up with only their tiny faces showing. They looked so cute, a mirror image of their mother.

Trudi refused to look at me. "You'll have to ride in the back. The car carriers take up everything. The rain's slacked off, so it won't be too wet."

I nodded and hopped into the truck bed, settling down with my back to the cab.

She drove away slowly.

I didn't pay any attention to where we traveled. I had faith in Trudi. She would keep her word. I gazed up at the gray November sky. I wanted to think about Wendy, but instead, I went through my mental checklist. I had gotten everything done that I needed to. I had even found more solar panels and had rigged them to power the pump again. At least for the short term, Trudi wouldn't have to carry water.

I must have dozed because I awoke as Trudi made a turn, and we started up a steep grade. I turned to look where we were going and recognized the park. I smiled, my excitement growing. *This was it!*

Trudi had to navigate around a couple of abandoned cars, but only a short time later, pulled into a large parking lot.

I remembered this. Wendy and I had parked here.

She stopped close to the trail and shut the engine off.

The rain had stopped, but the sky was gray and overcast, nothing like the day Wendy and I were here.

I grabbed my bag, ready to start. "Thank you, Trudi. I've got it—"

She cut me off and started to unbuckle the twins. "I promised I'd take you there, and by God, I will."

"But the twins—"

"Just shut the fuck up!" she said in irritation. "I *will* see this through."

She grabbed the handle of each of the baby carriers and started up the trail.

I followed a short distance behind. "I can carry—"

"No," she said through clenched teeth. "I don't need your help, Mister Dreal. You completed your side of the bargain. I will complete mine."

We walked in silence—the drips from the trees and a lone bird were the only sounds. We passed through the rocks I remembered and finally reached the cliff.

There was a safety fence, but we had a clear view across the valley. I walked slowly around the area, hardly believing I had finally arrived. I smiled. This was the place.

I turned to Trudi. "Thank you for bringing me here."

But she made no reply, only set the twins down beside her. She glared at me, her expression hard—yet sad.

I stood there awkwardly. I wasn't sure what to say to her. Goodbye didn't seem adequate. We stared at each other for several seconds.

"Trudi, I guess—"

She took a deep breath. "*Eyrian Dreal*," Trudi shouted.

I jumped in surprise. I could hear the sound echoing from the surrounding hills.

"I have completed my part of the bargain," she said formally. "All conditions have been met, and it is now concluded."

I nodded. "Thank you."

We stared at each other, and as I have many times before, I couldn't help but notice her piercing blue eyes. I hoped the twins inherited those.

Her expression suddenly softened. "Eyr," she said sadly. "I can't watch while you blow your brains out. I'm leaving now. But before I go, I need to tell you something. Something I've kept secret ever since we met."

"And what's that?" I asked.

"You're special, Eyrian. I've never met anyone like you—smart, handsome, and brave." She paused. Her hands curled into tight fists at her side. "I love you, Eyrian Dreal. I love you like I've never loved anyone." She picked up the twin's carriers and turned away. "I just wanted you to know."

She walked away without looking back.

I watched her god-awful pink jacket disappear into the woods. I longed to chase after her. Hold her one more time. My mouth opened to call after her, to make her stop, but no words would come out. I couldn't. I was married. And it was time to be with my wife. I turned back to the cliff.

I took out my phone, my special gun, and my book. I brought up Wendy's picture and propped the phone up on the fence post where I could see her. God, she was so beautiful.

I pulled out my special gun, loaded it, and set it beside Wendy's picture. Lastly, I took out the book and turned to the passage Wendy had requested. I balanced it in one hand while I picked up the gun and held it to the side of my head.

This was it.

I scanned across the valley, taking in the beautiful view for one last time. The air had a gray, misty feel, but I could see the sky lightening in the distance. Later, the sky would likely clear.

I wouldn't be here to see it.

My chest tightened. Like I'd never see Trudi again.

I closed my eyes and swallowed. I had delayed as long as I could. I had a promise to keep.

I looked down at the page and began to read aloud.

> *The Second leaned over the fallen Paladin— sadness gripped his heart. The battle was over. The Tainted Knight defeated. The people freed at last. However, the cost was the life of the man he had served. His master was slipping away.*
>
> *Tears fell across the Paladin's brow, and the Second used them to gently wash the blood from his hero's face. His savior was leaving, yet he owed him so much. He had not only given The Second freedom, but also taught him how to live and introduced him to his one true love. It would hurt to be without his master.*
>
> *The Paladin's eyes fluttered open, and he saw his friend's sadness, but he smiled up at him and raised a trembling hand to touch the man's face.*
>
> *"My Second," the Paladin whispered faintly. The man bent closer so he could catch his master's every last word.*

The hero took a tortured breath. "Thank you, my friend. My very best friend. You have sacrificed greatly for me. Before I go to meet the Great One, I give you one last command..."

The Second held his breath. Waiting.

"Go to she who waits for you. Your old home is no more, but she has prepared a new one." The Paladin took one last ragged breath. "Go to her... let her heal your heart, as you will heal hers... and be happy with her. Forever."

I was immediately reminded of Wendy practicing these lines aloud. They were her favorite. She had chosen well.

I tightened my finger against the trigger. Wendy was waiting.

But some phrases in the passage jumped out at me.

"Go to the one waiting for you..."

Unbidden, thoughts of Trudi played in my mind. It was strange that those words could apply to her, too.

"She has prepared a new home..."

I thought of Trudi's house. Eating at her table. The bed she'd made for me using her special quilt. The meals she'd prepared.

"Let her heal your heart..."

The night I held her while she trembled in my arms. And how I had come to care for her enough to risk my own life.

I reread the passage. Before I met Trudi, all I could think about was Wendy. But suddenly, I was no longer sure what my wife really intended.

I quickly put the gun down and fumbled for Wendy's letter, hurriedly unfolding it.

"Getting the right words is so hard."

"Follow the Paladin's last command... your true love awaits..."

"You will know what to do."

I looked out across the valley in disbelief. This was not what I remembered when I first read it. The meaning was different. *What had changed?*

The book was the same.

The words were the same.

The promise was the same.

The only thing that had changed...

Was me.

My hand began to tremble. I had gotten it all wrong. Wendy, somehow, in all her insanity, had still loved me and wanted the best for me. But she couldn't find the words. The craziness wouldn't let her. So she left me the Paladin's final command to say what she couldn't. And in my grief, in my depression, I had assumed she wanted me to join her. But that wasn't the message she wanted to give me.

She wanted me to live.

Tears blurred my vision. I stared at my wife's picture for several minutes. I brought it to my lips.

"Wendy," I said aloud. "I will always love you. But I realize now that I had your words all wrong. You wanted me to go on. To be happy." My voice broke, and I had to clear my throat. It took several moments before I could continue.

"My love, would it be okay if I waited just a little longer to join you? You see, there is someone here that needs me. And I guess, I need her too." I smiled. "Her name is Trudi. She's a little rough, and curses like a sailor, but she has a kind heart and a strength I've never seen." I nodded. "You would like her."

A gentle breeze skipped through the trees, gently caressing my cheeks and freeing the last drops of rain from the trees. I suddenly knew it was all right. Wendy was okay with this. She wanted me to be happy.

I turned my phone off and put it in my pocket, then carefully closed the book and put it in my backpack. One day, I'd show it to the twins and tell them Wendy's story.

I looked at my wedding ring. I removed it, kissed it, and placed it on the fence. It seemed like the right thing to do.

I heard leaves rustling and a snort. I jerked in that direction to see a black bear watching me. I think he was as surprised as I was. I carefully pulled my gun from my belt and pointed it upward, firing a single shot.

The bear, frightened, turned and ran away through the woods. I nodded and put my gun away.

I ran back down the trail. I was already planning what I wanted to say to Trudi. But as I rounded the bend, I spotted her on her knees between the two baby carriers, her head bent to the ground and both hands over her face. Heaving sobs racked her body, and her wails echoed off the trees. The sight broke my heart. She must have heard the shot and thought I was gone. I had caused her to feel that pain. And I resolved to never, ever make her feel that again.

"Trudi?" I called softly.

She looked up, her eyes swollen and her cheeks wet. She didn't hesitate. She sprang up and ran into my arms, clutching me so tight I couldn't breathe. "The gunshot. I thought... I was praying you wouldn't..."

I shushed her, holding her tightly in my arms. "I'm sorry I worried you. A bear came too close, and I scared it away."

She gazed up at me. "And Wendy?"

I smiled. "I made my peace. I finally realized that I had Wendy's last words all wrong. I think that in her rambling craziness, she was just trying to tell me to find someone else to love me. That's why she used the book's passage. To say what she couldn't."

I took her arms and gently pushed away from her. "But there is one thing I need to do."

She pulled back with a puzzled expression and wiped her eyes. "What's that?"

"I need to make a new promise. This time with you. But it requires you to make a promise, too."

She looked up at me, searching my eyes. A slow smile spread across her lips. "And what is this promise?"

I took her hand. "I promise to help you, to be by your side, and help raise our children. I will do my best to hold and protect you. And with God as my witness, I will do so until you tell me to leave."

There was a twinkle in her eye. "And what would my promise be?"

"I'd ask that you be my partner in return." I paused. "And not cut my man-parts off."

"I don't know," she said coyly. "Why should I go to all that trouble?"

I gazed into her eyes. "Because I love you too."

She grabbed my face with both hands and kissed me. Hard. When she pulled back, she looked up at me with her beautiful blue eyes.

The corner of her mouth curled up. "You know I want more children?"

"I thought you had sworn off sex."

"It's a means to an end."

"So you'll suffer through childbirth again?"

"If you'll be there to deliver them."

I shook my head. "Maybe I'll cut off my *own* man-parts."

She searched my eyes and grew serious. "Did you really mean it? That you love me?"

I kissed her again. "Yes. I have for a while now, but I was too messed up to see it."

As she met my gaze, her eyes welled with joyful tears. She pulled away and wiped at her eyes.

"Damn hormones."

EPILOGUE

——————————

"EYRIAN," I HEARD TRUDI call from the ground below, a note of disapproval in her voice.

I carefully stepped to the roof's edge to find her frowning up at me with a hand shading her eyes. She didn't look happy. "What the hell are you doing?"

With a wave of my arm, I indicated the chimney behind me. "I'm putting an illuminated Santa on the roof."

She stared up at me for a moment. "And why the hell are you doing that?"

I smiled. "Because it's Christmas."

Her frown deepened. "Do you actually expect me to believe that? From up there, that Santa will shine bright enough to be seen on the other side of the continent."

I sighed and surveyed the little farm around me. I'd hoped to surprise her. Less discussion that way.

"Because, my love, we're going to need other people close by."

"*Dearest*," she said tightly. I winced, knowing Trudi's patience was being stretched. "What if you attract the baddies?"

I eased over to the ladder and climbed down. I pulled her into a hug. She came reluctantly but still settled into my embrace. Ah, there was still hope of forgiveness.

"It's possible that some of the baddies are still out there."

She frowned. "Do you think that wise, *dearest?* Considering they tried to kill both of us."

"Then, if they show up, we'll have to be ready for them." I sighed and pointed to the empty fields. "We can't keep using the stuff from before the Judgement. There's still a lot left, but it's not infinite. We need to learn how to grow our food. Make our own clothes. All that stuff."

She considered me for a moment. "I can't argue with that. But what has that got to do with other people?"

I looked into her bright blue eyes. "What if the baddies do come back? We need people to stand with us. People we can trust. But to do that, we have to let them know we're here. By showing them we have electricity, courtesy of the solar panels, it means we're trying to improve things."

I pointed to the illuminated decoration and couldn't help but grin. "And if you put a Santa on your roof, how evil can you be?"

She shook her head and tried not to smile while she contemplated the tacky decoration. I could tell her beautiful mind was working. That's what I loved about her. She was quick and to the point.

"You have a tree to go with it?" she asked.

I held up a finger for her to wait and went to the truck. I brought back the tackiest, *biggest* Christmas tree I could find.

Trudi rolled her eyes. "You are a tasteless idiot." She put her arm through mine. "But I love you anyway." She leaned in and gave me a kiss.

She pulled back. But her expression quickly changed to puzzlement. "Do you hear that?"

I listened but shook my head. "What?"

She grabbed my hand and led me toward the front porch. With the cold weather, we rarely used it, but as we approached, I heard a squeaky animal sound. While familiar, I couldn't figure out what it was. Was an animal in pain?

Trudi squatted down and looked under the porch. She peered under it and broke out into a huge grin. I squatted down beside her and immediately knew what it was.

A medium-sized beagle lay on her side with several newborn puppies next to her. It was their newborn grunts we'd heard. The dog growled but made no motion toward us.

Trudi leaped up and ran to the back door. She returned a moment later with a bowl of water and some of Sammy's favorite food. The beagle didn't hesitate to lap at the water and then eat the food. When she was done, Trudi bravely leaned forward and extended the back of her hand. The dog sniffed her and then allowed Trudi to pet her.

While she was occupied, I looked over at the five puppies. I gasped. One of them had the same color and markings as Sammy. I shook my head. That old son of a gun had found him a mate. That's why the beagle had been making appearances.

Not liking my proximity to her pups, the beagle returned and lay down with them. We stood, and I put my arm around her. I guess our family had just grown again.

From inside the house, we heard Opal decide it was dinnertime. A few minutes later, Silas agreed.

Trudi gave me a peck on the lips. "I better go." She stepped away but turned, looking back at me while she walked. "And I want a real Christmas tree and lights in the den."

"Deal."

She shot me a smile and went inside.

I stepped away and looked up at the tacky Santa. Life was going to be rough for the next few years. But seeing the decoration gave me new hope.

And then it came to me.

We needed a new name for our future community. Something that would express the ideals we wanted.

I nodded and spoke the name out loud. "New Hope."

A breeze skipped through the trees behind me, and I couldn't help but smile.

I was sure Wendy would have approved.

Acknowledgments

As always, many people went into making *Last Promise*, and I am grateful to each and every one of them.

Lily did a fantastic job as my copyeditor. She saw things that I had no idea were there. Her suggestions definitely improved the book. Also, I want to thank my first readers—Nichole, Kasey, Callista, Rebecca, Kayla, and Daniel. Their input was invaluable. I also need to thank my local chapter of the Virginia Writers Club for their gentle support and encouragement.

Once again, my wife deserves major kudos for listening to me moan and groan while I was writing the novel. By design, this book is closer to her tastes in literature, and I was hoping she would like it. I knew I had hit the mark when she asked me, "Where's the next one?"

Books by Jessie D. Eaker

Last Promise

The Coren Hart Chronicles

Thief of Curses

Queen of Curses

Assassin of Curses

A Study of Curses (A series companion)

Unlikely Survivor Series

Monday After the Apocalypse

Vault of Silent Whispers Series

Midnyte's Dragon Kiss